Love, Lust and Lies

by

Deborah Caren Langley

Love, Lust and Lies

This edition published by Inscape Solutions Limited

Copyright © 2016 by Deborah Caren Langley

Deborah Caren Langley asserts the moral right to be identified as the author of this work.

A catalogue record for this work is available from The British Library

ISBN: Softcover   978-0-9935930-0-0

          eBook   978-0-9935930-1-7

My name is Deborah Caren Langley and I grew up in Blackpool, England. When I was at school I was always involved in school activities like choir, dance classes, even after-school events like weekends away camping, canoeing or hiking. As a child I enjoyed school, I had lots of friends and my parents always encouraged me in every way and in everything I did. I had a great childhood.

When I left school I worked in a sweet factory as a machinist wrapping lollipops and hated every minute of it. I decided to go to college, where I studied Childcare, and subsequently worked with children for many years. Even so, my real passion was creative writing and I really wished to be a writer. So one night I sat down and started writing this book (and then I put it away for many years).

I never in my wildest dreams thought it would ever be published – so you could say my dream has come true. I hope you enjoy reading it as much as I enjoyed writing it.

Acknowledgements

This book is dedicated to my Mum and Dad who are no longer with me. They would be so proud of me today, even though they might not approve of the language in the book. They would be right behind me and encouraging me as they always have. They always told me I had a creative nature. My dad always thought it would be singing, but knew I wanted to be a writer.

You are always In my thoughts and I wish you could be here to see this. Love you both so much. XX

I would like to thank all my family for the support they have given me when I was ready to give up.

Last, but not least, I must thank my friend Lorraine Fox for all the help and encouragement she has given me. I'd like to acknowledge the support she gave in aiding me and the time she spent proofreading the book. Hope it got you through any lonely nights LOL.

Thank you so much, *love you all*

Prologue

Deborah is an intelligent, beautiful young woman who ventured out on a journey that would not only change her life forever; but the lives of two handsome young men, who both fell in love with her. Through jealousy and spite she is thrown in to a bitter game of rivalry.

She loves just one man and they find a love that only happens once in a lifetime.

It's a bumpy journey but can the love they have for each other stay strong throughout? Can they ever be together without lying and hurting each other or are there just too many obstacles in their way?

This is her story.

Chapter 1

5th June 1995

Deborah stands in the bathroom gazing into the mirror, remembering when she first started out on her journey to America, her life, her loves, her fears, her hopes and expectations.

The only daughter of Katherine and Robert Carnell, she was always a happy, well-mannered, little girl, always smiling, the apple of her mum and dad's eye. They loved her so much they would have given her the world if they could.

She had enjoyed her school years. She was a good student, willing to learn and determined her education was going to give her the best opportunity to get where she wanted to be. When she left school she succeeded in getting into further education to achieve the higher qualifications she needed. She had grown into a bright and intelligent young woman with big dreams for her future.

Deborah had applied to get into Birmingham University. When her grades were announced, she had passed with distinction. Several universities said they would be happy for her to become a student and offered her a place. She was overwhelmed but her heart was set on Birmingham and she was ecstatic when they accepted her application…

London, England 1980

The charts are full of Punk and New Romantic music but there is a new underground scene where many new rock bands are emerging. Deborah wasn't into the chart music scene but she was into the rock music, having lived in a house which was dominated by the sound of rock from the 60s and 70s.

In all honesty, Deborah was only interested in reaching her goals. She threw all her effort into achieving her ambition, leaving nothing to chance. She was determined to succeed and for that to happen she had to study and work hard.

Between classes she was prepared to do any job she could to finance her studying. She worked in a local café, she cleaned home for a local business couple. She did as many hours as she could to raise the funds to get her through university. She didn't want to be a burden and be constantly asking her parents for financial support, they had already helped so much. They had even gone into debt themselves to support her chance to achieve her goals.

She needed the degree in economics to get the global qualification, ACCA, to become a chartered accountant. She not only wanted to work in accountancy she also wanted to be able to travel and this would enable her to do just that.

For a long time Deborah had been in a relationship with David, really her first love. They had met in the school playground. He stole the ribbons from her hair and teased her before finally giving them back. She was happy with David and, even after she went off to College, they managed to find time to see each other, mainly during holidays and weekends. Visits to the university presented some difficulties as Deborah shared a house with seven other young women so when he was flush, David would sometimes book them into a little boardinghouse. They had done so many things growing up together and it was David to whom she lost her virginity.

As David worked many evenings and weekends, they didn't get to spend every weekend together. He worked for Deborah's father as assistant manager at the car showrooms, earning a decent salary with some good bonuses. David also wanted to get his degree and he hoped to move into senior management one day.

They both worked hard, and wanted good careers. Deborah was more ambitious than David as she wanted to travel and see the world. David believed they would be married one day, he adored her very much and missed her while she was away, so when he did see her he made the most of it.

One weekend he managed get tickets to see the group *Roma* who had just broken in to the charts. David had wanted to go to see them so Deborah took the weekend off from the café. As the band was performing in Manchester they decided to make a weekend of it. David had booked them a little hotel, nothing extravagant just bed and breakfast. When they arrived they went to their room, Deborah looked around.

"This is great."

"Yeah… Come here," he uttered sexily, taking her by her waist.

Kissing her,"I've really missed you Deb."

"How much?" she giggled.

"Well… we have time… Why don't I show you," he said coyly.

He kissed her gently and moved her back towards the bed. She fell backwards reaching up and tenderly touched his face kissing him back, as he slowly moved his hands over the curves of her body. Sensually they undressed each other, touching each other. He pressed his thumb against the inside of her thigh making her body tremble as she gave out a moan of delight. She could feel his throbbing bulge pressing against her outer thigh. He looked at her, his eyes full of desire as he smiled softly and eased himself between her thighs, pushing himself down onto her.

They made love slowly and rhythmically, touching and feeling each other's bodies both feeling the pleasure of each other's touch as Deborah let out gasps of pleasures until they climaxed together.

David rolled off and they lay looking lovingly at each other, Deborah stroking his head and his face…

"You have missed me haven't you?" she smiled victoriously.

David smiled and nodded,"Oh yeah."

They lay in each other arms for a moment. David would have been happy to miss the concert and to stay right where they were but Deb had also been looking forward to seeing Roma.

"Come on… We'd better get ready," she said eagerly, jumping out of bed.

She had a quick bath and then dressed, pulling her jeans over her shapely legs. David watched as she pulled her tight, figure hugging T-shirt over her breasts. She slid her shapely calves and thighs into her new thigh length boots. To complete the look she put her makeup on. She always wore thick black eyeliner, she liked the way it complemented her eyes with their beautiful long lashes.

She decided not to wear her hair up, instead she left her beautiful, long dark hair flowing as she styled it to give her a great rock chick look. David looked at her appreciatively, grabbing her around the waist with one hand:

"Fuck me... You really wanna go out tonight? 'Coz I can think of something I'd much rather be doing."

"Down boy," she purred,"We've got a date with a rock band."

They went and grabbed a bite to eat then headed to the concert. The arena was already throbbing with excitement when they arrived and as the band came on stage the room went wild. Roma was a new rock group and had taken the British and American charts by storm. They gyrated around the stage sending their fans into frenzy, especially the young women. All too soon it was over, leaving their fans in a hot sweaty mess. Deb would have loved to have their autographs but they couldn't get anywhere near them.

Brooklyn, New York 1980

Danny Brooks was a young man of eighteen with the hormones to match. His first experience of the opposite sex was with an older woman who had shown him the art of sex and he just couldn't get enough of women.

He worked in a fruit processing factory with two of his friends, Simon and Tony. They had all left high school together and had gone straight into the local factory. In their spare time they were in a band called *Decade* with two other friends, Alan and Dave, who worked for the US Postal Service. They had formed Decade when they were about thirteen and they managed to get to play at high school proms and school clubs. They were all into rock music spanning the fifties to the seventies.

They hung out at Kool Kats' Diner on the corner of the boulevard near to where they lived. It was a grubby little place but the kids loved it, it had an old, fifties style jukebox in the corner that played good old rock n' roll. They wanted to be a rock band and dreamed of being famous like their idols and one day playing alongside them.

The guys were extremely talented, they wrote their own songs and all of them could play various instruments. Tony was the drummer, Simon and Alan played guitars, Dave played keyboard and Danny was the lead singer who also played guitar and piano. When they weren't at work they practised in Danny's garage. His dad had happily let them use it.

They started playing more and more proms, even weddings and birthdays, as they became a tighter outfit bouncing off each other, hoping they would get noticed.

Danny had a call to book them for a birthday party, a call that was going to change their lives. Russell Douglas had called to ask Danny if he could book the band for his son's sixteenth birthday party. Russell was in the music business and he'd heard about Decade who had been getting some rave reviews, even making it to the music press. This was no ordinary 16-year old's birthday party, some big names from the music business would be there. Everyone wanted to celebrate one of the current music scenes' top talent spotters son's birthday party. Artists offered their services for free as there would be some music figures who could turn budding artists into superstars – people like Alex Parks. It was *the* place to be.

Alex Parks was top of the new music scene. He had an eye for stars and what people wanted to hear see and buy. He was having an interesting evening, enjoying meeting some of the artists he had turned into superstars. When Decade came on he didn't pay much attention. Then one particular song, *Big City*, made the hairs on the back of his neck tingle. He broke off talking and went over to where they were playing.

He really thought they had potential. After they finished playing, he went over to Russell and asked him to pass his card to them. Russell passed over the card saying,"Hey Buddies.. think you need to get in contact with this guy – don't even think it over. Call him and get over and see him *as soon as possible.*"

Disbelieving, they dialled the number on the card and got excited to hear that the incredible Alex Parks wanted them to come to his office.

He told them he wanted them to go into the studios to cut a demo:

"I want to know what you can do – to see if you guys are as good as I think you are. Prove me right – I am going to give you a break and get you out there playing in every venue, all the bars and clubs across the country. It's going to be hard work, you're going to have to be committed and determined otherwise you won't make it."

The boys couldn't believe it:

"Where do we sign?" Said Simon.

In the studio

"Right let's get that Big City song down. I want to hear it like you played it last night" demanded Alex. He turned to the producer,"I want it raw. I also want them to put some other tracks down – the studio will be paid for four hours so they better make sure they get it right."

Alex went off and contacted the venues that would enable him to see how they performed and if they could go all the way. After the studio session the guys were told to go into the promotion rooms where they were met by Angelina who dealt with publicity and promotion, including how the bands looked.

They were typical hot-blooded young men and woman crazy. They all liked the women but they never stuck with them long. The band's motto was *'so many women and not enough time.'*

Danny had a mop of long mousey brown hair cut into layers with an unkempt look, that sat around his baby face and fell over his dreamy hazel eyes. He had high cheekbone and flawless olive skin that off set his sexy smile He knew he looked good in his ripped jeans and leather jacket and always had lots of young women chasing after him.

Simon was a love 'em and leave 'em type of guy. The guys called him Mr. Charm because he had the gift of the gab and he could charm the panties off any young woman.

Alan and Dave, the jokers in the band, were always messing about and playing tricks on everyone. Tony was the quietest of all of them. They called him Mr. Sensible, but he did like a good time and he loved the women, who went for his shy and quiet ways.

Alex had got them a few gigs in Valley Boulevard. It wasn't going to pay much but they didn't mind as they just enjoyed being on stage. As soon as they got up, women would swarm towards the stage shouting and screaming and hoping that at least one of the band members would look at them.

After they had finished their set, they all went for a drink at the bar and were talking when a woman came over :

"Hi there…"

"Hi… and what can I do for you baby?" Simon asked.

"Oh, sorry, I was talkin' to him." She said, looking sheepishly at Danny.

"Hi there," Danny laughed.

The young woman giggled giddily,"Hi"

"Sit your sexy ass down and join us." He smiled as he patted the seat next to him.

"My friends want to meet you," She giggled.

"Yeah… sure, we'll come over and meet your friends," Danny said with a wide grin on his face.

Danny's smile was enough to make any woman weak at the knees. They all went over and sat with her friends. Danny slid his hands slowly up her leg and seductively suggested they went back to hers. She didn't take much persuading so off they went. She had to sneak him in so as not to wake her roommate but they did anyway, with all the moaning and groaning she was doing. Danny couldn't believe how horny this woman was, especially when she went down on him twice.

Her buddy banged on the wall and shouted:

"For fuck's sake, if you are going to get laid Josie, do it quietly – some of us need to sleep."

Next morning Danny met up with Simon and Tony then set off in the direction of the factory. They had so much time off they thought they might end up getting sacked.

Simon casually enquired if Danny had scored.

"Oh Man, yeah!"

"You had a good night then?"

"Yeah, she was one horny chick. Man she was like a mechanical bull… What about you guys?"

"Simon got laid… the blonde chic" Tony laughed loudly.

"Way to go buddy." Danny cried out as they high fived.

After they had done their shift they headed off to the studios as they were meeting Dave and Alan there. They were all sat having a smoke talking about the previous night's events when Alex came in. They were still laughing and he asked what was funny. They started telling him about the night before.

"You guys are just hormones," said Alex as he chuckled.

"Yeah but we're having fun, Man," Danny said, smirking.

"Yeah I can see that."

"I bet you were the same when you were our age," chirped up Simon.

"Suppose I was…"

"See, Man"

"…Yeah but I'm married now." he laughed.

"I'm not getting hitched." Danny stated

Simon agreed with Danny."Fuck em and split that's our motto. Who the fuck wants to get married when there so much pussy out there?"

Danny sniggered,"Yeah right on … you said it, Man"

Alex shook his head and rolled his eyes,"You guys kill me."

Alex suggested they cut this track so he could play it back. Tony started knocking out the beat to *Wild, Wild Girl*. Simon and Alan joined in, strumming the chords on their guitars. Dave then played it on the keyboard while Danny went in to the vocal booth and blasted out the words loud and hard. Hitting the high notes he sounded strong and sexy. Simon was lost in the riff of the guitar. Tony was on fine form, the drums sounded fantastic, there was some good old rock 'n' roll going down.

Alex was rocking out in the recording booth. His foot was tapping, his head was banging – he really liked what he was hearing. He just knew he could make them into superstars worldwide – they just needed that big break. They had it all: looks, sound, and that bad boy image.

Birmingham, England 1983

When the time came for Deborah to sit her exams she sat through them hoping she would pass. In the back of her mind she wondered if she had done enough… She really needed those results.

The months waiting for her results were anxious ones. She stayed in Birmingham and carried on working in the café. When the day came to find out she went with nervous expectation and was so relieved that her hard work had not been in vain. She and her friends jumped for joy with excitement as they had all passed their chosen subjects. They were all so enthusiastic about their futures.

She rushed to phone her parents to tell them the good news:

"Mum is that you? She screamed down the telephone excitedly.

"Yes… Deb… well…?"

"I've passed…, I've really…really… passed", she said, over the moon.

"Oh Deb, that's fantastic, you clever girl."

She could hear her dad in the background shouting:

"Is that Deb?"

"Yes its Deb and she's passed her exams"

Her dad took the phone:

"Deb well done, we knew you could do it, we're so proud of you"

"Thanks dad"

"When and what time are you back?"

She told him she was having a night out with her mates from university and that she would be returning on Saturday.

"Can you meet me at the station at 4.30?"

That night she celebrated with her friends and partied the night away. She hadn't been on a good night out for ages and there was a big group of them enjoying the evening together after the hard work they had all put in for the past three years. She had a great night. Such a shame about the bad head next morning.

When Saturday arrived, her mum and dad were there to pick her up from the station and take her home. When they arrived she went up to her bedroom, dumped her bags on the floor and looked round her room. It was just how she had left it, with the Brad Cannon posters still on the wall – Brad Cannon, the film star she was crazy about… She considered herself a little too old for posters now.

She was so excited to be home, she couldn't wait to see her Nan. She always wanted to look good and spent an age getting ready, putting on her blue jersey dress. Her dad then took her to see her Nan while her mum got her surprise party ready. All her friends were there waiting for her.

"Where are we going?" She asked

Her dad told her they were just stopping at the club. He needed to see the barman about something.

"OK, do you want me and Nan to wait in the car?"

"No, we'll have a drink while we're here"

She helped her Nan from the car, holding her arm firmly. When they walked into the function room:

"SURPRISE." everyone shouted as they jumped out at her.

She jumped out of her wits. She was not expecting that at all, she was so happy to see everybody. David stepped out:

"Welcome home, babe," he said as he kissed her lovingly.

He had his own surprise. In fact he had two.

He couldn't wait any longer to give Deborah his surprise. He handed her a box containing a pair of gold earrings with little diamonds in the centre. She opened the box. She was so delighted she threw her arms round him, and kissed him tenderly.

"Oh David, they're lovely."

"You like them, then?"

"Oh, Yes."

Then he handed her an envelope. She looked puzzled as she opened it. Tickets to Paris. David had booked it weeks before she came home.

Her mum and dad were so proud of her. They had missed her so much and were glad she was home.

Deborah really enjoyed herself at her party. Lots of family, many friends – some old, some new.

"You all knew and never said a word – how the hell did you manage that?"

"It was hard, but we did it," Kelly said smiling

There were some friends whom she hadn't seen for ages but her parents had so wanted it to be special party and they'd contacted everyone they could think of. Deborah loved seeing all her friends again.

Her old mate Maggie tapped her on the shoulder.

"MAGS!" Deborah bellowed.

"SURPRISE!" Mags shouted back. They flung their arms round each other and hugged tightly.

They had talked on the phone but hadn't seen each other for ages.

Mags was with her boyfriend Ryan. She had been with him as long as Deborah and David. A good-looking lad with short mousey brown hair and big green oval eyes, medium height and medium build, he was good-natured and liked a good laugh. Ryan had always liked Deborah and he still did. He and David had known each other for a long time and that's why he'd never asked her out.

Mags and Deb talked and talked. They both agreed that now Deborah was back they would be going on holiday together and invite a few of the girls.

Deborah thought that was a great idea.

"Where shall we go?" Mags asked.

"We could go to Spain for a week. It could be a real girly holiday."

"I'll start looking."

"Who are we going to ask to come with us, Mags?"

"What about Mel, Shaz, Libby, and Beth?"

"Yeah, that'd be great," agreed Debs.

They went over to the girls to ask them and they thought it was a brilliant idea.

The following weekend Deborah and David left for the airport. They left Heathrow at 8:25 am and arrived in Paris at 9:27 am. The flight itself was wonderful. Deborah was so excited she wanted to see everything.

They got to their hotel, threw their bags into the room and did a quick change. They both put on their jeans and t-shirts. The weather was beautiful. They went for a walk to look around and bought a few items.

They felt quite hungry when they found a bistro on the corner of a little cobbled street. Inside, the walls where adorned with old French scenery paintings. It was filled with fresh flowers and had trailing roses and some pretty little yellow flowers in Parisian vases. You could smell the beautiful fresh fragrances of the different flowers as what could only be described as fruit loops sweets with a touch of mint. After eating they took a leisurely walk back to the hotel.

When they got back to their room David took hold of Deborah and kissed her and told her he loved her. He gently laid her on the bed and kissed her again, this time more passionately. He pressed his body against hers as he ran his fingers through her hair and down the sides of her curves. He slowly moved his hand up her T-shirt gliding his hand over her breasts then trailing his fingers down her stomach to her navel.

He flicked the button and pulled the zip down opening her jeans and slipped them off slowly. Moving his mouth seductively up her legs, he worked his way up her body. She sighed deeply as she removed his T-shirt and opened his jeans. He pulled them off swiftly and threw them across the room.

They made love tenderly as he told her how he had missed her so much. Now she was back, he had so many plans. She'd missed him too and was intrigued and couldn't wait to hear his plans.

They got up and she changed into a white skirt, black blouse with red shoes. She put her makeup on and lifted her beautiful long dark hair onto the top of head. Deborah was a pretty petite young woman with big emerald green eyes.

David put on a blue suit. He looked handsome with his sharp features, tall with thick wavy black hair and piercing slate grey eyes.

They went for dinner at the Eiffel Tower. The view was amazing. They went on to see the show Moulin Rouge, the home of the cancan. After the show they strolled hand in hand back to the hotel. They talked about the future and what they wanted to do. When they got back to the hotel they went to the bar for a drink. They talked some more about the future. David was thinking more about marriage and children. Deborah was thinking more about travel and a career… They were thinking worlds apart.

The next day they took a tour and visited the valley of the Loire. It was the land of wine and castles and a former playground of French kings. Deborah could speak a little French so she could understand the tour guide when he spoke in French.

They enjoyed the day and that night they went to see the Bluebell Girls at the Paris Lido show, *C'est Magique*. Deborah thought it was great and thoroughly enjoyed her weekend. The next day they went home.

When they got back to Deborah's house, David stayed for a cup of tea then headed back home. Whilst travelling back she remembered the conversation that she and David had had about the future and she started to think more about it. Deborah told her mum and dad about her trip.

She told them she wanted to do more travelling and that she wanted to learn to drive. Her dad thought that was a great idea. He had been saving this surprise for when she got back from Paris. He had got her a car. This was her present for how well she'd done at university.

She hugged both her mum and dad and thanked them.

She wanted to get going with driving lessons as soon as she could. Her Nan gave her some money she had put away for her for this very occasion, she was so proud of her.

She told her Nan that as soon as she had passed her driving test she would take her out for the day to anywhere she wanted to go.

"You better get your test done then because I know where I want to go"

"Where, Nan?" Deb asked, laughing.

"I'd like to go to the seaside, for an ice cream." Deborah kissed her Nan lovingly.

"Anywhere you want Nan, anywhere."

Chapter 2

Deborah started her new job at Sparkman and Son Accountants. She planned to do so much with her life – she liked her new job and she'd already made some new friends. She'd started her driving lessons and couldn't wait to pass her test. She wanted to pack in as much as she could.

David was planning to ask her to her to marry him. He had bought her a trilogy engagement ring and was going to ask her that evening. He was so sure she would say 'Yes.'

He took her out for a special meal. It was quiet and dimly lit, shimmering on the beautiful decoration of the walls, romantic music was playing in the background and the staff couldn't do enough for them.

They had just finished their meal and he looked at her lovingly.

"What's on your mind David?" she asked looking at him closely.

"What makes you think I've got something on my mind?"

"Well…"

He interrupted her.

"Actually, I do have something on my mind…"

"OK, what is it?"

He took a deep breath.

"Will you marry me?"

In that moment her future flashed before her eyes. She felt far too young. She wanted to travel and see the world. It was just too soon.

"No David…I'm sorry…I just can't… I'm sorry…"

He couldn't believe it. He was certain the answer would be yes. He didn't even get chance to give her the ring. The evening came to a complete standstill and he told her would take her home. He was devastated.

Everything between them changed after that.

They drifted apart and their relationship ended. They stayed friends but both wanted very different things out of their lives. She wanted to have some fun. She'd worked hard for the past three years and she was only 21, plenty of time for marriage and children.

A few months later she passed her driving test. Her dad came good on the car he'd promised her and, in turn, she kept her promise and took her Nan to the seaside for that ice cream. They went for a fish and chip supper and sat on the Promenade. They both enjoyed the sea air and it was a lovely warm sunny evening. They walked to the harbour and visited some local landmarks, like the Victoria Pavilion – where Nan used to go when she holidayed there as a young girl. Together, they had a great time.

Now it was time for that holiday with the girls.

They flew off to Spain, leaving Eastbury behind. Their hotel looked fabulous as they stepped off the bus. They could see the harbour front from their balconies. Mel wanted to check out the bars as soon possible so they all got changed and went to explore, sussing out the pubs and nightclubs because they intended to have a fun packed week. Six young women, partying every night – they were going to be loud and rowdy and they were on the pull.

On the second night, they got talking to a group of lads. Mags really fancied one of the them.

"Look at him girls, look at them muscles, look at that body, he is sooo fit" Mags drooled.

"Sooo is his mate," Mel laughed.

"They're on holiday and they're after getting shagged." Beth said

"Yeah and that's definitely going to be me." giggled Mags.

"What about Ryan?" asked Shaz.

"What he doesn't know won't hurt him"

"You can't do that."Deb murmured, loyally.

"Oh Debs, you've not turned in to a prude have you?" Mel sniggered, mocking her.

Libby laughed,"And how's he gonna find out?"

Debs shrugged,"It just doesn't seem right."

For Mags, Mel and Libby the holiday just got better and better.

Deb and Beth wanted to do some sightseeing as well while they were there – they didn't just want to be drinking and sleeping it off over the course of the week. Beth asked if they could go on a boat tour and Deb said she would. The others just wanted to sunbathe round the pool and drink sangria all day. Beth got seasick and was ill most of the trip although she was fine once she got off the boat. They went for something to eat then went for a mooch round the markets to find some great bargains. Deb thought she might have to buy another suitcase, she bought that much stuff.

They met up with lads every night. One of them fancied Deb but she had not long since broke up with David and she wasn't looking for any sort of romance. Mags, on the other hand, had a holiday 'romance' with one of lads even though she had Ryan at home.

Mags, Mel, Shaz and Libby partied all-night and sunbathed all day; their holiday was over too quickly and before they knew it they were heading back to Eastbury

Two months after they'd arrived home, Mags found out she was pregnant. She knew the baby wasn't Ryan's but she simply couldn't believe her bad luck. What was she going to do? In the end, she was going to have to tell him about her fling. He was furious when she did.

"Why the fuck would you do that?"

"It just happened…"

"No… you went on holiday with that in mind."

"No… no…Ryan…"

"YES." He shouted angrily.

He told her right there and then that they were finished and he didn't want anything to do with her. She rang Deb and asked if she could come round. Deb could tell she been crying and told her she would put the kettle on.

When she arrived at Debs she was crying uncontrollably. Deb put her arms round her and just hugged her friend and asked her if she was alright.

"I'm pregnant"

There was an awkward pause for a spit second.

"Have you told Ryan?"

"It's not his…"

Deb passed Mags a mug of coffee and sat down.

"Oh… the boy you met on holiday?"

"Yeah" she sobbed, "Ryan was so angry with me – he's finished with me."

Concerned about her friend, Deb asked her what she was going to do.

"I-I'll…" Mags spluttered as she began to cry again, "I'll have the baby on my own." Salty tears rolled down her face.

"Are you going to manage?" Deborah asked, concerned.

"I'll have my parents, they'll help me"

"I'm so sorry about Ryan, Mags"

"I can't blame him. I cheated on him, it's my fault"

Deb gave her friend a big hug and said it would all be fine

As the months rolled by, Mags' pregnancy was advancing and she asked Deb to go to the hospital with her – she needed her best mate to be there with her for her first ultrasound scan. Mags missed Ryan and wished that he had been the baby's father. How could she have been so stupid? Deb had been right when she said it wasn't right having a fling on holiday.

When they saw the scan and they saw those little fingers and toes they both gasped with excitement.

"Oh Deb, look at my baby"

"That's amazing… , Oh My God"

Mags was glowing, she looked amazing. She was positively radiant – pregnancy agreed with her.

1983 in Brooklyn, New York

Danny and the guys were getting booked for regular shows in many clubs. They were very popular with the crowds, really building up a fan base. They still had their day jobs and were working hard to fit everything in.

They started going on the road at the weekend but they didn't earn a lot from it. Alex had got them some recording time and they got a two-song demo together. One song had had some airplay on the local radio but unfortunately it didn't get far.

Danny decided to change his hair colour. He went to streaky blonde and had a shaggy perm – it seemed to be all the rage with rock stars. He looked really different and the girls seemed to like him even more so Alan thought he'd do the same. Pretty soon, they all changed their appearance one-way or another.

They went on more and more gigs and the more they went on the more women they had. The guys were having a great time. They weren't earning much money and they had to sleep on the bus and eat takeout food but they were doing what they loved most. They now had a mobile shagging wagon, a tour bus they would take the women back to on nightly basis.

All the touring was paying off and they finally got their big break. *Roma*, the British rock band, had seen them and asked Alex if they would be the support band on their tour. Alex told the guys and they jumped at the chance. They would have to give up their jobs, though, as the Roma tour would be for over six months.

It all went really well, so when they got back Alex arranged for them to do another demo in another local recording studio. They got offers to support more bands such as *Tiger eye* and *Demon light*.

It was a tough schedule and hard work but they thought it was worth it. They were getting better money than in the clubs – and they were loving it.

Deborah was very excited at an unexpected opportunity to go and work in America through a friend of her dad. In the end, she jumped at the chance.

She had to go for an interview at the American Embassy to get her Green Card, Resident's Visa and request a social security number. Her mum and dad helped her get organised. Her new boss, Mr. Parker, was to be her sponsor and, soon, everything was sorted out.

Sparkmans were sorry to see her leave but they could see what a great opportunity it was. She insisted on working out her notice. By now, Mags was ready to have the baby and Deb had agreed to be her birth partner. They were both so excited.

When baby did arrive she was beautiful, tipping the scales at 6lb 12oz. Deb asked Mags what she was going to call her.

Mags looked down at her beautiful baby girl and said:

"Natasha, Natasha Eve Rankins"

Deb smiled,"Yes, that suits her beautifully."

Now she was all set to go. She said her goodbyes to everyone. Kath and Rob told her they would get over to see her as soon as they could. Her Mum, Dad and Nan took her to the airport, telling her how much they'd miss her.

After they kissed their goodbyes, she looked back and waved with tears in her eyes. Although she was looking forward to her new start she would miss them so much. She wondered what was in store for her. This was a whole new chapter starting in her life and she was so excited.

She boarded her plane and settled down for take off. Everything looked so tiny. She had something to eat. It was nearly a seven hour flight so she had plenty of time to read and watch a film, she even had a nap.

As the plane started its descent, Deborah became more and more excited. She took her first steps off the plane in New York. She smiled to herself and headed for passport control and then for her luggage. She found a cab and headed for the Royals Hotel where she was to meet her dad's friend, Mr. Parker.

She had never been this far from home before and on her way to the hotel she saw some amazing sights. She was taken aback by the size of the buildings – especially the biggest of them all, the Empire State Building. She was so excited and couldn't wait to see the rest. She was really looking forward to visiting Central Park.

On arrival at the hotel she paid her cab and went in. She asked for Mr. Parker and a few moments later he came out.

"Deborah, I hope you had a good flight. How are your mom and dad?"

"They're both fine" She replied.

"I sure hope you'll be happy here."

Deborah smiled:

"I'm certain I will be – and I have to thank you for this opportunity."

"I'm sure you are exhausted. Let's show you to your room and we will talk tomorrow."

On entering her room Deborah flopped onto the bed, weary from the journey, and slept through to the next morning. When she woke Deb made herself some fresh coffee before showering.

She dressed, putting on a navy blue suit with white blouse and navy blue shoes. She looked smart, and as usual she piled her hair on top of her head.

She went downstairs to meet Mr. Parker who then took her on a tour of the hotel, including the restaurant, where she was introduced to Sue, who was in charge of the restaurant and introduced her to the chef, waitresses, and the rest of the kitchen staff.

Sue was a friendly person, with beautiful long fiery red hair, and big grey eyes. She worked hard but also liked to party and they hit it off straight away.

Finally Mr. Parker took Deborah to her office introducing her to Trish who was to be her secretary. Deborah beamed with real pride to see she had her own office with her name on the door: *Deborah Carnell, Hotel Manageress.*

Mr. Parker and Deborah talked for a while before he left her in her office. She felt so giddy she sat on the swivel chair and spun round and round, giggling to herself with excitement.

She rang her mum and dad, forgetting the time difference. She woke them up but they weren't bothered. They were just glad to hear her voice. She told them she thought she would be happy here and would settle very quickly. They told her they would get over to see as soon as they could.

Sue asked Deborah if she wanted to go for a drink after work. So after they had both finished they headed off to a little bar that Sue knew. They had a few drinks and Deborah asked Sue if she was hungry because she was starving. They went for something to eat, had a few more drinks then headed back.

"See ya tomorrow" Sue shouted.

"Yeah see you in the morning"

They got on well. They both liked to party, both had the same sense of humour and they both worked hard.

Chapter 3

She had settled in really well. She'd made some new friends and was going out enjoying life, exactly as she should. In particular, Sue was fast becoming her best friend and they did many things together.

It was Sue who had seen *Decade* advertised on the billboard outside the club as she passed on her way to work and wondered if Deb wanted to go and see them. When Deb went down to the restaurant to give Sue some paperwork, she waved at her:

"Do you wanna go out tomorrow night?"

"Yeah… where are we going?"

"See *Decade*"

"Who are they?"

"They're a new rock band – I've heard they are awesome"

"Yeah… Why not? I've never heard of them though…Should we ask the girls if they wanna come too?"

"Sure thing…why not…?"

Kim and Tiff worked in the restaurant. Deb asked if they wanted to go too and they said 'Yes' so she got them all tickets on her lunchbreak.

After work they all got ready in Deb's room. Deb put on her jeans with her *Roma* T-shirt and let her hair down.

"You look fantastic – a proper rock chick...I dig the look of your eyes" Sue said, looking at them closer – then asked her if she would do the same for her.

The girls had a few drinks first and then took a cab to the club. They found a table and sat down. Deb went over to the bar where the band members were having a drink before they went on stage. Deb didn't realise that they were the band and smiled at two of them. They both smiled back at her and one of them, Simon as it turned out, said: "Helloooo baby."

Deborah laughed, "Hello baby – right back at ya."

Danny the singer gave an amused haha at Simon:

"She's sure got your number Si."

"Think she could be my kinda girl" Simon came back, smiling. "Can I get ya a drink, babe?"

"If you want to buy me a drink you have to buy them one." She said, pointing to her friends.

"But it's you I want to get in the sack" laughed Simon.

"Fucking hell, Si" Danny said.

Simon gave in and ordered drinks for Deb and her friends and sent them over to the table. Deb thought both men were cute – but the singer, Danny, more than the other.

Danny and Simon watched her as she went back to join her friends. Danny seemed to stare at her for ages. Sue saw that Danny couldn't take his eyes off her.

"Yeah, yeah – he's gorgeous."

But when she turned round to check him out again, he'd disappeared. Deb wondered where he'd gone. She was disappointed because she'd really quite fancied him. She was still wondering when the band came on to play. She looked over and realized she had been talking to the band members.

"Look." she shouted to the girls, "We've just had a drink off the band."

"Any good looking ones?" asked Tiff.

"Yeah but he's mine. So hands off girls."

At that, everyone seemed to surge to the front of the stage so Deb grabbed Sue and pulled her on down with her. Danny looked down and spotted her. He put his hand to his chest and sighed, giving her such a sexy look. Deb smiled right back at him. She decided he had the most beautiful smile she'd ever seen. It was pretty obvious that Danny was very taken with Deb. What she hadn't noticed was that so was Simon. Meanwhile, Sue was eyeing up the drummer.

The whole place was rocking. Women screaming in frenzy… they were reaching out at the band trying to get noticed.

As ever, they were a big hit with the young women but Danny wanted to get Deb's full attention after the gig. After they'd finished their set, Danny told Simon about the beautiful girl he'd been flirting with.

"I saw her. She was the one from the bar, one sexy young woman.
"I'm going to try my luck and give her the old Simon charm." He said, confidently.

Danny said, "Well buddy good luck with that – she hasn't had the full Danny charm yet."

Tony shouted, "Hey guys – we've got a Danny and Simon competition – they both dig the same chick."

Simon got to her first and asked her if she would like a drink.

Deborah smiled and said, "Yeah… thanks", while looking round for the singer. As Simon headed off to the bar, the young women just smiled to each other. Sue winked and left for the bar where Simon was.

Danny casually walked over and sat down.

"Hi there, I'm Danny," he said and gave her that sexy smile. That did the trick.

Simon reappeared with her drink.

"Hey Danny, this is Deborah from England"

Looking straight into Deb's eyes, Danny said, "I've already introduced myself.."

Simon sat down next to Deb and passed her the drink. He started asking all sorts of questions, all the time cracking jokes and playing the fool. He succeeded in making her laugh. Danny finished his drink and went to the bar. He returned with a drink for Deb and gave Simon a lemonade as a joke.

He was hoping that Simon would have to leave them alone while he got a proper drink for himself.

Danny turned to Deb:

"I hope I guessed right" He said, passing her the drink

"Yes you did. Thank you." She was impressed that he knew what she was drinking.

They were all talking at once when Sue came back over. She whispered in Deb's ear that they going on somewhere else and asked if she was coming as well.

Danny heard and turned to Sue,

"Hey, No – don't steal her away. I'll see she gets home safely."

Deb made up her mind and asked Sue if she minded if she stayed.

"No, but can I just mention the fact that you don't really know them. Are you sure?"

Deb looked at her, "I'm sure"

"OK.. but be careful – we'll catch up tomorrow."

Deb said she would and the gang left, leaving Deborah behind with just Danny and Simon.

Deb didn't normally take risks but she felt safe somehow. She liked them. They were funny and charming. When the rest of the band came over to say they were heading off to another club they asked if Danny and Simon were coming, Danny said,

"No, no, I'm fine where I am."

Deborah smiled and blushed at the same time.

"Excuse me" she said, "I've got to go to the bathroom."

"You're coming back, right?" asked Danny.

"Yes, of course," she replied.

When she'd left and headed for the rest room Simon said that he was going with the guys as it was plain to see who Deb was most interested in. When she came back, Simon said that he was splitting.

"It's been awesome meeting you" Then he left with the guys.

Danny offered Deb another drink and she smiled her thanks. She watched him walk over to the bar and back and thought this guy was *so sexy.*

"Now I want to know everything about you." Danny relaxed back in his chair.

"What exactly do you want to know?"

"Everything"

"Well my name is Deborah Carnell. I'm British, my parents are British. I work and live at the Royal Hotel here in the City and I'm 22 years old".

"So what do you do at the hotel?"

Deborah told him she was the manageress.

"Awesome," he said, then he hesitated, "have you got a boyfriend?"

"No I haven't," she said wondering where this was going

"Why not…?" he asked smiling, "You're a very sexy woman."

She blushed, " I haven't been here long."

"Do you want a boyfriend?" Danny asked, watching her carefully.

"If one comes along then maybe we'll see."

"Oh"

Now it was Deborah's turn to be curious.

"OK, so tell me about you, Danny."

"Well, I'm in a rock band as you know, trying to hit the big time. I've got two brothers. My name is Danny Brooks and I'm 22 years old." He hesitated, "I think you are beautiful and I think 1984 is going to be my lucky year."

Once again Deborah blushed.

"And why is 1984 going to be your lucky year?"

"I've met you, that's why."

"Does that mean it's my lucky year too?"

"Sure does," Danny said raising his eyebrows and smiling.

"You have the most beautiful smile I have ever seen on a man."

"Awesome. Is it sexy?" He said, curiously.

"Ohhh, Yeah" She said, looking downwards then straight into his eyes.

Danny was pleased. He really liked Deb and hoped that he could see her again – very unusual for him.

They talked and talked for hours. Finally, Deb noticed the time and said she had to go. Danny asked if he could see her again. She smiled and wrote her number on his cigarette packet and told him to call her.

Chapter 4

Next morning, Sue went to Debs office and knocked on the door before bouncing in.

"Hi Deb. I'm dying to know, did you have an awesome night?"

Deb simply smiled and nodded.

"Are you seeing him again?"

"Ohm…, I hope so – I gave him my number."

"Hmm" Sue mumbled.

Deb looked over at her friend. "And what does 'hmm' mean?"

"You like him a lot don't you?"

Now Deb was a little puzzled.

"How do you know which guy I was talking about?"

"It's obvious," Sue replied

"Oh no, not so obvious I might have put him off?"

"Hey, don't worry – he'll call."

"How do you know?"

"I'm sure. He couldn't take his eyes off you. He'll call."

Over in Brooklyn, Danny had gone in to work. The guys were eager to find out if he'd got laid and when they found out nothing had happened, Simon and Tony were astonished. Danny told them how much he liked this British chick and wanted to see her again. He had her number and was going to call her. He loved her accent.. she was so intelligent.. she was *so hot.*

Simon and Tony looked at each other in amazement. This had to be a first.

"Wow" said Simon and Tony at the same time.

"I dig her"

"Fucking hell, Dan"

"Why don't you fuck off and get some fuckin work done." He stuck his middle finger up.

Danny thought about Deb all that day and the next. He thought he'd better play it cool so he was going to wait a few days before calling her.

For her part, Deb thought her rock singer had forgotten her. Then, a few days later, the phone rang. It was him. She was so pleased but tried to play it cool.

It lasted until Danny asked if he could see her the next day.

"Yes" she said.

"Awesome. I'll pick you up at noon. See you then"

After hanging up Deborah jumped up with excitement, clapping her hands together. She giggled and danced around her office. If anyone had seen her they would have thought she was crazy. She was so pleased her heart was pounding. She was already planning what to wear – she needed to look really good but casual. She wanted his undivided attention.

On Friday, Danny was waiting at the staff entrance to pick her up – showing her the basket he was holding.

"Hope you haven't been waiting long? – So what's in the basket?"

"Not telling you. It's a surprise."

"OK then, where are we going?"

"Can't tell you that either – that's another surprise! You're looking very sexy" he said, looking at her shapely legs and her perfect bottom.

"What, in jeans and sweater?"

"Yeah, they show off that extremely sexy ass of yours." he said smiling.

"Oh so you've looked then?" she smiled back.

"Hell Yeah." he said with a cheeky grin.

They went to Central Park and got a rowboat. They had a lovely picnic on the lake by a bridge. They were surrounded by beautiful trees and the sun was shining through them – it was such a beautiful day. He impressed her with his knowledge about the park and impressed her even more when he told her about the Bethesda fountain sculpture, *Angel of the Water*. She was thoroughly enjoying herself and didn't want the day to end.

When they came off the lake they went for a walk. He took her hand and they strolled hand in hand through the park. Danny made her day so sweet. He made her laugh, he was the perfect gentleman and she thought he was so gorgeous. She couldn't believe this man was interested her.

When he took her back home she thanked him for a lovely day.

"Pleasure was all mine."

He asked her if she would like to see him that night as he had a gig and suggested that they could do something after. She said she would love to.

"Awesome I'll pick you at 6. 30. See you then."

Right on time, Deb went down to meet Danny. She had put on her black jeans and a pink glittery top and piled her hair on top of her head. He was there waiting.

"Hi there. You're looking mighty sexy."

"Thank you… that's twice today you've called me sexy."

They headed to the club where she met the rest of the band: Tony, the drummer, Dave who played keyboards and Alan, the other guitarist. Simon she already knew. They sat and had a drink before they went on stage.

Deb was allowed backstage to watch. They were great. All through, women were screaming and shouting at them, trying to grab them. They had quite a fan club now. They finished the gig and she had really enjoyed it.

"You were fantastic."

"I like this chic. She has taste." Tony laughed.

"Sure she has, she's with me." Danny said, smiling his sexy smile just for her. Deb shook her head and laughed. Danny asked if she wanted to go or stay.

"Hey guys – you got to stay for a drink." Said Alan

"Stay for a drink it is then" Deborah said willingly.

"OK…I'll go to the bar." Danny smiled at Deborah touching her cheek gently. "Look after this beauty for me"

Just then Simon appeared and sat down.

"Hey there pretty lady. It's sure nice to see you again."

"Hi… Simon."

"Has anyone ever told you how beautiful you are?" Simon asked confidently?

"Well, now you have."

Tony butted in, "Here he goes. Mr. Charm himself."

Danny came back with the drinks and said, "OK, what are we talking about?"

Dave said, "Well Mr. Charm is at it again"

Danny turned to Deborah and said,"Simon is the charmer of the group – He changes girlfriends like underwear."

"Come on guys… you are making me sound bad in front of this beautiful young woman."

Deborah just laughed and said, "I bet you're a big softy really"

"Oh Deb, don't encourage him." Tony said, shaking his head.

"Hey, the lady knows what she's talking about."

"Deb look what you've gone and done.," Alan laughed and winked at her.

They spent the whole night with the guys and on the way home Danny apologised for not getting away.

"That's OK. I like your friends, they're great and it was fun. I really enjoyed myself."

"Are you sure you didn't mind?"

He smiled, brushed her hair out of her face and leant over to kiss her gently on the lips.

"Can I see you tomorrow?" he asked.

"Yes, I would like that."

Chapter 5

Over the weeks, Danny and Deb saw more and more of each other. He was falling for her in a big way and the feeling appeared mutual. They were getting closer and closer but still Danny had not made a move on her, even though he was obviously getting horny.

Danny was puzzled. He didn't do relationships, one-night stands were his thing. He wasn't interested in marriage or living with anyone. All he had ever wanted was to be a rock star, have lots of chicks and lots of money. But Deborah had changed all that. He just wanted to be with her. He could see himself spending the rest of his life with this young woman.

The time arrived when Alex told Danny and the guys he had set up gigs in Boston, Baltimore, Ottawa, Cleveland and Newark – they would be away for a good few weeks. They would be performing in stadiums and parks with *Roma*, *Vintage Warrior* and several up-and-coming bands.

As the lights went on in the stadium and music started to blast out, the crowds went crazy, screaming at the bands. When Roma came on all you could hear was the crowd chanting Nick's name: " Nick… Nick… We Love you, Nick.."

Simon couldn't wait until it was *his* name the crowds were chanting.

Dan told Deb he would call her while he was away and he did, every night.

The guys had a great time with different women every night but he just wasn't interested. He would party but he left the women alone. The guys asked what was wrong – there were horny young women everywhere. Alan asked him if he was sick or something.

Tony looked at Danny, "You've got it bad, Dan"

"Tony, she's awesome… I like her."

"*Like* her? I think it's a bit more than like Dan."

Deb was spending her evenings with Sue while Danny was away. They went to the health club in the hotel. She wanted to keep trim and fit. She also rang her mum and dad to tell them all about Danny. They told her how pleased they were and how much they would love to meet him when they came over.

The night before Danny came back he called her. He told her he was missing her like crazy and couldn't wait to see her. She told him she had missed him too and was so excited he would soon be home. He said he would pick her up at Eight the next evening.

When she finished work the next day she rushed to get ready. She had picked out a burgundy silk dress with a split up the front revealing her gorgeous shapely legs, she planned to knock Danny for six. She plaited half of her hair up and wrapped it round into a bun on top of her head. She left the other half down.

As soon as she was ready she went down to meet Danny. He was there sat casually on the wall and he had dressed up for her. He had put on his black trousers and a white shirt – usually it was just jeans and t-shirt. He looked very handsome and she was flattered he'd made the effort.

He jumped off the wall, stubbed his cigarette out with his foot, took her in his arms and kissed her.

"You look so beautiful," he told her.

"You look sexy." she smiled.

"Well you have made me feel much better. I didn't think this looked right – tell the truth, I thought I looked a bit of a prick" he laughed.

"No you don't," and she kissed him gently.

They had dinner in a cosy little restaurant in Little Italy. Inside it looked like it had a fishing net draped from the ceiling with trails of ivy hanging from it.

The atmosphere was romantic, with candles on each table and a beautiful aroma of tuberose – a sweet smell of almond – a very exotic, sexy and rich fragrance. Danny reached across the table and took hold of her hand and he just gazed at her. Quizzically she asked him what he was looking at.

"You… You're so beautiful"

"Thank you"

"I just love being with you"

Deb smiled at him her eyes shining, "I'm glad… I love being with you too."

They left the restaurant and strolled through the park, hand in hand. Danny stopped and pulled Deborah towards him. He kissed her. Her heart started racing as his lips kissed her softly.

"I've got something for you…"

He handed her a box, there was a necklace inside that was engraved with 'MY HEART IS YOURS. '

"Oh, it's so beautiful Danny",

She asked him to put it on for her. She turned round and lifted her hair so he could put it round her neck. He wrapped his arms around her waist and whispered,

"I've really missed you…"

"I've really missed you too, Danny. "

She turned round to face him, gently tracing his lips with her fingertips, smiling up at him all the time. Danny pulled Deb close to him and kissed her slowly. She could feel her legs turn to jelly.

"Oh man… come on… I'll take you home before I get carried away, and not want to let you go."

Deborah didn't want him to let her go.

There was nothing Danny wanted more than to take her home and make love to her. He wanted to feel her body next his and wake up to her in the morning.

He took her back to the hotel, pulled her close and gave her a slow smouldering kiss.

"Good night" he whispered softly.

That kiss told her he wanted her. She wanted him too.

The next day at work Deborah went into the restaurant with some menus. She showed them to Sue who couldn't wait to ask about her date with Danny.

"He gave me this. Isn't it beautiful," she said, showing her the necklace.

"That is so nice."

"Yeah," she paused then she whispered, "The most he's done is kissed me."

"He's a nice guy. There are not many guys like that these days." Sue said.

"No. You're right there, there aren't many guys like Danny."

"I bet he's romantic," Sue said with a dreamy look on her face. "I Wish I could meet someone like that," she said.

Danny had finished his shift and was heading for rehearsals with the guys when Tony asked him if he'd seen Deb.

"Yeah"

"She must be quite a lady in the bedroom." Tony said grinning.

"I don't know I haven't tried yet. I like her Tony, I like her a lot. I don't want to mess up, so I am waiting."

"You sound like you're in love, Dan."

"I think I am Tony. I've never felt like this about any other girl before. I'm crazy about her."

"I'm happy for you, Dan."

"Thanks man. I'm thinking about asking her to go away for a few days, or do you think it's too soon? Like I said, I don't want to mess this up."

"No pressure on her."

"Yeah that's good – I've just got to get the nerve to ask." Danny said looking a bit apprehensive.

"Just ask, Dan."

"OK – I'll ask."

A few days later Danny and Deb had the same day off so they went in to the village for a burger. They sat talking, until Danny coughed slightly.

"I've got something I wanna ask you. I've been thinking…"

"That's brave Danny"

"Ha, Ha Deborah" then he paused, "Right, here goes. You can say no, but do you wanna go away for a few days, what do you think?"

Deborah looked at him, "Yeah" she said.

"Wow you said Yeah" he said, sounding very surprised.

"Why wouldn't I? Where are we going and when?" she asked.

"What about going to the Rockies?."

"OK. The Rockies sounds great."

"Great"

"Oh I can't wait."

"Really...? I thought you would say No."

"Why?" she asked as her eyes levelled up with his.

"I don't know really. Too early I guess?"

"No it's the right time."

Danny was excited about the weekend away. He couldn't wait. He just hoped he could live up to expectations. Whatever they were. Deb told Sue about the weekend. She told her she was nervous, she had only ever been with one man. Sue reassured her and told her it would be great, that Danny was a nice guy – she was sure he would be awesome in the bedroom too.

Deborah couldn't wait. She was so excited and she was driving Sue crazy. But she wasn't the only one driving everyone crazy. Danny was driving the guys mad too.

"When you going?" Tony asked.

"Why?"

"Well..., soon I hope, you're driving us fucking crazy." Tony laughed.

"Fuck off, Tony."

"Go get laid. You obviously need to get laid."

"You will tell Deborah to be gentle with you." Alan said sniggering.

Danny laughed.

"You really dig this chick don't you?" Simon butted in.

"Yeah Si"

The time passed quickly. Danny went to pick Deborah up and they set off as they had quite a long drive. Sue came down and waved them off.

"Have a great time"

They had booked an authentic cabin. When they arrived, they put their bags inside and had a look round. There was a big bed made of oak and a big log fire. It looked very cosy. They went down to the creek for a while and had a snowball fight. Danny chased Deb around and grabbed her.

He pulled her down in the snow and fell on top of her. He looked deep into her eyes and kissed her longingly. Tony was right, he was in love with this beautiful woman.

He took her for something to eat at the restaurant on the other side of the lake. They had a great view of the mountains – they looked beautiful with the white snow glistening on them. They had a beautiful view of the lakes and the trees surrounding the cabin. This was just perfect – this was the right time.

They strolled back to the cabin hand in hand. Danny opened the door and said,"After you." Deb went in, grabbing Danny's hand to pull him after her.

Danny lit a fire while Deb opened the wine. He turned the lights off so there was just the fire blazing and the logs crackling. It was so warm and cosy. They sat in front of the fire, talking and drinking wine and he made her laugh by telling her corny jokes. He kissed her, telling her how beautiful she was.

He put his drink down and removed the glass from her hand. He kissed her passionately pulling her close, he made everything perfect. Kissing her gently he ran his fingertips down her neck and over her breasts. Sensually,he caressed the curves of her body, removing her clothing slowly.

He reached the 'v' of her thighs. She allowed him to push himself between them and he made love to her beautifully. He didn't rush as he caressed her body. She could feel his lips kissing her gently as his hands created a fantastic excitement in her. She had never felt like this before. They lay limply across each other, breathless, looking into the fire. He stood up, took hold of her hand and led her to the bedroom. He kissed her and caressed her body then he made love to her once again.

They lay in bed cuddling each other, murmuring gently before they fell asleep in each other's arms.

The next morning Deb woke, made some coffee and lit a cigarette. Danny was still asleep. She looked at him, realising she was in love.

Danny opened his sleepy eyes stretched and reached for her.

"Morning sleepyhead, want some coffee?" she asked.

He took the cigarette from her, inhaling a long drag, blowing the smoke into the air. He smiled lustfully into her eyes.

"Yeah, but I want you first."

He grabbed her hand, pulled her back into bed moving his hand up her thighs. Her body surged.

He hovered over her, bending his head to kiss her, moving his body between her thighs. Making love to her once again, he made her feel so special.

They lay in each other's arms, smiling at each other.

"Can I ask you something?" Deborah asked.

"Sure"

"Why did you wait so long?" she asked curiously

"Because I..." he paused for a moment."I wanted our first time to be special."

"Was it?"

"Yes, yes it was" he paused a second time."Very special... I'm in love with you... I've never felt like this about any woman."

She was so giddy she blurted out, "I love you too"

He leaned over to her and kissed her.

They finally got up, packed up their stuff before going down to the trout stream where they watched the trout swimming in the river.

They went horse riding for a while before they went for some lunch, then set off back home. Danny dropped Deb outside the hotel. They were like two lovesick puppies as they stood kissing and staring into each other's eyes. Danny wrapped his fingers around a strand of her hair that had fallen, not wanting to let go.

When they eventually pulled apart, they arranged to see each other the day after, as they needed an early night. They both had work the next day.

Chapter 6

Next day, Danny met up with the guys after work. All he did was talk about Deb and how lovely, how beautiful she was. Simon interrupted him.

"We've got a gig in Washington DC."

"Awesome. When…?" Danny asked.

"Next week," Simon said moodily.

Simon felt jealous when Danny mentioned Deb for the very simple reason that he had fallen for her as well – but he didn't know why. Yeah she was sexy but Danny had been out with some pretty hot girls in his time and he'd never found himself wanting them, so why her? It wasn't as if he found girls difficult to get so he couldn't understand why he felt like this about her.

Deb went on her lunchbreak and met up with Sue, who wanted to know all about the weekend.

"Did you have good time?" she asked.

"The best time ever. I'm in love. Now all we need is to get you a man!"

"That weekend certainly worked for you." Sue said, smiling.

They had their lunch and chatted some more then went back to work. After work Deborah rushed to get ready. Danny was taking her to a party.

He got there early so Sue took him up to Debs room.

"Danny's here," she shouted.

Sue waved,"See ya later I've got a date"

"Oh ...why do I not know about this?"

"We'll ... catch up tomorrow"

Danny walked in and instantly took Deb in his arms, kissing her longingly.

"Let's not go to this party." He murmured suggestively.

He started to open her dressing gown, brushing her nipples with his fingertips, his lips caressing hers... he laid her down onto the sofa, his erection pressing hard against her. He opened her dressing gown wider, pressing his body down on hers. He moved his hands tenderly up and down her body.

She moaned and pulled his T-shirt over his head, moving her hands down his back and round to the front of his jeans. Unzipping them he peeled himself out of them. He bent his head, kissing her passionately. He pressed against her as she braced her hands on the back of the sofa he slid down between her thighs.

As they made love she arched her back and moaned softly, their bodies trapped in rhythm. She felt a burning sensation in the pit of her stomach like electricity shooting through her as she felt his body spasm as they orgasmed together. They lay on the sofa breathlessly, looking at each other.

Danny was still caressing her body as he told her he wanted them to move in together. Deborah was over the moon she jumped up said 'Yes.' straight away. She told him she would start looking straight away.

"Come on, we'd better get to this party," she said.

"Do we have to?"

"Yeah."

"Why...?"

"The guys are expecting you."

"Oh well, I'd like it better if I were all cosy in bed with you."

As Danny got up Deb slapped his butt with the back of her hand.

"Ahhhhh. Your gonna pay for that."

"Really...? Come on then Danny Brooks, show me what you got."

"Oh right you wanna play." he said cockily and proceeded to grab her.

They fell on the sofa and he began to tickle her. She laughed so much. She couldn't speak.

"Come on, let's get ready." she choked out when Danny finally let go.

They got dressed and went to the party, obviously later than planned. Simon spotted them and came over.

"You're late"

Danny and Deb just looked at each other and smiled.

"Let's get a drink, come on Deb," he said, getting hold of her hand.

They started talking to Tony. Danny and Tony got into a discussion about songs so Simon asked Deborah to dance. She told Danny she was going to dance with Simon. It was a slow song so Simon wrapped his arms around her.

He could smell her perfume. It was light and feminine, she smelt good. How good she felt. It took him all his time not to kiss her as he was so close to her. It wasn't just Danny who had Deb on his mind.

"Danny is so lucky having you."

"Oh… Simon thank you."

"I think you are so beautiful, I…"

He stopped suddenly as Danny came over and stepped in, taking over. Simon stood back and watched.

"What do you think you're doing?" Tony asked.

"Nothing." Simon snapped.

"I know you Si. You need to snap out of it – this is the real thing for Dan."

Simon turned to Tony and said,"I don't know what you're talking about."

"Si, I know."

"You know Fuck All… , now can we talk about something else?" he snapped moodily.

Just then a young attractive young woman came over to Simon. He looked over at Deborah and Danny. They only had eyes for each other.

Simon was a good-looking young man. He had a beautifully toned and tanned body. He didn't have trouble getting women. He just couldn't understand why he felt like he did.

'Oh just go for it Si.' he thought and turned on the charm.

The young woman was putty in his hands. She had been watching him from across the room and his long dark hair and brown eyes had attracted her. This was only going to end in one place, and he charmed her straight into bed.

Deb and Danny decided to split. They told the guys they were off and went back to Deb's. Danny stayed the night and left early for work in the morning.

Chapter 7

THE BAND LEFT for Washington for the gig. Deborah rang her parents and told them she and Danny were moving in with each other. They were so pleased for her and said they would love to come over and meet Danny.

"You will love him as much as I do when you meet him."

"You sound very much in love." her mum said.

"I am mum. He has the most beautiful smile and you will love him"

"He sounds lovely, Deb."

"He is. How is my Nan? Tell her I love her and that I miss her."

"I will Deb. We will see you soon."

"Yeah see you soon. Oh mum, you'll meet Sue as well."

"We can't wait to see you and meet everyone. See you soon… your dad says hello."

"Tell dad hi. Sue is going apartment hunting with me now so see ya. Love you all."

As soon as Sue arrived they went looking for apartments. They went round so many apartments they got tired of looking. Then Deb saw a promising one advertised in the paper and dragged Sue with her.

"It's perfect… The rent's right, the location's right, everything is right." Deb cried excitedly.

It was nothing special, just a first floor apartment with a lounge, a kitchenette, a bedroom and a bathroom.

"Yes it is nice. Sue said, exhausted,"Please say you like this one."

"Yes I do, Sue." Deb laughed.

Sue was so relieved, she thought they could have been doing this for days, weeks, even months.

"I love you to bits, Deborah – but we have seen so many apartments I thought I might stop loving you."

"Did you not enjoy looking with me?" Deb said smirking at her.

"Oh yeah…I loved going here there and everywhere, covering New York."

"Come on Sue, let's go and get us some lunch."

"Oh my God … LUNCH."

Deb put the deposit down on the apartment and took Sue for lunch. When Danny got back she took him to see it.

"When can we move in?" Danny asked.

"Any time – we just need to get the keys."

He took hold of her and kissed her.

"Can we get them now?"

"Yeah I think so"

"Good – we move in this weekend."

They moved a truckload of stuff into their apartment that weekend. He let Deb sort out where everything was going seeing as how she kept telling him where to put things.

Danny thought it was time for Deb to meet his parents. Danny's parents loved Deb and thought she was perfect for Danny. They could see how much their son loved her. For her part, Deb thought his parents were lovely, she really liked them. She met his brothers, John and Michael, as well. They told her that they have never seen him like this with any girl before and asked her what she had done with their brother.

Deb rang her mum and dad. They told her they were planning to come over in a couple of weeks, so Danny arranged for his parents to meet hers as he planned to ask Deborah to marry him.

The two weeks flew by and Deb's parents arrived. They were so pleased to see her and they finally got to meet Danny. He wasn't at all what they expected. They thought he would be something like David. Deb's dad looked him up and down and noticed he had his ear pierced. Kath thought he looked gorgeous in his ripped jeans and t-shirt.

They liked him and they could see how happy he made their daughter. They could see that they were madly in love so they were happy. They knew their daughter was in safe hands.

Danny had arranged a meal for them to meet his parents. He had booked a table at the restaurant for 7 O. clock so Rob and Kath went to their hotel to change. Danny made sure he was dressed smartly as well.

They all met at the restaurant. Danny introduced his parents, and his brothers to Rob and Kath. They had a lovely evening as the evening was drawing to a close, Danny went pay to the bill. Rob followed him.

"No, let me." He said."We don't see Deborah much, so let me pay."

"No sir... I can't do that"

"Yes, you can I insist," Rob said firmly.

Danny thanked him then asked if he minded if he asked Deb to marry him.

"Haven't you asked her yet?" Rob asked, nearly choking.

"No, not yet I wanted to ask you first." Danny said.

"That's very respectful. Welcome to the family, Danny."

"Is that an OK then?"

"Yeah it is, when are you going to ask her?"

"Now … if that's alright with you sir…?"

"OK, let's order some coffee and some champagne."

"Champagne?" Danny asked curiously.

"Coffee for now… champagne for when Deb says yes."

"If she says yeah."

"Oh, she'll say Yes, Danny"

They got back to the table as the coffee came.

"There's something I want to ask Deb while I have got us all together," Danny said as he got down on one knee and took a deep breath.

"Will you marry me?"

Deb looked at him lovingly.

"Yes…Yes… Yes … she said, kissing him.

He pulled a box out of his pocket and placed the beautiful solitaire ring on her finger. He had been putting money away secretly.

The waiter brought the champagne over right on cue.

"We need more champagne, we sure have got a lot of celebrating to do."
Pete said as he kissed Deb on the cheek.

They celebrated for the rest of the evening.

Rob, Kath, Pete and Marie got on so well they met the evening after for dinner. Danny and Deb were so relieved. Before her parents went back home, Danny and Deb decided to have a party. Everyone came, the guys from the band and Sue and her boyfriend. Deb introduced Sue to her mum and dad. They loved Sue and told Deb they were adopting her. Sue said she would happily let them.

Rob asked Danny if they had set a date for the wedding.

"Yes we want to get married 22nd of April, next year."

"Gives me time to save then" Rob said laughing.

Simon, however, was devastated. He just could not shake these feelings he had they were getting worse if anything. He couldn't understand why he still felt this way about her. He knew how much Danny loved her and he was happy for them. But he just couldn't keep his mind off her.

The next morning everyone had bad heads but they'd had a good night. It was time for Rob and Kath to go home. Deb and Danny took them to the airport to see them off.

"See you soon," her dad said, kissing her good-bye."Look after my daughter, Dan."

Danny said, "You can be sure of that."

Kath gave her daughter a kiss and then Danny.

Tearfully she said,"See you soon."

Danny and Deborah went home and after they made dinner they chilled out in front of the TV and talked about the wedding. They made up a guest list and discussed where they wanted to have it.

After the party, they were exhausted. They got into bed and cuddled up to each other and soon fell asleep

Two days after her mum and dad got home Deborah got a phone call from her dad with some bad news. Deb's grandmother, her Nan, had died. She was devastated but told her dad she would get a flight back home as soon as she could. Danny got home and she told him about her grandmother and said she had to go home.

Danny immediately said,"I'll come with you."

They got a flight straight away. It seemed to take forever. When they arrived in England, Rob was there waiting for them. He took them home, where Kath had made them something to eat and drink. They talked for a little while before Danny and Deb went to bed. They were so tired and as soon as their heads hit the pillow they were asleep. The next morning Deborah went to the chapel of rest to see her nan and kiss her good-bye.

After the funeral Deborah and Danny had to go back home to the States for work. Deb's dad gave Danny a cheque to cover the flights.

"It's OK, Rob."

"No take it. You can't afford all that money"

"Rob, its fine… really"

"We are going to give you some money for the wedding as well"

"Thank you Rob but you really don't need to. All we want is you there." Danny said.

"We'll be there. I've got to give my daughter away."

"And you will"

"Danny take the money – and before you head off back I will make sure you have another cheque for the wedding"

"Thank you Rob. Thank you so very much,"

Danny and Deborah had an early night that night ready for their journey back.

They set off back on their journey to the states. Another 6 hours and, again, by the time they got home they were exhausted. They had a coffee and fell into bed. They both had work in the morning and when they got up they were still so tired. They had breakfast and set off to work. At lunch Danny met up with the guys and Deb met with Sue.

"Are you OK?" She asked Deborah.

"I loved my nan so much." Deborah told her."I will miss her."

Chapter 8

When Deb got home Danny was already there and had made dinner. He was really impressed with himself. He'd made salad and Macaroni cheese.

"Oh Danny thanks for dinner – I've had such a shitty day." she said as she flopped on the sofa, kicking her shoes off.

Danny sat down next to her, reached for her feet and started rubbing them.

"Ohm that's nice …" she sighed, relaxing heavily, "Ohhhh Danny, that's fantastic keep doing what you're your doin baby… hmm, thank you"

"I want to bring the wedding forward."

"Why?" she asked.

"I want to"

"But the band has just got noticed."

"Yeah, but I'm not marrying the band."

Deb mentioned the fact that the girls would go crazy over them and if he was married it might have an effect on the band.

"What girls? I don't care about girls."

"Oh, I know what I mean."

"I'm glad you do." he said looking very puzzled." I love you. I just want you to become Mrs Brooks."

"I love you too Danny, but I know what the band means to you" she said, touching his lips and kissing them.

Danny smiled at her and said, "I don't care quite as much now."

"Oh Danny, I know you want this, you've worked so hard for this – and the women are gonna go crazy over that smile of yours. You could win any heart with that smile."

"I don't want any heart. Just yours baby."

"You've got mine".

"Well in that case Mrs. Brooks to be, take me to bed, rip my clothes off and make love to me. After all I did make dinner."

"Oh Danny, I love the sound of that"

"What?."

"Mrs. Brooks"

"Good"

"Come on sexy let's get those clothes off."

"Now you're talking, babe" he gave a cheeky laugh.

They went to the bedroom and she pushed him down on to the bed ripping his shirt open. She kissed him hard biting his bottom lip. Removing her clothes she moved her hands seductively over her breasts and down her body. She was driving him crazy.

"Oh Deb" he sighed, as she pulled down the zip on his jeans.

She moved her hands in to his jeans, "Hold on to your seat, baby – it's going to be a bumpy ride"

Danny's face began to beam like a lantern, "Ohh… baby… yeah… that's good… that's making me so horny…"as she moved her hands over his manhood back and forth inside his jeans.

He tossed his clothes aside until they were both naked. She gradually moved her mouth down his body. Her lips were on his skin. She looked so sexy looking up at him. He just wanted her. His hands reached out to grab her. He pulled her closer, sliding his hands slowly down her skin to send ripples through her entire body. His hands moved from the nape of her neck to her breasts. He caressed them gently, moving from a deep intimacy into hot carnal lust.

Excitement ran through her body. She arched her back and gave a long-drawn-out groan. He was so hard, she turned him on so much. She eased herself on top of him, grazing her lips over his, teasing him more and more. She gripped his lip with her teeth, staring into his eyes making him want more. They were hot and sweaty. He crushed her breasts into his chest, moving together in rhythm as they made love. They made love for some time. He gripped her legs as they moved together, moaning and groaning as they reached their orgasms. They fell asleep with their legs entwined round each other.

Next morning she woke first. Looking at him lying there, all the lust she had felt the night before re-surfaced. Running her tongue over her lips, she slid her head under the sheets. Slowly she moved her mouth down his stomach, over his manhood, reawakening him. He awoke excited. He was so hard he thought he would explode. Turning her over with some urgency, he gripped her thighs. Swiftly he entered her from behind and they had hot, passionate sex until they came together once more.

"You can wake me up like that every morning if you want to."

"Oh really…? You liked that did you?"

"Oh yeah …. You may take it upon yourself to do that any time you want."

"Come on stud, let's get breakfast."

They had breakfast and went to work. Deb had a busy day ahead with a really important guest arriving at the hotel, only the film star Michael Lee. He was shooting a scene at the hotel. She had to make sure everything was just perfect. She and Sue went through the menus with the chef. They were both going to be there late. She called Danny to let him know.

"OK, babe – see you later."

They were both so excited, they were going to get the chance to meet Michael Lee. Deb wished it had been Brad Cannon. She was still excited though.

Danny had rehearsals after work so he met up with the guys. They went over some new songs that Danny and Simon had written and wanted to hear what they sounded like after Tony, Dave and Alan had put the music to them.

"Sounds great."

"Dan, let's take that one again."

They went over the songs again…again… and again.

Danny had had enough for one day.

He told the guys to wrap it up.

"I'm beat" he said wearily, stretching his arms up before moving his fingers through his hair, pushing it back.

Danny took the guys and their girlfriends to their apartment and they ordered take out. Simon came on his own and Deb brought Sue back with her.

"Hi baby" Danny said, taking hold of Deb and kissing her.

"Pizza girls?" Tony asked, looking at Sue who nodded and smiled.

Simon spent most of the evening with Deb. Danny noticed and became very jealous. He did not like the way Simon was looking at her, he knew that look. When Deb started laughing at Simon's jokes that just made Danny worse. She seemed to be enjoying his company a little too much. Simon was definitely flirting with her and Danny did not like it, not one little bit.

By the time everyone had left, Danny was in a foul mood and couldn't stop himself mentioning that Simon had spent virtually all night with her. Deb pointed out that he was on his own.

"And your problem is what, Danny?"

"Oh I know he was on his own but why is he always round you? He's got a thing about you."

"No, he hasn't"

He pointed at her and shouted angrily, "You encourage him."

"I beg your pardon, what the hell is that supposed to mean?" she shouted back.

"You know what I mean."

"Are you accusing me of something?"

"Yeah…I am." He said matter of factly.

"Oh I see …" she shouted outraged by his accusation."How dare you" she yelled prodding him in the chest with her index finger. He stumbled as she pushed him back.

"How dare you." She repeated, slapping him across the face so hard she left a red mark on his cheek.

"Fuck you Danny." She shouted, charging across the room to the bedroom slamming the door behind her.

Danny hit the table with his fist.

"Shit. Shit. You handled that well, Danny boy." He said out loud.

He went over to the bedroom door and knocked gently.

"I'm so sorry" he whispered, "Deb…?"

"Go away Danny – I don't want to talk to you."

"Deb … I'm sorry."

They had never argued like that before and Danny slept on the sofa. He felt stupid because he knew she wouldn't do anything like that and it was pure jealousy that got the better of him.

The next morning Deb got up and got ready for work. Danny was sat at the kitchen table.

"Coffee, baby?" he said, sheepishly

"Just don't fucking talk to me…"

"Deb…" he grovelled.

"I don't want to talk to you Danny"

"I'm sorry, I really am sorry."

"How could you think such a thing?" she asked.

"I was so wrong I'm so sorry. Please don't stay angry with me"

Deb looked at him and he smiled at her.

"Don't think you can get round me with that smile."

"Sorry. I really am".

She leaned over to him and kissed him.

"Am I forgiven?"

"Yeah, you're forgiven" she said smiling.

Danny dropped Deb off on the way to the studio. When he got there, Simon and the guys were already there. Simon was very quiet. He couldn't get Deb out of his head. If anything it was getting worse. He didn't know what was wrong. It was driving him crazy and he didn't know what to do. He knew he couldn't have her but he just couldn't shake this feeling off. It hadn't helped being with her last night. Danny noticed how quiet Simon was and asked him if he was OK.

"Yeah I'm great bud, why?"

Danny mentioned that he was so quiet.

"Oh got some stuff to sort out that's all"

"Do ya need some help?

"No buddy, I'm good"

"Sure?"

"Yeah sure, and thanks"

They went back to their rehearsals, Tony was thrashing out the beat to *'Dream of me'* on the drums and Alan was hammering out the bass. Simon grabbed his guitar and started to play. Danny shouted out they needed to go over *'On a rainy night'* and *'Rock me'*. Dave started with *'Rock me'*, mixing the synthesizer in, giving it a whole different sound.

"Try this beat" Danny said, playing the first chords and belting out the lyrics.

"Oh man. Feel that riff" as Simon played.

"Dan man, you nailed it" Alan said, beating the rhythm out on his guitar.

"Yeah… That's fucking awesome." Danny said, impressed with the way the song had turned out.

They had always planned to do as many of their own songs as they could. They all knew the songs were coming together nicely. *'Rock me'* was going to be a major hit. It was a good hard rock and metal fans would love it.

Christmas 1985

Deb's parents were coming over for Christmas so Danny and Deb decided to have a party. Danny's mom and dad came round as well, along with his brothers. Sue came with her date and the guys from the band and their girlfriends. Even Simon brought a girl.

Tony kept looking over at Sue even though he was with someone else. He couldn't seem to keep his eyes off her. Deb noticed him staring and made her way over to him. She asked him if he liked Sue.

"Why?" he asked.

"You keep looking at her…"

"Do I?"

"Yeah you do."

"Oh, I didn't realise."

He did like Sue but wasn't sure if she liked him so he'd decided to leave it alone.

The guys had a surprise for Danny. Their record *'Big City'* was racing up the charts fast. Tony told Danny that they had been lots of airplay. It was selling like crazy and they had hit the top 10.

It had gone in at No 9 and was still expected to go on climbing higher. They might just make number 1. *Rock Down Records* wanted to sign them. They were going on tour in the New Year but now they would be the Headline Act – no longer the support band. A national music paper had made a big splash about them, giving them a big centre page spread.

"Will you look at this?"

The guys showed Danny the paper and there it was – a big poster of them.

'THIS IS THE HOTTEST NEW ROCK BAND'

"THIS BAND IS GOING TO BE BIG'

'THEY ARE *SEXY BAD BOYS*.'

"When were you told?" Danny asked excitedly.

"Alex called you tonight – He tried to get you but you didn't pick up"

"That's great." Deb clapped her hands together, so excited for them.

Danny took hold of her and swung her round.

"I love you Deb. Our future is mapped out, we're on our way baby." he said with a big smile on his face.

"Oh Danny I'm so pleased for you. Well I'm pleased for all of you. You've all worked so hard for this."

They celebrated till the early hours. It was an amazing feeling and they got drunk on the excitement and the alcohol.

Because they had taken off in such a big way Deb suggested that they put the wedding back a couple of months.

"No Deb...no way."

"I just think it would be better for the band." She explained.

"Why?"

"– only till July."

"No...I really don't want to."

"Danny...You're going to be touring and other stuff."

"Yeah...but we can still get married."

"You are going to be busy with all that."

Sue came over and asked what was wrong as she'd seen Danny's face drop.

"She wants to put the wedding back"

Sue looked at Deb and asked why so Deb told her.

"Oh…Look at his little face." Sue teased.

"Yeah…Look at my little face." Danny said smiling at Deb. She shook her head and laughed.

"Poor baby."

"I'm not happy with this" replied Danny, "but I'm OK if it's only a couple of months"

"Yeah…July" Deb responded.

"That's three months."

"Yep, you surely do know your months" she laughed

Danny smirked and agreed on July he wasn't happy but he went along with it

They told Rob, Kath Pete and Marie that they were putting the wedding back to July. They asked why, so they explained together.

With the band taking off in the way they had it was going to be impossible to fit the wedding round the touring and all the promotion. Danny was quick to point out that it was Deb's idea. Rob and Pete could understand why it would be so difficult.

Kath and Marie were disappointed but went along with it. Danny told Deb that she had some making up to do.

"What do you want me to do to make it up?" she asked.

"Well…Let's see…First you can kiss me." he grinned.

Deb kissed him.

"Hmm…I haven't finished yet." He said, waving his finger at her as he pulled her close and whispered in her ear.

"You can take me to bed and make hot passionate love to me – I want you to be a bad girl."

"What *now?*" She asked incredulously.

"No…Later…But you can kiss me again now." And he pulled her closer and kissed her.

"I love you"

Deb smiled affectionately and whispered "I love you too, Danny Brooks."

They smiled at each other and Danny ran his fingers though her hair.

"You are so beautiful." he murmured huskily.

The band had taken off in a really big way. The tour was scheduled for six months. They had bought new equipment ready for the tour. There was so much stuff to take and so many people going on tour with them – tour manager, production manager, sound crew, lighting crew and back line crew. Alex had had T-shirts and sweatshirts printed, with Tour Mags and key rings. You name it, *'Decade'* was all over it.

Deb and Danny missed each other desperately – but at least Simon thought he had finally got over his feelings for Deb.

While the band were away, Deb spent time with Sue or worked late. Kath flew over to help Deb pick her wedding dress. Deb, Kath and Sue were going to make a day of it. Deb asked Marie to go as well, she wanted as many opinions as she could get.

When they got to the boutique she tried a number of wedding dresses on until she found the perfect one – a white lace, figure-hugging bodice, dipped and buttoned at the back and feathering out at the bottom. Kath filled up with tears.

"You are so beautiful Deborah"

Marie and Sue both agreed and it was settled. That was the dress Deb ordered and she ordered her veil and shoes. She was so excited. She suggested they went for lunch, her treat. While Kath, Sue and Marie ordered, she gazed at her engagement ring. 'Mrs. Brooks…, Mrs. Deborah Brooks …' she said dreamily. Kath, Sue and Marie just smiled at one another.

When Danny and the band came home, they took some time off before going back to the studio to make their album. He and Deb spent time on their wedding plans as it wasn't far away, only a few weeks before July 22nd and they still had lots to organise. Preparations were going great and they were both really happy and excited.

Things were about to go terribly wrong.

One evening Simon came round looking for Danny. Deborah opened the door and Simon just stood there, staring at her.

"Si, Hello…Earth to Si, come in Si."

"Hi Deb, sorry I was zoned out just then. I'm looking for Dan" he said.

"He's not in but you can wait if want"

"Yeah, great" he said just staring at her again. He realised at that moment he hadn't got over her at all.

"Look Deb I'll catch you later"

"Simon wait – Danny will be here soon." She pulled him back in by his arm. Simon felt uneasy.

"Simon, you're so tense… what's wrong?"

"Nothing… I know your wedding is close"

"Hey, it's me that's getting married"

"Yeah I know that's the…" he stopped abruptly

She started talking about the wedding like any normal bride to be. Simon could feel himself getting jealous.

"Shut the fuck up about your frigging wedding!" he shouted

Deb looked at him confused.

"What's wrong Simon, this is not like you."

"You… It's you. Don't you know by now – I… I'm in love with you." He said grabbing her. He kissed her hard and wouldn't let go as she struggled to break free.

"Oh fuck Deb… Deb… I'm so sorry. You weren't ever meant to know. Just forget what I said." Simon said nervously seeing the look on her face.

"You can't, Simon you can't"

"Shit. Deb just forget that this happened" he cried as he rushed out of the apartment.

Deborah sat down. She couldn't believe what had just happened. She didn't know what to do. Should she tell Danny or was that not a good idea? She didn't want to ruin their friendship – she didn't want to come between them. This could split the band up.

She started pacing the room. Danny had been right when he'd said that Simon had got a thing for her, but she had not seen it. Why had she not seen this?

"Oh … shit what do I do?" He couldn't have these feeling for her. 'How?' She thought to herself, starting to pace the floor again. "What do I do?'

She decided to go home back to England. It would be better all-round if she wasn't around complicating things. She had started to pack when Danny came back looking really pleased with himself.

"Deb where are you?" He went into the bedroom and put his arms round her waist, kissing the back of her neck.

"What are you doing?" He asked curiously,"Why are you packing? Is there something wrong back home?" he asked.

"No, I'm leaving," she said as the tears started to roll down her face. She had hoped to get out before Danny got back

At this point Danny was looking very confused

"Leaving? Why? What about our wedding. I don't understand."

"There is no wedding. I'm leaving. Please don't make this any harder than it already is."

"What the fuck is going on? What has happened? What have I done? You can't leave me. I love you. We can sort it out whatever it is. Deb, please." he said desperately.

"It won't work, so let's end it here and now" she said with salty tears rolling down her face even faster.

"Why? Deb, don't do this please. Don't do this I'm begging you, Don't."

He grabbed her bags trying to stop her walking out of the door.

"Tell me what the fuck happened"

Deb turned to Danny.

"You are going to be a big rock star, it just won't work. There will be loads of girls." She put her hands to his face and kissed him. "I'll love you always."

Danny grabbed her arms and pulled her close and kissed her tenderly as he begged her not to leave. Deborah pulled away grabbing her bags and she started to walk towards the door. Danny followed and grabbed her again.

"Please Deb, don't."

Deb walked out of the door. She had to get out of there and she couldn't stand seeing Danny like that. He chased after her, grabbing her by the arm. She pulled away to get into the cab and it drove off.

"Deb … Deb …."

Danny's head dropped. He couldn't believe this was happening. He dragged himself back into the apartment, slumped to the floor and put his head in his hands. Tears rolled down his face as he tried to work out what had gone wrong.

What had happened? Everything had been fine before he'd gone out. Was it because he was going to be famous? That had never bothered her before. It had to be something else. Nothing made sense.

He reached for a bottle of booze and started to drink himself into oblivion.

Chapter 9

Next morning, Danny was still on the floor with one hell of a hangover when the guys came round. He let them in reluctantly. Simon was a bit worried after what had happened the day before but never thought for a minute that Deb would have left.

"You look like shit Dan. What you been doing?" Tony asked.

"Leave me alone… What you here for anyway?"

"Rehearsals, Dan"

"I don't fucking give a shit."

"Are you OK?" Dave asked, concerned.

"She's dropped me. Just up and left…Checked out."

"Deb?" Tony asked

"Yeah, that's right, who else?" Danny barked.

"But you two are crazy about each other…"

"So what's happened? Deb wouldn't just go like that. Something has got to have happened." said Alan.

"You tell me what the fuck happened. When I went out she was fine."

Simon looked at Danny

"It's my fault," he blurted out. "Oh Dan, I'm really sorry."

"Why Si, why is it your fault?"

"I'm sorry."

"Simon – *tell me what you did*"

"I'm sorry I didn't mean to."

"What the fuck have you done?" Danny asked again looking confused.

"I told her…"

Tony put his hands to his head,"Oh no."

Trying to put all the pieces together, Danny said "Keep talking"

"I told her. I didn't mean to."

"What the fuck have you told her, Simon?"

Tony stepped in front of Danny. He knew Danny was going to blow any time soon and there was no way of stopping him. Danny started to shout.

"What did you fucking tell her?"

"I told her I love her. I love her Danny."

Danny pushed in front of Tony and swung his fist at Simon, hitting him on the left side of his jaw. Simon put his hand to his mouth. His lip was bleeding. Danny raised his fist to hit him again, but Alan and Dave stepped forward and grabbed him.

Alan shouted at Simon,"What the fuck were you thinking Si?" and, forgetting, he let go. Danny took full advantage and hit Simon again. Alan and Dave pulled Danny away. They kept hold of him, they knew if they let him go he'd kill Simon.

"I knew it. I fucking knew it. You've been hanging round her since we met. You've been after her all this time. What she do, fucking freak at you?"

"No, no, I told her I loved her and then I grabbed her and kissed her."

Danny went for Simon again and this time his fist made contact with his face. Simon didn't retaliate. He took what Danny gave him. He knew how much he had hurt him. Tony pulled Danny away.

"You fucking bastard. You have fucked up my life – Stay away from me."

Dave suggested it was time Simon left. Danny turned round and shouted,

"Yeah, just fuck off."

Simon left shaking his head in despair. He knew he had messed up but he couldn't take it back and it didn't change the way he felt about Deb.

Tony asked Danny if he wanted him to stay.

"No – I need to find out where she is. There is one thing though, Tony. Did you know?"

"I had a feeling, but no, I didn't know for sure."

As they left Danny, Alan said,"I don't fucking believe Si."

The guys left and Danny called Sue.

"No, she's not here. Why?"

"I thought she might have come to you but I think she got a flight home,"

"What's happened, Danny?" she asked.

"Fucking Simon, that's, what happened. He told her he was in love with her."

"He *what?* Look Danny I'll get off the line so you can ring her mum and dad."

"OK Sue. Oh and… Sue if she shows at your place please let me know."

"I will Danny, or if I hear anything I'll call you."

Danny wandered in to the bedroom looked round in despair. Her beautiful wedding dress was hanging on the closet door he buried his face in it. He inhaled deeply and sighed:

"Oh Deb… baby, please come back"

He moved his hands down her wedding dress. He could smell the newness of it. And again he sighed, 'Oh baby… baby please come back'. Danny's world was on the point of collapse. She had brought her dress home before taking it round to Sue's. She never got the chance before Simon had turned up.

Danny decided he must call her parents.

Rob answered."Hi Danny."

"Is she there Rob?" Danny asked.

"Yeah, she won't talk to anyone though. She is so upset we have just left her alone. What's happened?"

Danny explained what had happened.

"I see. Look Danny, let me talk to her and I'll will ring you back later"

"OK…it doesn't matter what time it is, just call me."

Tony went round to see Simon. Simon let him in.

"You prick. What did you think you were doing?"

"It just came out. She was banging on about the wedding I just blurted it out. I grabbed her and kissed her. I think I scared her, I wouldn't let her go."

"Oh Si, you had to fall for the same chick"

"How is Dan? I didn't plan this Tony." Simon said. He had a busted lip and his black eye was starting to come out.

"No, I know you didn't plan it but Dan is really angry. Pissed off. Hurt. … you name it."

"What about the band?" Si asked.

"I think the band will be alright. Your friendship with Dan is another matter."

The next day the band had a meeting with Alex to discuss future tours and the new single. After their meeting Simon went over to Danny.

"Can I talk to you Dan?"

"Fuck off and stay away from me. The only time I want you around me is when we have to be together."

"Dan I didn't do this to hurt you. I didn't mean any of this to happen."

Danny moved his head in close to Simon.

"Keep the fuck away from me," he growled.

Tony went over and pulled Danny away. The tension between Danny and Simon was electric. They carried on with business but their friendship had taken a real blow. Alex took Tony aside and asked him if the band was going to be alright or if this was going to break them up.

"No, I think we will be OK. I think the band will be OK"

"Will he forgive him?"

"I don't know. It's going to take some time before Danny forgives Simon – if he ever does. I hope so though. We've all been buddies since we were kids but he loves Deb so much."

"Danny's so angry with Simon he looks as if he wants to kill him."

"Yeah, but we'll be OK."

"I need to know, Tony, if things don't improve…"

"They will, Alex. They will."

Back in England

Rob took some breakfast in to Deb. She was sat at the window crying.

"Danny rang last night Deb,"

"Is he alright? I left in such a rush – I didn't know what to do."

"He told me about Simon."

"All this is his fault. He shouldn't have told me that he loved me. He's ruined everything. I'm not going back to Danny. He should forget me." she said, spluttering and crying.

"Simon shouldn't have told you, but maybe that's how he feels, and maybe, he's been holding that in for a long time."

"He shouldn't feel like that."

Her dad gave her a hug and said, "You can't help who you fall in love with Deb."

Rob went downstairs and found Kath.

"She's not going back. It's just one big mess. We'd better ring Ed and tell him she's not coming back to work."

Rob rang Ed Parker at the hotel. He was a good friend of Rob's and he was very sad that Deb wasn't coming back.

"That's such a shame, Rob. She was a great manageress. If she ever changes her mind let me know."

Rob said, "Thanks Ed, and I am sorry for leaving you in a mess"

Next, Rob rang Danny and told him what was going on.

"Danny…"

"Rob…"

"Deborah isn't coming back… and she told me that you should just get on with your life."

Danny's heart sank. " I can't Rob. I need her in my life. Should I come over? Can I talk to her? I just need to talk to her."

"I'm sorry, Danny, she just won't talk to you."

"Ask her again Rob, please."

Rob shouted up to Deb and told her Danny was on the phone.

"No dad. Tell him to get on with his life and forget me."

Danny heard everything.

"Rob, please get her to the phone."

"I'm so sorry Danny," Rob sympathised.

Deb just couldn't see how it would all work if she went back. She'd made her decision and was sticking to it no matter how hard and painful it was.

That night she woke up screaming in a lot of pain and was losing a lot of blood. Kath and Rob rushed her to the hospital. The doctors seemed to be in with her for ages. When they finally came out, they told Kath and Rob they were taking Deborah to theatre.

"Mr Carnell, your daughter was pregnant. Unfortunately she lost the baby and we need to take her to theatre to check that everything has come away"

"Tell me she's alright."

"I will let you both know when she comes back from theatre, and then you can see her."

"Thank you, doctor." said Kath.

"I wonder if she knew." Rob said. He was really worried about his daughter. "This is going to hurt Deb even more. I wonder if Danny knew."

The next day Rob and Kath went to see Deb. She was so unhappy. Tears were streaming down her face as she tried to come to terms with what had happened. They stayed for a while and then went home. Deborah was sat looking out of the window when she heard a voice from the past.

"Hi Deb"

She turned round and there was David, her first boyfriend. They talked and talked and he told her he was getting married.

"Probably not the time to tell you is it?"

"Don't be silly. That's great news. I am really pleased for you."

After a few days in hospital she came home. Everyone seemed to know she was back and all her old friends rallied round. She rang Sue, and told her why it had taken her so long to call.

"I knew you would call me when you were ready. I am so sorry Deb."

"Things have gone horribly wrong. This was not meant to happen."

"Danny is in pieces, Deb."

"I didn't want to hurt him. I love him."

"Deb I'm sure this would work out fine if you just come back."

"No Sue. I just want Danny to get on with his life and be happy."

"I don't think that's gonna happen"

"He will, he'll be fine."

Deb told her she wanted her to come over and said she would send her the fare. Sue said she would love to.

"… but I will save the money."

"No, it will take forever that way."

"It's just a loan then."

"No Sue, I just want you to come over please. I need you."

"OK Deb. I will be there as soon as I can."

"Oh Sue, what am I going to do?"

"Well, I know what I think you should do."

"Oh, I just don't think I can."

Chapter 10

Deb was still very down but decided she had to put her life back on track for her own sanity. She got herself a job with Fletcher and Fletcher Accountants. She started going out with the girls again and eventually got her own place. She sent Sue the fare so she could come over.

Sue came over for two weeks and in that time Deb introduced her to all her friends. They all liked her. Deb introduced her to David as well.

"Who's he?" Sue asked inquisitively,"one of your ex-boyfriends?"

"Yeah David was the first." Deb smiled.

"Oh. When you say *first?*"

"Yeah…he took my virginity." Deb laughed.

"He's good looking. I wouldn't say no."

"Yeah, but he's taken, he's getting married." Deb said wistfully.

"Hey, shit happens."

"Oh Sue, this is why I need you here." she said laughing.

Deb's mum and dad moved house whilst Sue was there. They moved from Eastbury to Sonning on the river Thames. Sue helped them with the move

Sue had a great time in England. Deb took her to all the places she wanted to see. They went to London and stayed overnight so Sue could see Buckingham Palace. They went to see *'Mystery Lover'* in the West End while they were there.

She didn't want to go back but eventually she had to. Deb took Sue to the airport on the day she was going back. As they drove they talked about Danny. Deb said she had seen him on Top of the Pops.

"I miss him," Deb confessed.

"Why could you not just have come back?" asked Sue, exasperated.

"I couldn't see how it would have worked with Danny and Simon, knowing that Simon had said what he had."

"Yeah I could see how it would be awkward. But you should have given it a chance. I am so going to miss you, Deb."

Deborah hugged her friend and said"I'll miss you too, but we will see each other when we can."

"It's just not the same though." Sue said with tears filling her eyes.

"Oh Sue don't. You'll make me cry."

Sue left and went in to passport control.

Deb was so sad, she really didn't want Sue to go.

Chapter 11

1987

The band had been on tour all over the world. They had even been to England. Danny had hoped he could go and see Deborah while he was there and had even gone round to Deb's old house in Eastbury. When he got there he discovered they had moved. He was so disappointed, that was his last hope of changing her mind.

"She's moved. I don't believe she's not there." he cried at Tony.

"Dan you really need to move on."

"I just wanted to see her"

"I know"

"Why did she leave me?"

Tony didn't say anything. He didn't want to upset him yet again. Alex asked Tony if Danny had dated anyone since Deb.

"Nnah …." Tony said. "He's never with them long enough to get to know 'em. It's just no strings sex. He doesn't give a shit. He's worse than Simon. There were three of 'em last night"

Danny still wouldn't have anything to do with Simon. He wouldn't even be in the same room as him if he didn't have to. When they were together, he would snipe and growl at him at every opportunity. And Simon took it, until one day when things came to boiling point. Danny had been digging at Simon all day in the studio and he'd had enough

"I know I fucked up, Dan"

"Fuck you"

"Dan we need to deal with this once and for all"

Danny went over to him, getting right in his face, pushing his forehead into Simon's head.

"Fuck off"

Tony stepped forward to part them. Simon shook his head at Tony

"Come on then, Danny – let's deal with it. If you wanna hit me then DO IT"

Dave and Alan rushed over. Tony put his hands out to stop them. Alan yelled that Danny was going to hurt Simon real bad, if they let them do this. Tony told them that they probably need to do this to sort themselves out, Dave shook his head in dismay.

"We grew up together, we were like brothers," Simon muttered.

"If we are supposed to be like brothers then why the fuck would you do that to me?"

Simon started to tell him what happen that night that he was going to leave but Deb wouldn't let him and was going on about the wedding and he couldn't take it anymore and that he just blurted it out and it was never meant to come out.

"So it was her fault?"

"No … Dan, No… it was my fuckin fault"

Danny started to walk away. Simon shouted he would do anything to make it up to him. Danny turned round and told him that when he fell in love with someone he hoped he would end up hurting like him and their friendship will never be the same again

"For fucks sake, Danny – if I could make this right I would"

"Listen Simon understand this, I will do whatever it takes to get her back"

The band had been on tour for nearly a year. They had toured all over Europe and now they were tired out. It had been a tough schedule but they'd enjoyed every minute of it. The cheering crowds, all the gorgeous girls, partying all the different countries they had visited and all the fans they had met – they were due a little time to recharge their batteries.

After they had finished the tour, the guys decided that they would move to Beverly Hills. If they were going to be at the top then they needed to be where they could be seen and taken seriously as artists and that was in the company of other top artists. They all bought their own places. Danny, Tony, Alan and Dave had penthouses but Simon had wanted a house with grounds and a pool so he bought a fabulous mansion with gardens. There were orange and apple trees in the orchard and rose trees surrounded masses of lawn and a beautiful big swimming pool. It was gorgeous.

Danny and the guys asked why he wanted such a big mansion.

"Because I can." was his reply

"Well he has got a point," Alan said

"We have worked our asses off for this, and I wanted this house." Simon said.

They had worked hard for the fame and they wanted to be famous rock stars. They had got what they wanted. They were a worldwide sensation. It had taken a long time to get where they were. Crowds would chant their name now *D E C A D E… D E C A D E…* they were a big hit with the girls, particularly Danny and Simon. Fame. Money. Girls everywhere. What more could they possibly want?

Simon decided to throw a big party to celebrate his new house. Lots of famous people were there. A gorgeous blonde model called Candy had her eye on Danny and was trying to get his attention. She went over to him dancing suggestively, rubbing herself against him as she gyrated. He was getting turned on by it and took her by the hand towards one of the bedrooms. He pushed her gently onto the bed as they were kissing passionately.

"Come on then just bang the hell out me." he said over-confidently.

"You could have put that so much better," Candy said huskily.

"Come on darling, this is what you came up here for, wasn't it?"

"Just fuck me …"

He kissed her and she kissed her back. His hands started to wander and before she knew it they were up her dress and down her panties. She writhed to his every touch. He laid back

"Sit on it baby." he cried.

He pulled her panties to the side. She was so excited as she mounted him quickly, screaming out with excitement as she rode him. She moaned loudly as she neared the brink of orgasm he swiftly changed positions not losing the rhythm as he took her from behind. She just couldn't get enough. Loudly they came together, their hot, sweaty bodies entangled.

Silently she moved to the edge of the bed. Grinning at Danny she straightened her dress and rejoined the party.

"Where've you been Danny?" Alan asked.

"Doinkin her." Dan said cockily.

"What, the model?"

"Yeah, that's right buddy."

"You lucky bastard."

"Horny chick. Man she couldn't get enough," he smirked, winking at Alan.

A few nights after the party the guys had some time off and they were relaxing at a night club. Simon and Danny were getting on better, not like they had before but at least they were talking to each other. They were all having a laugh when Dave pointed out that a girl was eyeing Danny up.

Danny looked over and she smiled at him. He looked at the guys.

"That's my cue, see ya later."

"Fuckin hell, he's worse than me." Simon sniggered.

"Yeah he fucked that model at your party" Alan smirked.

Danny made his way over and got talking to the girl. She told him her name was Chris. He told her his name was Danny.

"I know who you are."

They talked and talked and he decided he liked her. He ended up telling her all about Deb.

"You must have loved her."

"Yeah I did."

"I'm glad you said you did and not still do," Chris said.

"Why?"

"Because I like you." she replied.

He went back to her apartment and stayed there all night. Chris didn't look unlike Deb. She had the same longish, dark hair and brown eyes though she was a bit taller. She asked if she could see him again.

"Yeah … why the hell not"

Danny started seeing Chrissie a lot. She was fun to be with, she made him laugh. The guys thought he was finally getting over Deb but they couldn't have been more wrong. Deb was always at the back of his mind.

Deb had also started dating again. Ryan always liked Deb but never asked her out because she was David's girlfriend and he was with Mags at the time. He'd really liked her at school and couldn't believe his luck when he asked her out and she said Yes.

They got on really well and liked each other's company but he wasn't Danny and she just couldn't get round that. She wondered if she would ever get over Danny. She missed him and wondered if he still missed her. She rang Sue and told her she was dating again

"That's great Deb."

"Is it? Why?"

"Yeah, it is Deb. It's good to know you're getting back out there."

"What have you been up to Sue?"

"Not a lot. But I'm going to see Danny and the guys in concert."

"Are you…? Are you going with the girls?"

"No this guy I'm dating,. he's a big Decade fan."

"I hope you have a good time. Tell me all about it next time we talk. When are you going?

"This Saturday," Sue said excitedly.

Sue and her boyfriend Max went to the Decade concert. It was awesome. The guys really got the crowd going and the girls were going frantic. Later, Sue and Max went into the bar where the bands go after the gigs. Max worked in the industry so they got to mingle with the VIPs. What Max didn't know was that Sue knew the band and when Danny spotted her through the crowd he shouted excitedly to her.

"Danny." she cried, giving him a hug. "It's so good to see you"

"It's great to see you Sue. You're looking good too"

"Yeah, I'm fine," Sue replied.

Max stood with his mouth wide open then he nudged her discreetly.

"Oh, Danny this is Max. He is a big fan."

Danny asked him if he'd enjoyed the concert.

"Yeah awesome. , You rock…"

"Thanks. Look I'm not being rude but I haven't seen Sue for a while."

"No… sure that's fine."

"So Sue, have you seen Deb?"

"Yeah I've been over."

"Is she OK? What's she doing ?"

"She's doing alright. She's got a new job, new home."

Then he asked the question, "…is she dating anyone?"

"Yep"

"Really?" he asked, looking disappointed.

"What about you Danny?"

"Yeah, yeah I'm dating"

"Is she here?"

"No."

Just then the rest of the guys came over. "Sue."

"Hi guys."

Simon gave her a big hug and asked how she was.

"I'm good Simon"

"You're looking good babe." he grinned.

Danny laughed sarcastically and said to Max, "You better watch your girlfriend." Simon threw him a stony look.

"What…?" Danny asked innocently.

"Hey Guys, you were wicked."

Tony thanked Sue and asked if she and Max wanted to come to the party back at their hotel.

"Yeah, that would be great."

Tony gave Sue two passes and told her how to find the hotel.

"See ya there."

"It's really good to see you Sue," Danny said, wistfully.

"Yeah, it's good to see you too, Dan."

"Is Deb happy?"

"I think so, Danny"

"Good"

"How about you, are you happy?

"I suppose so…"

"Danny…?"

Just as Sue was about to speak, Tony reappeared.

"Dan, we're splitting."

"OK, coming."

Danny turned to Sue. "You are coming to the party aren't you?"

"Yeah…, we'll be there Danny"

Sue and Max went along to the party.

"Why didn't you say you knew them?" Max said incredulously.

"Don't know really," Sue replied.

Danny looked for Sue and when he saw her he went over to her. Tony had also seen her but he just watched her. Secretly he was attracted to her but he had never made a move on her. He'd always felt she was out of his league.

"You made it then." shouted Danny over the music.

"Yeah, thanks Danny."

Danny just wanted to sit and talk to Sue about Deb but people kept grabbing him. There were a lot of girls there and they were all over Danny so he obliged. As Sue was leaving, Danny grabbed her by the arm.

"You weren't going without saying bye were you?"

"No, but you seem to have your hands full." she laughed.

"Girls everywhere… not enough of me though."

"Danny I thought you were dating." Sue said in surprise.

"Yeah, but I'm not married."

"No, that's true. Give me a hug"

Sue hugged Danny and he kissed her cheek.

"Look after yourself, Sue."

"You look after yourself, Danny"

"Sue… when you see Deb will you tell her I…." he stopped, shaking his head sadly.

"Yeah Danny I will." She knew what he meant.

She waved at the rest of the guys, then she and Max left. Danny went back to the party, but didn't feel like having fun after that. Tony asked him if he was OK

"Yeah… no sweat."

He wasn't, though. Deb was totally on his mind – he wondered if she was really happy or was Sue just saying that…

He told Tony he was bailing, he'd had enough. He went to bed thinking of Deb, he just couldn't get her from his mind. He pictured her face, those big beautiful flirtatious green eyes looking back at him, the way her eyebrows were perfectly arched over them and that beautiful big smile she had. He could see all the contours of her face. He just wanted her back.

Next morning he went for breakfast. The rest of the guys were raw, they all had hangovers. Danny, on the other hand, felt great.

"Morning…. You all ready for rehearsals?"

"Fuck off, Dan." Dave grunted, holding his head.

"What… Come on guys, let's have a good breakfast and get to it."

Toast come flying at him from every angle

"Fuck off." they roared together.

Back in England

Deb was at home doing some work she'd brought home when there was a knock on the door. It was David. He had brought a wedding invitation round. She thanked him and he asked how things were going with Ryan.

"OK"

"Just OK, Deb?"

She looked at David and gave him a funny little look. David knew that look and knew what it meant.

"It's not working, is it?"

"No… it's me. He's so nice. I like his company and we got on well but…"

"I know what you're saying. That look you just gave me says it all."

"Why don't you go back, Deb?" David asked.

"Oh... David."

"You're not happy."

"What am I going to do?"

"Look I will leave you to it, I'm meeting Sally. But I think, you should think about going back."

Deborah kissed him on the cheek.

"See ya," she said, affectionately.

She called Sue that evening. She needed to talk to her friend, they were really missing each other. Sue told her she had spoken to Danny at the concert and that he had gone over to talk to her specially.

"Is he OK?"

"Yeah... he says so"

"Is he...hmm," she stopped. "Is he dating?"

"Yep.... I told him you were too."

"Is she nice?"

"I don't know. She wasn't with him."

"Why?"

"I don't know – but she wasn't there..." she paused, "He did talk about you, though."

"Did he?"

"Yep, a whole lot. He still loves you Deb."

"Oh, he must have dozens of girls round him"

"Oh yeah, he has... but..."

"No Sue, please don't say it."

Deb just couldn't get into that conversation yet again. She knew what Sue was going to say, that's why she stopped her. It just hurt too much. It was easier to believe that Danny was having a good time and not thinking of her even though, deep down, she wanted him to.

She asked Sue if she and Max had enjoyed the concert.

"Yeah Deb they were awesome, but I'm not seeing Max again."

"Why not?" Deb gasped.

"He was such a jerk."

"OK, I'll take your word for that," she laughed.

"Yeah, I pick up all the jerks." Sue giggled.

Deb laughed uncontrollably." Oh Sue, you make me laugh so much."

They talked and talked for hours. Deb's phone bill was going to be huge but she just didn't care.

Chapter 12

David's wedding was getting closer and so, after work one day, Deb went shopping for an outfit to wear. She had her hair cut to shoulder length and permed. She'd never had her hair cut that short before and it felt strange. She bought a light pink dress with a short lace jacket and a couple of days later the day of the wedding arrived.

David's bride Sally looked amazing and David looked really handsome. The wedding was beautiful,they looked so in love. Deb's mum and dad were there and they thoroughly enjoyed it, although at one time they had thought it would be Deborah and David getting married.

Ryan looked very handsome in his suit and he got Deb up to dance.

"I think I'm in love with you Deb..."

"Ryan."

"Yes, I really think I am." He kissed her and said,"I am falling for you."

She smiled at him. "You are so sweet Ryan, but please don't fall for me."

Ryan looked at her, "I want to stay with you tonight."

Deb wasn't sure she wanted that. She wasn't sure about the whole relationship at all. She left Ryan talking to David and went over to her mum and dad.

Her dad wasn't looking at all well. He was very grey in the face and kept rubbing his left arm. Deb asked her mum if he was alright.

"He's been like this a few weeks."

"That's not right, mum." She suggested that he needed to go to the doctors.

"No I know… but he won't go to the doctors."

"He needs to go mum. I'll make him an appointment"

"Yes, you're right. If he has an appointment then perhaps he'll go"

"I will ring on Monday"

Her mum and dad went home early. Rob still didn't feel good and Deb told her mum that if he wasn't any better in the night she should ring for an ambulance.

"I will…Now you enjoy yourself"

"I will but if you need me call me"

"Go have fun. See you tomorrow."

They left and Deb did enjoy herself as Mags was there with the girls.

"Are you OK with me being with Ryan, Mags?" Deb asked.

"Deb yeah, course. Don't worry."

"Where's that baby girl of yours?"

"She's with my mum."

Natasha was such a pretty little girl, the spitting image of Mags. She was growing up so fast. Ryan had seen Deb talking to Mags and made his way over.

"Hello Ryan"

"Mags, how ya doing?" he said, placing his arms round Deb's waist.

"I'm great"

"How's your little girl?"

"I was just telling Deb, she's with my mum and she's growing up so fast."

Ryan smiled and told them he was thirsty and suggested they went to the bar.

"Come on Mags," Deb said, taking getting hold of her hand

"You two go… I'll make my way over in a minute."

Deb got quite drunk and started fooling about with Ryan. They'd been dancing most of the night and were having a really good time together.

Ryan took Deb home and as he kissed her she responded passionately. She had turned him on with that kiss.

"I want to stay." he whispered huskily.

She kissed him again and they went in. Slowly his lips traced their way down her neck his fingertips teasing her breasts. She put her head back as he pressed against her. She could feel his heart pounding in his chest as his erection exploded into life. He looked at her longingly and told her he wanted to make love to her. As he picked her up and took her to the bedroom. His hands stroked the shallow curves of her stomach. Slowly he undressed her, his hands moving over her breasts as she began to move her hands seductively over his body. He groaned with pleasure, he wanted her so much. He moved between her thighs and made love to her passionately. It was hot and frenzied and it seemed such a long time since anyone had made love to her like that

The next morning he had made breakfast by the time Deb appeared from the bedroom feeling pretty rough.

"Hi there, I've made bacon and eggs." Ryan said enthusiastically.

"Oh… really…? I don't feel so good." she said, shaking her head.

"Come on eat something you'll feel so much better."

"Hmm…Don't know about that."

"Look, I've got to go in to work, when I've finished I'll get us a take away."

"Yeah, OK."

"What would you like, Chinese or Indian?"

"Hmm, surprise me." The way she was feeling, she really wasn't bothered about any food.

After Ryan left, Deb rang her mum to check how her dad was. Her mum told her he was feeling a bit better. Deb said he should still go to the doctors and that she would make the appointment on Monday. When she got off the phone with her mum she got on with some work that she'd brought home.

Later, Ryan came back with an Indian takeaway. They sat and ate it watching TV. The next day they went to work and Deb called the doctor's to make the appointment for her dad.

Three days later her dad died suddenly of a heart attack, before he even got to the doctor. The paramedics had tried to revive him but they couldn't get him back. When she got the news, she rushed to her mum and put her arms round her and hugged her tight.

Deb was devastated. She was a daddy's girl and her world had fallen apart. What would she do without her dad? She helped her mum with the funeral arrangements. Ryan was a big help to them. Deborah needed him and he made sure he was around for them when they needed him. There were a lot of people at the funeral. Sue sent flowers as she couldn't get over.

Her mum found it hard coping without Rob, even more so after the funeral. Soon after, Sue called them to see if they were OK.

"Oh Sue, I just can't believe this has happened."

"No, neither can I. It was such a shock."

"It's my mum I'm worried about."

"Yeah it will be difficult for her"

"I don't know how she's going to cope without him."

"I wish I could get over for you both" Sue said.

"I know you would be here if you could. Don't worry, we'll be OK."

"Deb, I'm really sorry but I've got to go I'm covering for someone at work."

"OK Sue. Look after yourself and I'll call you soon."

Deb had got to go back to work but she was really worried about her mum. She was so sad and Deb didn't know what to do for her. Although she was still seeing Ryan and enjoying his company, she still wasn't sure if she wanted to be with anyone really.

Ryan felt she was slipping away from him and made a big romantic gesture by arranging a special meal at a posh restaurant. He was very attentive, which she enjoyed and very romantic.

When they got back home he leaned in to kiss her. She kissed him back and he pulled her firmly against him. He kissed her more passionately now and she responded. They made love passionately and afterwards they lay in each other's arms, content. Deb asked Ryan where he saw himself in the future.

"I don't know… married maybe."

"Is that what you really want…? I don't ever want to get married"

"What… never?

"No." she turned over moodily. "Goodnight Ryan"

"Yeah…, goodnight."

He lay in bed next to her staring at the ceiling. He knew what was coming next.

Over the next few weeks Deborah realised that she didn't want a boyfriend and told Ryan that she didn't want to see him anymore. It wasn't because he'd done anything wrong it was just that she wasn't really ready for another steady relationship. Ryan was upset and disappointed but he knew, he had felt it for a while.

Deborah decided to give men a miss for a while. She didn't need one. She went to work and had nights out with the girls but she missed her dad. He was the only man she needed.

October 1987

The girls in the office were talking about going on holiday to Italy and asked Deb if she fancied going.

"Yeah I'd love to… but can we all get the same week off ?" Deb said enthusiastically.

"Yeah…We're not all in the same department." Mandy replied.

"Well in that case…Yeah, count me in." she laughed.

"Great."

Deb's first thought was to go round to see her mum and ask her if she would be OK if she went on holiday.

"Yes of course…You go and have a good time."

The girls booked a cheap deal holiday to Italy and a few weeks later they headed off. When they arrived and got to their hotel they got changed and went for something to eat and to have a look round. There were talented musicians playing in the streets and they booked a show for in the middle of the week.

There were loads of bars, cafés and street markets. One night they went to a jazz club. They went to local pizza place and had beautiful authentic Italian pizza. They also visited the Neptune's fountain and they went to all the art museums as Becky loved anything to do with art. They found the mall and had a great time doing lots of shopping. Deb bought some beautiful clothes and bought her mum and Sue a beautiful dress each.

Mandy bought some shoes and clothes and Becky bought hand bags and shoes. They packed in as much as they could. Deb rang her mum every night to make sure she was alright and found time to give Sue a ring.

Sue asked her if she was having a good time.

"Oh yeah – it's great but I wish you were with me"

"Yeah…I wish I was with you too. Is it nice in Italy?" Sue asked.

"Totally… It's beautiful…I got you such a beautiful dress."

"You bought me a dress – Oh Deb thanks, can't wait to see it."

"I'll ring you when I get back home." Deb promised.

"Yeah…Enjoy the rest of your holiday…Bye."

Before the girls went home they managed to visit the Cathedral and Santa Maria del Fiore. They'd had a wonderful time and had met lots of lovely local people. The week after Deb got back, Danny and the guys were in Florence doing a concert. Danny would have kicked himself if he had known she was there. It was the chance he'd been waiting for – and he missed it by a week.

1988

Deb's mum had taken ill suddenly and had been rushed to hospital. They did a lot of tests on Kath to find out what was wrong but Deb put it down to the stress of her mum losing her dad. When the results came back, however, it was to bring more even upset. They diagnosed Kath with cancer and told Deb she only had months to live. The cancer had spread everywhere and there was nothing they could do except to make her comfortable when the time came.

Deb took time from work to be with her mum. She wanted to spend the last months with her as she hadn't been able to do that with her dad before he was taken from her. She made sure she was there for her mum.

Kath deteriorated quickly but Deb was there for her and nursed her through it. It was one of the hardest things she had ever had to do. Seeing her mum in so much pain along with everything else she was going through was very distressing. The nurses that were coming had to increase the morphine and did everything they could but it wasn't enough and Deb watched as her mum slipped away in her sleep.

She had to arrange the funeral on her own this time.

She felt so alone. She'd not long since lost her dad and now her mum – the two most important people in her life, She felt that she was being punished but for what she didn't know. She had no brother or sisters, no family at all to speak of. She didn't know what she was going to do.

She called Sue and told her how she was feeling and Sue told her to come back.

"I'm not sure Sue," Deborah said, mulling it over in her mind.

"So what's keeping you there Deb? Just come back."

"There's nothing…, I don't suppose."

"So you'll come back?"

"OK, but I need to sort things out here first."

She put her mum and dad's house and business up for sale, and spent her time sorting everything else out. She asked David if he was interested in her dad's business and, although he wasn't sure if he could raise the money, he said he would try.

America 1988

Danny had now been seeing Chris for quite a while and she had fallen head over heels in love with him. She asked him to marry her.

"Married… OK, why not?"

"Really… Do you mean it?"

"Yeah we've been seeing each other for some time now – it seems to be the next obvious step."

"Oh… Danny. I love you so much."

She was so happy she glowed with happiness and she thought that Deb must be well and truly in the past now. Well, why else would Danny marry her if she wasn't?

"I don't want a big white wedding, though."

"Oh." she said, sounding disappointed.

"We should go to Vegas tonight and get married there."

"No family or friends?"

"No, just us."

"OK then," she said thoughtfully.

"Are you OK with that Chris?"

"Yeah, let's get married." She said, suddenly getting excited.

They flew to Vegas, pulled two witnesses in off the street and got married in the Little White Wedding Chapel in Vegas.

Next day, Danny had made the front page.

Rock star Danny Brooks married his girlfriend in Vegas last night at the Little White Wedding Chapel

FULL STORY PAGE TWO

Danny's mum, Marie, read the newspaper. She was so angry. She immediately called Simon

"Have you seen the papers?" she yelled down the phone.

"No, why… what's wrong?" he asked.

"Read it."

Simon got hold of the paper and there it was on the front page about Danny.

"Did you know about this Simon?"

"No I had no idea. He never even mentioned marriage to me. I didn't think it was that serious." he spluttered.

"Wait till he gets back." Marie threatened.

"Let me talk to Tony, Marie, and see if he knew." Simon rang Tony.

"Have ya seen the paper?" he asked.

"No, why?"

"Read it Tony." Si said urgently.

Tony read the paper. "Holy Shit." he cried.

"I take it you didn't know anything about this neither?"

"Did I fuck."

"What about the rest of the guys?"

"Not that I'm aware of. I'll ring Alan and Dave and see."

"Right OK…I need to call Marie back. She is so not impressed."

Simon called Marie back and told her no one knew what was going on.

"What is he playing at?"

"I don't know, Marie.

"He likes her, I know… but does he love her?"

"I honestly don't know."

Simon spoke to Tony again. Alan and Dave knew nothing about it either and it had come as a bit of a shock.

Chapter 13

Back In England

Danny was married. Deb couldn't believe it when she read it in the paper. She nearly changed her mind about moving out but Sue convinced her it was the right thing to do.

Her mum and dad's house and business sold quite quickly. A young couple had bought the house. David had managed to get a loan from the bank to buy the business. His dream had finally happened for him.

She said her goodbyes to her friends and she was ready to go. Ryan asked her to stay but she said No, she wanted to go back to America.

She called for a cab to take her to the airport and was on her way. She had a good flight and passed the time by reading, watching the in-flight movie, having a few drinks and eating on the plane. She arrived in New York at 12 noon.

She immediately called Sue.

"What time you arriving?" Sue asked in excitement.

"I'm here.... I'll be with you soon. I'm just jumping in a cab."

The cab took her the long way round and charged her for the pleasure but she didn't mind, she was just so happy to be back. The cab pulled up at Sue's and Deb paid and went in. Sue put her arms round her

"It's so good to see you. I've missed you Deb"

"Oh Sue, I've missed you too it's good to be back. Hey, I've got that dress that I bought you in Italy"

"Oh Deb."

They sat and talked and talked. They ordered takeout and after two bottles of wine they fell asleep on the floor. Next morning they were both a bit stiff and a bit hung over but they didn't mind. Deb was so pleased to be back.

When Danny and Chris came back from Vegas, Marie was waiting.

"What have you done?"

"I got married."

"Do you love her?"

"I must do, I married her."

"Don't take that tone with me Danny Brooks. Do you love her Danny?"

Danny wouldn't answer his mum. He just nodded and shrugged his shoulders.

"That's not an answer."

"Mom, get off my case."

"I don't think you do" she accused.

"I'll never love anyone as much as I loved Deb. She's gone and she's never coming back – so let's just drop this."

"That's it right there Danny."

"What?"

"Deb… "

He left his mom's and went to the studio to meet the guys. He knew his mom was right but he had to forget any hopes he had about Deb coming back because it wasn't happening or so he thought. He met up with the guys at the studio and they had put a big banner up

CONGRATULATIONS DANNY AND CHRISSIE!

"I didn't think it was that serious Dan." Tony confessed.

Alan came over and said, "Fucking Hell, Dan…Marriage…?"

"Yeah it had to happen sometime."

Simon and Dave congratulated him.

"Come on guys, let's run through some songs." suggested Danny, reluctant to talk about Chrissie.

For a newly married man he wasn't very excited and the guys noticed how unwilling he was to talk about his wedded bliss. They ran over some songs and changed a few lyrics. Danny had written a new one called 'Gone Away'. The guys loved it and they wanted to release it to the charts.

"That's what I wrote it for but we need to put the music to it now."

"Not a problem," Tony said.

So they got to work on the music for the song. They worked on that music for that song all night. Danny called Chris and told her he would be working all night and not to wait up. They finished the song and played it for Alex. He loved it and it went straight into the charts at number 15 and soon made it to number 1 in the American and British charts and it stayed there for 5 weeks.

The band went on tour to England. Chris was clearing some stuff away of Danny's, as they had just moved in to their new house. She found some photos of Danny with Deb. There were quite a lot. She sat on the floor looking through them and couldn't help thinking to herself how stunning Deb was and that Danny looked so in love with her. She put the photos back as if she hadn't seen them.

She had done most of Danny's things but not the box with the photos in which she'd left Danny to put away himself. Chris was hoping that Danny would show her the photos but he didn't. She was disappointed because she had caught him looking through them when he was putting them away and it was the way he looked at them that really bothered her. She had asked what was in the box but he just said 'stuff' and so she didn't mention the box again.

Chris loved Danny and hoped her marriage would work. She was very unsure of their relationship at times and Danny only ever really told her he loved when he had to.

Deb had managed to get tickets to see the Broadway show 'Starburst' on West 43rd Street. The show was a sellout so she had been really lucky to get the tickets.

She and Sue really enjoyed the show. As they were coming out, Deb and Chris bumped straight into each other. Deb apologised but Chris just smiled at her. She carried on walking but then she stopped, turned and looked round but Deb was out of sight by then.

"That was Danny's ex – I'm sure it was." Chris said to her friend.

"No, it couldn't be. You said she was back in England."

"I'm sure that was her."

She didn't mention it to Danny. She was sure it was Deb and she didn't want Danny to find out that she was back. If it was her, she thought that he would head straight back to her if he found out.

As the weeks passed, Deborah looked for a job. She thought she would never find one but finally she was taken on at the Sharringdon Hotel as Manageress. She also looked for a place of her own as she was still living with Sue. Sue didn't mind, she liked having her there but Deb needed a place of her own.

Sue had started dating Martin and she was quite taken with him. Martin mentioned he had a friend called Shane.

"What about fixing Deb up with him?" he suggested.

"Nope… I can't see Deb hooking up with him."

"Why?" Martin asked.

"She's not ready for dating yet." she replied.

Martin introduced Shane to Deb. She liked him, but only as a friend.

Deb was sat all cosy one cold and rainy night in her pyjamas, watching a film starring Brad Cannon with her popcorn and soda when she got a call. Sue was at the hospital.

"Hi can I speak to Miss Carnell?"

"Speaking"

"I have a Miss Anderson here and you are down as her next kin."

"Oh my God – is she OK?"

"Yeah… could you come to the hospital?"

"I'll be right there."

Deb rushed to the hospital thinking all sorts of things, her mind was doing somersaults. She rushed in and went straight to the desk and asked about Sue.

The nurse came out to see her. She told her that Sue had been beaten and took her in to see her. She was a mess.

Martin had broken two of her ribs, bust her lip and blackened her eye, she was bruised all over her body. Sue was so upset, she was crying when Deb reached her.

"Oh my God... Sue."

"Oh Deb, please take me home" she sobbed.

"Can I take her?"

The nurse said it would be OK but that she would have to take time off work. Deb took Sue home and got her into bed. She gave her the pain killers the doctors had given her.

"Why Sue? Why did he do this?"

"I don't know. We argued then he hit me... he just kept on hitting me"

"Oh God, has he hit you before?"

"No."

"Get some rest."

Deborah left Sue to sleep. She made some hot chocolate and watched TV for a while before she went to bed herself. The next morning Martin came round and banged on the door. Deb opened it carefully.

"What the fuck do you want?" Her tone was aggressive.

"I want to see Sue"

"Well you're not."

"Who the fuck do you think are?" he shouted in her face and tried to push his way in.

"Do you want me to call 911?"

"I wanna apologise."

"Why? Have you seen what you have done to her?"

Sue came out of the bedroom holding her ribs, clearly in a lot of pain.

"I never want to see you again."

"I'm sorry. I really am," he cried.

"Never come here again"

Deb slammed the door in his face. She turned to Sue

"Are you OK?

"I've finished with men for a while," Sue said as she struggled to get back to the bedroom.

Deb rushed over to help her get back in to bed. She got her some more pain killer and a glass of water. She told her not to worry about Martin anymore, she would never see him again. When Sue recovered she went back to work. Deb decided they needed to get away so she suggested that they go on vacation.

"Yeah let's go have some fun, men free. Where do you want to go?"

"Let's go on a cruise."

"A cruise…. You want to go on a cruise. Can we afford a cruise?"

"Yeah I always wanted to go on a cruise. How expensive can it be?"

They agreed on a cruise. They booked their vacation at work and booked their cruise. It wasn't as cheap as they had hoped but they were really looking forward to it.

They had a great time. It was a week of total relaxation on the ocean. Lavish saunas that they visited every day. There was great entertainment, hi-tech night clubs, glittering Broadway shows and comedians. There was tennis too, which neither of them could play, but they sure had fun trying. Sue couldn't control her laughter when Deb tried to hit the tennis ball. She had tears rolling down her face with laughter.

More food than they could eat even though they gave it a good try. They must have tried everything on the menu. And fashion shops everywhere. They had a great time but by the end of the week they had spent more money than they had intended to.

"I've done more with you, Deb, than I have in my whole life." Sue grinned.

"Stick with me kid you're gonna do a whole lot more!" she laughed.

Sue looked at her. "You're crazy. You are absolutely kooky but I love you."

"I know." and they both laughed in unison.

When they arrived home, Thanksgiving was just round the corner. They made plans and decided they would go to Macey's Parade. Deb loved it: all the giant balloons in the sky, the floats, the marching bands, the rockets. Even Santa's sleigh was there. There were some surprise celebrity appearances – and Decade was one of them.

Deb didn't want to get too close as she didn't want Danny to spot her. She thought he looked so hot. As she turned to look at Sue her eyes started to fill up and her lips trembled as she realised she had made a big mistake running back home. She had let him go, the only man she really loved. Now someone else had got him.

Sue grabbed her by the hand and squeezed it and smiled at her. Deb tried to put a brave face on, to mask her feelings as she smiled back at her

"Come on Deb, let's get away from here"

They headed towards the Stargazer diner for something to eat. They played karaoke there which was always good fun and the bonus was they only played rock music. Deb and Sue loved it in there. After they had eaten and had a few drinks they decided to join in and do a duet on the karaoke they were now in full swing the place was now buzzing. They even joined in as backing singers for some guys who got up and sang 'Crazy Baby' by Tiger Eye.

The guys introduced themselves.

"I'm Tristan and this is Corey… and the drunken guy is Dylan."

Tristan asked what they were drinking and called the waitress over and bought Deb and Sue a drink. They spent the whole evening with them.

Chapter 14

With Christmas approaching, Deborah went shopping for Sue's prezzies. She bought her a gold necklace with a bracelet to match and some other little bits. Sue had bought Deb a friendship ring, earrings, the usual perfume, body lotions and some big fluffy slippers. Deb loved stuff like that.

They went shopping for their Christmas food together and bought a big Christmas tree. They trimmed it together and with good timing the snow started to fall down. It was going to be a great Christmas and they were looking forward to it even though they were both at work a lot of the Christmas holiday. They had Christmas Day together and lounged around in their PJs, opening their presents.

"Merry Christmas Deb"

"Yeah, Merry Christmas Sue"

They had a big Christmas breakfast and spent the day drinking, pulling crackers and playing board games – the fun they had playing twister. Later they had their Christmas dinner together and carried on drinking and playing more games. They had a great Christmas day. They both had Christmas parties to go to so they went to each other's and each other's friends, and ended up going to twice as many. They were having so much fun.

They also got invited to two new Year's Eve parties. One of the guys that Sue worked with invited them to his and one of the girls that worked for Deb invited them to hers so they decided to go to both. They had a great night and then they headed to Times Square to see the new Year in. As time counted down every one in Times Square held their breath and a big cheer went up as the clock struck twelve. 'HAPPY NEW YEAR' they shouted at each other and anyone else that passed them.

1989 a New Year

Deb moved in to her own apartment. Sue got a new job in the same hotel as Deb as restaurant manager. Life was changing for them both again.

Sue had gone up to Deb's office with some paperwork, but that was just an excuse. She was so excited. She had only managed to get tickets for the new exclusive night club that had just opened. Anyone who was anyone was going.

"You're great," Deb said excitedly. "When and how did you get them?"

"Saturday, and it's not what you know it's who you know."

"OK, so you met someone in the restaurant that could get tickets." Deb laughed.

"Yeah sure did."

After work off they went for some retail therapy. Deb bought a black dress, to the knee with spaghetti straps at the back. Sue's was blue which was off the shoulder. They had to have shoes and bags to match.

On Saturday they got ready at Deb's. They got a cab and got in line for the club. Finally they were allowed in and they got a drink. They had been in the club for about an hour when someone tapped Deb on the shoulder.

It was Simon. He and Tony had come over to new York because they'd been given VIP tickets. He'd seen her from the other side of the club and nearly choked on the ice in his drink. He simply could not believe his eyes.

Deb turned and there was Simon, looking astonished to see her.

"Simon." she said, looking round nervously.

"Relax," he said, smiling at her. "Danny's not here"

"Who are you with?" she asked curiously.

Before Simon could answer Sue rushed up to her in a blind panic.

"Guess who I've just seen."

"Who…?"

"Tony. So who is he… aagh. Simon, H-hello…." Sue spluttered, taken by surprise.

Tony appeared from the back of the room."Hey… Girls."

"Hi Tony." they said in unison

"I would like it if you didn't mention me to Danny, I know he's married."

"Sure," Simon interrupted.

Tony looked at Simon and shook his head."Danny won't like it if he finds out"

"He won't find out will he…?" Deb questioned.

"Not from us." Simon said, interrupting again.

"Is that what you want Deb?"

"Yeah… I don't want him to know I'm back, Tony."

"OK Deb, if that's what you want."

They spent the whole evening together, talking about the old times and all the new stuff that had happened in their lives and later they went for a meal together. Tony talked to Sue a lot. He had always liked her and she liked him too. Simon asked Deb if she was with anyone, like a boyfriend. That was what he really wanted to know.

"No Simon. There's no-one."

Simon still wanted Deb and he'd realised it as soon as he'd seen her. He was going to play it safe, though. He didn't want to blow it this time and she wasn't with anyone. So when they left the restaurant Simon asked if she would go out to dinner with him some time.

"Yeah, that would be great"

She gave him her cell number and then she and Sue got a cab and went back to her place.

"What are you doing?" Sue asked her

"What do you mean?"

"Seeing Simon."

"Nothing… It's just a meal."

"As long as you know what you're doing Deb."

The same conversation was going on with Tony and Simon.

"What the hell are you doing Simon?"

"Why? What have I done?" he replied innocently.

"You are going to bring up some really bad vibes."

"Look Tony. I don't want to hurt anyone but Dan is married. I still want that woman."

"It just doesn't feel right."

"Look. Danny got married."

"Yeah I know that, but…"

Simon shook his head"no… no Danny got married

Si and Tony flew back to Beverley hills the next day for rehearsals. Simon was on such a high and in a really good mood. Danny noticed how exuberant Simon was and mentioned it.

"I am in love."

"Wow Cheryl sure is a lucky chic." Alan said, nudging Danny.

"No… no that's all finished"

"New chick?" Danny asked curiously.

"Yeah, I met her last night."

Just then Dave shouted. He seemed to be in a rush to get rehearsals started.

"Come on guys I wanna get out of here today."

"Friggin hell Dave, we're comin." Danny shouted back.

"Yeah, you can talk about Si's sex life after."

The guys all turned on Dave and shouted, "Someone didn't get laid last night."

"Fuck you."

The guys laughed at him. Dave just turned his lip up at them and stuck his middle finger up.

Chapter 15

Simon called Deb and asked her if she was free for dinner the following night.

"Yes"

"I'll pick you up at eight."

He flew back to New York and booked himself into a hotel. He was so happy that she had agreed to meet him. Deb finished work at six, went home and got ready. She put on a blue velvet dress and let her hair down. It had grown back lovely and thick and flowed down her back in tresses.

Simon picked Deb up at eight as he had promised. They went to a little exclusive restaurant that he knew well and they had a great evening.

"I am really sorry for what I did," Si apologized.

"It's all in the past," said Deb.

"Yeah, but I ruined things for you and Dan. I hurt you and I hurt Dan. I never meant to do that. It was never meant to come out."

"It doesn't matter anymore. Danny is married and that's that… Is he happy?"

"Yeah, Chrissie is awesome."

"That's good. We all had to move on."

They had a coffee and Simon took Deb home and asked if she would go out with him again.

"Yeah that would be nice"

"Great"

Over the next few weeks Simon flew back and forth to New York and saw a lot of Deb. She liked his company and they got on really well. Sue mentioned the fact that she was seeing a lot of him and hoped she knew what she was doing. Deb told her that they were friends and that was all.

"Yeah? What happens when Danny finds out?"

"He won't find out"

"Deb, you won't keep this a secret."

The next day in the studio Danny asked Simon if he was still seeing the same girl.

"Yeah"

"Wow fuck me that must be some sort record … you must be in love."

"Yeah… She's amazing."

"Why haven't we been introduced to her?"

Tony butted in, "She's shy."

"You've seen her?"

Danny turned back to Simon. He wanted to know all about this lady that could make Si want to see her again and again.

"Come on Si. What's this girl like? Come on Si tell"

"Yeah Si, come on," said Alan, intrigued by the secrecy, "have you banged her yet?"

"No."

"You haven't banged her yet." Danny started getting very curious.

"What's her name then? What's she like? You haven't told us anything about this girl." Danny started shooting questions at him.

"Why don't you bring her to the Awards?"

"I don't think she'll come."

"Why? All girls love the fame shit. That's what gets you into their pants."

"She's not like that."

"Yeah… right," Danny gave a loud laugh.

"What's her name Si?" He was getting really suspicious about this and he had an uncomfortable feeling about this girl.

"OK Dan, Deborah."

Danny looked at Simon, his eyes began to narrow and crinkle at the sides, his nostrils started to flare.

"What? … Deborah? as in my Deb?"

"Yeah… it's Deb"

"Fuck."

He pushed his hand in to Simon's head grabbing him by his shirt.

"You're jerkin my chain right?" pointing his index finger at him.

"Why didn't anyone tell me she was back?" he shouted. "I should kick your fuckin ass"

"Dan… Dan… I…" Simon spluttered, putting his hand up in front of him.

"You must be lovin this." Danny interrupted angrily. "I'm out of the fuckin way."

"We bumped in to her. We're friends… friends that's all …."

"You said you were in love." Dan shouted, poking Simon in the chest.

"Yeah I am. She's not…" Si answered.

"You want her though?" Danny shouted, getting really angry.

"Yeah… but it's not happening."

"Tell her I know she's back and bring her to the Awards."

"She's not going be happy Dan. She didn't want you to know she was back."

"I don't give a fuck. You tell her. And she better be at the Awards."

He turned and started to walk away, he was so angry and upset. He just couldn't believe it. Tony went over to him.

"I'm sorry Dan. I told Si this would happen."

"Tony."

"They are just friends"

"I love her Tony."

"You have Chris now, remember."

"I care about Chris, But Deb. I've never loved any one like her – no one. What the fuck do I do? Oh shit… Chris."

104 | Deborah Caren Langley

Danny went straight home and told Chris that Deb was back. Chris got very upset and asked Danny if he was leaving her.

"No...Why?"

"I know you love her," she said with tears rolling down her face.

"Don't be crazy Chris...I'm married to you. She left me. It's all over." He said gently, wiping the tears from her face.

"Really...? Do you mean that?"

"Yeah..., but she will be at the awards with Simon."

"She'll be with Simon?"

She was taken aback for a moment by that. Chris was worried... She knew deep down Danny still loved Deb and he would feel it as soon as he saw her. When Simon told Deb she was really angry as well. He also told her that Danny wanted her to go to the Awards.

"Why? Simon... Why?"

"He wants to see you I guess?"

"Why?

"Will you come?"

"NO... No...." she shook her head.

"Please Deb. he would have found out sooner or later."

She sighed heavily and said,"Yeah I suppose you're right."

"Will you come then?"

"I am not sure this is a good idea."

She was worried about how she would feel seeing him with his wife as well. She wanted to see him though, she couldn't help herself. Next day, Simon told Danny that Deb had agreed to come to the Awards.

"Good...I need to..." He stopped.

"You need to what, Dan?" Simon asked.

"Nothing...It doesn't matter"

"Si leave it. I told you this would stir things up again." Tony accused.

"Yeah Tony, he's married."

Danny didn't want to see her with Simon, he just wanted to see her.

He hadn't forgiven Simon even though they were now talking again. He still blamed Simon for the break up and, although he had recently got married, he always knew if Deb ever came back his marriage would seem like second prize. He had never got over her and now he was faced with a major crisis in his life. His marriage felt like a sham and for the first time he felt a huge anxiety about his future and what it meant for those that were close to him – including his new wife who hadn't done anything wrong but she was not Deb and that was a major problem. He felt terribly guilty and yet he was excited at the thought of seeing her again.

Deborah finished work and waited for Sue to finish.

"I'm taking you to dinner"

"Great… Errrrr, why?

"Do I have to have reason to take my best friend out to dinner?"

"Hmm… No."

They headed off in the direction of Peggy's Diner. They went in, sat down and ordered. Sue lay back in the leather seat and looked directly at Deb.

"I'm not convinced, I know you too well, so explain to me what is going on in that head of yours."

"Nothing"

Sue tilted her head and said, "You are not convincing me, Deb"

"OK…OK … Danny knows I'm back"

"I warned you Deb. What are you going to do?"

"I know Danny's moved on so I have told Simon I will go to the Award ceremony with him."

"I wish you luck." Sue said shaking her head. "I think you are going to need it if you think he's over you and you can just turn up – especially on Simon's arm.".

"Oh Sue, I really want to see him"

"Yeah I know…this could get very messy"

"Will you help me pick something to wear and get ready?"

"Are you sure you want to do this Deb?" Sue asked.

"Yes and No?"

"Yeah, course I will".

"I want something really special."

"Who is that for, Simon or Danny?"

"For Me," she stated.

"You are sure?"

On their day off they went shopping. Deb found the dress she wanted. She fell in love with it straight away. It was beautiful and it cost her more than she intended to pay but she had to have it. It was a black, floor length dress with natural shoulder straps which crossed at the back, decorated silver diamanté from the bust line right round to the waist line and over the straps. Sue said she was going to have them both fighting.

The Awards were being held in New York. Alex had booked the band into the Plaza Penthouse Suite. It had everything that anyone could possibly wish for. It was massive, with stunning hardwood floors, five luxurious bedrooms, four poster beds in the two master rooms and the biggest of round beds in the other three, each with their own luxurious bathrooms. Each was distinct from the others – one with a guitar-shaped bath, another with a gold-encrusted bath, tiled and illuminated. They all had their own hot tubs. It was just incredible.

The centre of the penthouse was the dramatic lounge which included a huge, cinema-type TV with a sound system linked to state of the art lighting surrounded by huge settees. Outside the French windows there was a rooftop pool with a bar and wicker sun loungers. The pool looked amazing and when it was lit up at night it looked spectacular, facing Central Park. The view of the sky line was amazing.

The guys made plans to meet up with family and friends and the penthouse was the perfect setting.

On the day of the awards, the guys arrived in the city in style. As the limo pulled up outside Plaza, their fans were chanting their name DECADE... DECADE ... There were Decade banners waving around everywhere, and flashbulbs flashing in every direction. The guys stood signing autographs and waving to their fans for a good twenty minutes. The girls were draped over the barriers trying to grab Danny and the guys trying to get their attention, screaming their names over and over.

They were shown up to their penthouse. Chris told Danny she was getting in the tub. She was feeling uneasy and on edge about meeting Deb. Danny was too, he hadn't seen her for so long.

On the other side of town, Deb was also very nervous. After work she went home and showered. Sue came round to help her get ready, she'd been on edge all day as well.

Even so, Sue told her everything would be fine. She started on her make up, putting a silvery white eyeshadow on her eyes before finishing them with black eyeliner – making her look like a fifties film star. She piled her hair up on top of her head leaving wisps dangling at the sides, framing her gorgeous face.

'What am I doing?' she thought as she put her dress on. She looked sensational, the dress showing off her slender figure beautifully. She slipped on a pair of black, satin, high stilettos. She looked and felt great. She did a quick turnaround for Sue.

"Ta-Dah…"

"You look beautiful." Sue exclaimed admiringly. "Who's this for again?"

"Me."

"Are you sure?"

Deb looked at Sue and gave her a cheeky grin showing her pearly white teeth. Just then Simon knocked on the door. Sue made a quick exit.

"Sue… thanks."

"Have an awesome night babe."

Simon told her she looked so beautiful.

"You don't look bad yourself"

Simon smiled and took her hand.

"Come on, let's go." As he led her to the limo the driver opened the door for her. She smiled and thanked him.

"I've never been in a limo before."

"Are you nervous about seeing Danny?"

She sighed heavily, "Yes I am."

"Do you know what… so am I"

Simon and Deb pulled up at the entrance in their big silver limo.

The crowds were going crazy at all the stars, shouting and screaming. Deb peered through the tinted windows.

"Oh my God." she was so overwhelmed

As they stepped out of the limo flashbulbs were flashing everywhere.

The press rushed over wanting to know who his latest lady was.

"Simon tell us about your new love."

Simon just waved and made no comment and led Deb into the building

When Danny and Chrissie arrived they made their way over to Tony, got a drink and started talking. Then Dave and Alan made their way over

"It was great to see her back," Alan blurted out.

Simon and Deb were on the dance floor when he kissed her on the cheek. Danny looked over and felt sick, he wasn't sure he could do this.

"Hi… Tony. Simon's here then?" Chris asked nervously.

"Sure is"

"Is that Deborah?" Chrissie asked.

"Yeah." Danny said abruptly.

"She's beautiful."

Danny's heart was beating so fast he thought it would jump out of his chest. All he wanted was just to talk to her, just to get near to her.

Chapter 16

Simon saw Danny and pointed him out to Deb. Suddenly she felt very nervous indeed.

"Let's get this over with Simon."

Deborah took a deep breath and looked towards Danny.

"Come on, before I change my mind."

She got hold of Simon's hand and held it tightly as they walked over. Danny watched every step she took. Her heart was beating so fast she thought she might have a heart attack.

"Hi Dan," Simon said.

"Simon…. Deb…." Danny exclaimed, not taking his eyes off her for a minute.

"Hi Danny," she said nervously.

They just starred at each other until Danny finally asked how she was.

"Oh … I'm great. I heard you got married"

"Yeah …. Oh Deb… meet Chrissie my wife… Chrissie, I would like you to meet Deb…She's ……she's…" he said stuttering, not knowing what to say.

Deborah interrupted, "I'm an old friend. It's nice to meet you."

"It's nice to meet you too. I've heard so much about you," Chris replied.

"Oh God, I hope not." Deborah said, feeling awkward.

"I'll get some drinks." Simon said, leaving Deborah with Danny and Chris.

There was an awkward silence until Tony rescued her.

"You're doing great," he whispered.

"I'm shaking Tony," she shuddered.

"Yeah I can feel you. Just take it slow… Everything will be OK."

The awards were about to get going so they were shown to their table. The band won Best Rock Band. When Decade's name was announced the guys jumped for joy and went up to the stage for their award, thanking Alex, their manager, and above all their fans.

After the awards it was party time. Plenty to drink, lots of dancing and eating. Simon asked Chris to dance.

"I think they need some time don't you?"

"Yeah I think you're right…There is a lot of tension," she added nervously.

"Don't worry Chris" Simon said, trying to convince himself as well as her that there was nothing to worry about.

While Simon and Chris were dancing Danny moved over to Deborah looking at her searchingly and asked how her parents where.

"They both died." she said sadly.

"Oh God… I am so sorry."

"That's why I came back. I only had Sue left – I'd lost my parents…my baby… you."

"Your baby?" he asked curiously.

"I was pregnant when I left…I didn't know."she quickly said

"You were pregnant… I was going to be a dad… ? WOW."

They were both silent for a moment just staring at each other. Danny couldn't hold back any longer.

"I missed you Deb," he blurted out, looking straight into her eyes.

"I missed you too, Danny"

"We could have sorted it out…"

They stared into each other's eyes, both feeling the pain of the past.

"You and Simon…?" he asked hesitantly.

"We're friends." She replied.

Simon and Chrissie came back from the dance floor but Danny wanted to talk to Deb some more without everyone around them. He grabbed hold of Deb's hand.

"Come on let's dance. We haven't finished our conversation yet."

As he led her to the dance floor the guys and Chris watched them intensely… they were very close they could feel the heat between them. Danny's arm wrapped round her so tight that she could feel his hand on her skin. He could smell her perfume, a sensual smell of ylang ylang. He just wanted to keep her there in his arms.

"Oh Deb, It's has been so long since I put my arms around you, you feel so good. You are still beautiful."

He kissed her on the cheek and they stared deep into each other eyes. Deb could feel Danny's body against hers… he was so close

"We'd better go back," she said, feeling very flustered.

"Why?" he asked

"We are being watched Danny"

"So… I don't care. Let them…I haven't seen you for so long I just wanna…"

He sighed heavily. "Oh Deb. Why did you leave me?"

"I just thought it was for the best."

They seemed to stare at each other all evening. They couldn't take their eyes off each other and although they both tried to hide it, it was noticeable. At the end of the evening Tony pulled Deb to one side.

"You were awesome"

Deb took a deep breath and smiled at Tony. She knew Danny was still in love with her but there was nothing to be done. Deb looked back and saw Chrissie kissing Danny. She shook her head sadly.

They all made their way to their limos, hugged and said good night. On the way home she was so quiet Simon asked if she was OK. She said she was but she was thinking about Danny.

He had made his choice and moved on, just like she had told him to do all that time ago. She needed to do the same.

When they got back to Deb's Simon went to kiss her and she pulled him closer and kissed him back. He looked at her longingly"

You know I want you, don't you?"

Deborah smiled and kissed him passionately. He sent the car away and they went inside and she kissed him again. He scooped her up into his arms and took her to the bedroom and laid her down on the bed. Huskily he asked her if she was sure about this, kissing her seductively at the same time.

She whispered,"I'm sure."

"I love you Deb…"

She kissed him and unbuttoned his shirt, moving her hands up and down his body. She could feel him against her and knew he was very excited. He removed her clothes slowly and very gently caressed her body. Clasping her hands he moved between her thighs. She kissed the nape of his neck. She sighed and began to breathe more heavily. His lips brushing against her ear, then slowly down her neck he moved his lips down her body.

"Ohhhh ahhhhhhh"

She moaned as he started to make love to her. He moved slowly and rhythmically, letting her know how much he wanted her. He made her feel good and she knew he loved her. Maybe, she could fall in love with him…

The next morning Simon woke Deb up with breakfast.

"Good morning," he said with a very jolly tone.

"Are you always this happy in the morning Simon?" she grumbled as she tried to wake up.

"Hell No – you are the reason I'm happy."

"Why?" She stretched out

"Last night was just awesome."

Deborah started to laugh and Simon looked at her suspiciously.

"Why are you laughing?"

She grabbed him and pulled him to her to kiss him. He kissed her back softly.

"So, why were you laughing?"

"I think you are so funny. Go on…Go meet up with the guys."

"I want to just stay with you. I'll see you later won't I?"

"Yeah."

Simon left and Deb got ready for work. She met up with Sue on her break.

"Well? How did it go?"

"Good…Danny is still Danny and his wife is nice, unfortunately. Danny wouldn't have married her if she wasn't"

"Simon?"

"Simon… Mmm…he stayed last night" she mentioned casually

Sue looked at her with her mouth open, speechless.

"Stayed as in… ?"

"Yes…As in…"

"I've gotta to ask Deb… Is he a good lover?"

"Yeah… he is actually" she grinned.

"You do know what you're doing right? Simon is in love with you, you know that don't you?"

Shaking her head she replied,"I'm just hoping for the best. Danny is married and I need to get on with my life.

Simon met up with the guys and Chris at breakfast. He was extremely happy. Danny, however, was in a foul mood. He knew Simon had stayed with Deb. He knew because he had called Simon's room in the early hours and there was no answer.

"Good morning, Simon"

"Morning, Chris"

"Are you having breakfast?"

"Hmm, actually, I'm good Chris."

"Why?" Danny asked, "You like breakfast."

"I'm good, Danny." I'm going to get changed. I'll be with you guys in a sec." Simon said as he left.

They headed for the new York studio. Chris went off and did some shopping.

Danny kept forgetting his words and losing his temper. 'Fuck…fuck… fuck…', hitting the microphone stand before storming out of the recording booth.

"Let's take a break guys," Tony said, shaking his head.

Danny stormed out of the building and sat outside. He lit a cigarette with his head down in his hands. Tony went out to him.

"Dan?"

Danny looked up.

"Yeah, yeah – I'm fine," he said, with a doleful look in his eyes.

"No you're not; and I know why."

"He stayed with her Tony. I can't handle the thought of him being with her. I'm gonna go outta my fuckin mind I can't even about him thinking about him fuckin touching her."

"You don't know he stayed with her, Danny."

"Yeah I do. He did. What do I do? I'm married. Chris knows I still love Deb she's not stupid. She knows"

"Oh Dan, I'm so sorry buddy......"

"I'm in a fuckin nightmare. This isn't happening."

The day went from bad to worse for Danny. He couldn't concentrate, he couldn't get Deb out of his head – all he could see was her and Simon together.

Deb had only just arrived home from work when Simon knocked on the door. He had bought her a present. As he gave her the box he whispered, "This is for you." She opened it and gasped at the most beautiful bracelet.

"Simon this is beautiful, but why? You don't need to buy me gifts."

"I know, I wanted to"

She kissed him"thank you"

Simon smiled at her and said hesitantly, "So… Are we together Deb or was last night just last night?"

"Do you want us to be together?"

"You need to ask me that?" he said incredulously.

"Looks like…we are together then," she grinned.

Simon smiled, "Really? he breathed slowly as he took hold of her and kissed her. He took her hand tenderly, lead her to the bedroom and started kissing her very passionately. She started to undo his shirt and moved her hands over his body. Soon they were skin to skin

"Oh baby… hmm…you are the hottest woman I have ever seen." he sighed as she kissed his neck moving her lips down his body.

The more she kissed the more he moaned. "Ohhhh yeah baby". She was driving him crazy. Quickly he reversed positions – he could feel her breasts against his chest. He brushed his lips over her nipples, making her arch her back. His mouth made its way down her body, his tongue flicking over her flesh making her want more, her legs stiffening as she built to orgasm.

Slowly and tenderly they made love for some time until they lay smiling and satisfied in each other's arms…Deb was first to move, getting some wine out of the fridge. As she got back in to bed Simon turned to her and more urgently this time they made love again.

They lay in bed Simon resting on his side with his arm under his head putting his finger though her hair feeling very satisfied.

"I want to you to meet my dad… Will you come?"

"Yeah – It would be nice to meet him."

"I've told him all about you."

"Have you?"

"Yeah – I told him about you when you were with Dan"

"WOW."

Early next morning they got up and got dressed. Simon went off to meet the guys and Deborah headed in to work.

Danny asked the guys if they wanted to come to a pool party on Saturday night. Danny wanted to see Deb again and that was the only way he could think of doing it.

"We'll come" Simon said, then added, "Dan, can I talk to you first?"

"Yeah, what is it?"

"I've got something to tell you and I don't want to hurt you or make things bad between us again but things have moved on with me and Deb…We're not just friends anymore…we're together."

Danny looked at him. "I know," he replied

"Are you OK with that?"

"She's got to get on with her life – You love her don't you?"

"You know I do Dan."

"So…It's time to move on,Si."

Danny was hurting and jealous. It had taken him all his courage to say what he did. Tony had overheard and went over to Dan.

"I know that hurt you"

Danny turned, shaking his head. "What do I do? What the fuck do I do?"

"I don't know Dan…

"She could tell me she still loves me."

"How can she do that, Dan?"

"I don't know. This is a fucking mess. I do know one thing – this is going to drive me fucking crazy." he cried as he hit the wall…

"Dan…Bud…"

Danny took a deep breath and sighed. "Come on Tony, lets fuck off outta here – let's get hammered."

They went off to a bar and Tony started talking about the party on Saturday.

"So this pool party – I guess Deb will bring her friend, Sue?"

"Oh Tony…buddy…you wanna hook up with Sue?"

Tony just spluttered. "Hmmm, I really like her."

Danny went on to drinking shots. He'd ordered some more when a young lady and her friend came over to them.

"You're Danny from Decade aren't you? Can I get your autograph"

Danny's eyes widened and he told her she could have anything she wanted and patted his lap. He didn't have to tell her twice. Now his hands started to move higher up her leg and he kissed her neck. She couldn't believe her luck she was going to get laid by Decade's Danny Brooks. He grabbed her hand and led her out the back where he pushed her up against the wall. He pushed his hand up her skirt.

"Oh baby, no panties!"

She purred like a kitten as he turned her around and lifted her skirt up round her waist. "Oh, man… yeah". He pulled his manhood out of his jeans and banged her right there.

When they went back in Tony looked at him and shook his head and simply said, "Chris"

"Come on Tony, shit happens"

Danny was so rat faced Tony had to shove him in a taxi.

When he got home, he nearly beat the door down, he hammered on it that hard. Chris looked down at him as he fell in.

"Fuck…" he managed as scrambled to pick himself up off the floor

"Where have you been?"

"Out"

"Yes I can see that – but where?"

"Out…out…"

"Danny"

"What… what? Fucking hell." He pushed past her and went to bed, totally dismissing her

The next morning, Chris wouldn't talk to him, she was so angry. He asked her what her problem was and she told him she didn't like the way he was behaving. He just shrugged his shoulders at her.

Simon was taking Deb to meet his dad, Gary. He was a lovely man and he told Deb all about Simon's mom and how she'd died of cancer the year before. Deb told Gary that she had lost her mum to cancer and her dad from a heart attack. He told her he knew only too well how much pain losing someone caused and how he missed his wife.

Deborah, Simon and Gary went out to dinner at classy restaurant. While Deb went to the restroom Gary told Simon how nice Deb was and he could see why Simon was in love with her.

"How's Danny taking this news?"

"Good." Simon said, relieved.

"Simon, are you sure? he was really hooked on her."

"Dad, he said he was fine."

"Hmm." Gary wasn't as sure as Simon.

The evening came to a close and they dropped Gary off on their way back to Debs. He had told her she was a breath of fresh air.

On Friday Deb and Sue flew out to Simon's for Danny's party. Their mouths dropped when the saw Simon's house

"Oh my God, Deb – this house is beautiful

Deborah looked round nodding her head and they stepped out in to the garden thought the sliding doors In front of them was a beautiful round swimming pool with sun loungers round it and freshly-mown lawns They could smell a rainbow of flowers, there were so many different flowers.

Simon's housekeeper had arranged a spectacular meal for them – a rack of lamb with all the trimmings and banoffee sundae for afters. Simon had secretly invited Tony and he was quick to say 'Yes'. They all spent a pleasant evening together. Tony was going to ask Sue if she want to go out to dinner with him, but he bottled it.

Next day, they headed over to Danny's. They went in Simon's new convertible and Deb sat dreamily looking up at the sky watching the clouds past by while Sue looked on in amazement at the at the mansions. 'Oh, what would it be like to live here?' she thought.

Simon pulled in to the drive. Deb and Sue stepped out of the car and looked at Danny's house from the outside.

"Come on ladies." shouted Simon.

It was a glorious hot day, the sun was beating down. Deb had bought a new high-cut white bikini which was very revealing and a short beach dress with flip flop sandals. She certainly knew how to get attention if she wanted it. Sue had played safe with a blue strappy bikini.

Danny spotted Deb straight away, 'Now, how to get close to her,' he thought. Danny pointed out to Tony that Sue had arrived. They'd set the barbecue going and the drink was flowing. Chris spotted Deb went over.

"Hi"

"Hay Chrissie – hello"… Oh, this is Sue, my best friend."

"Hi Sue… I hope you've both brought your bikinis… and call me Chris please. Chrissie is what my mom and dad call me."

Sue smiled and said hello, at the same time having real good look at Chris. She couldn't deny that she was very attractive. Just then Simon appeared

"Hi Chris," he said as he slid his arms round Deb's waist.

"Are you two an item then?" she asked, visibly relieved when Simon confirmed that they were.

"Oh It's so hot… Right I'm going in the pool."

Deb pulled her dress over her head revealing her shapely body. Danny watched her intensely… his eyes fixed on her.

He had pulled his sunglasses down to the edge of his nose to have a better look. He remembered that body, how it felt to the touch. He needed to figure out how he could get close enough to touch her again

"Who's coming? Si, come on…" Deb laughed as she got hold of his hand.

"Hold on. I need to get changed."

"No you don't." Deb said pulling him nearer to the edge of the pool.

"No… no… Deb…."

Deb started to laugh uncontrollably and Sue called him a pussy.

Simon stood eyeing Sue. "Pussy…eh." he said throwing his hands up.

"Yeah ,pussy." she laughed.

"You are going to regret that." he smiled at her and then said, "I'm gonna get changed"

As he walked away Sue again shouted"pussy" until Simon turned.

"I'm going to set Tony on to you."

Sue smiled. She could think of worse things.

Deb jumped in the pool. Danny was still watching her and then BINGO. He had it – he knew how he could work this. Sue was stood at the side of the pool bent over talking to Deb when Danny came up behind, her grabbing her round the waist. Picking her up , he threw her in –she didn't even get a chance to take her dress off.

"You wait, Danny Brooks." she shouted.

"Come on babe," he said provoking her. Tony was stood at the edge of the pool laughing. He couldn't help himself.

"What are you laughing at?" Sue asked as she grabbed his leg, pulling him in too.

Next, she pulled at Danny's leg but she couldn't get him in so she got out and chased him round the pool until she finally got him. He did make it easy for her to push him in – he just needed the excuse to get in the pool with Deb.

Danny swam underwater, over to where Deb was, and grabbed her. Slowly moving his hands up her legs, he suddenly pulled her under the water, moving his hands up her body as he got very close. She could feel his hands gripping her thighs then slowly moving up her body brushing over her breasts

Everyone else seemed to notice too. Simon and Chris seemed clearly worried.

Tony scrambled out of the water and looked at Sue.

"I'm coming back for you. I've not finished with you yet."

Danny and Deb shouted in unison, "Oh yeah." Danny added, "Let's get this party going, Tony."

"I'll be waiting." Sue said confidently

"Oh yeah baby …,." Danny shouted.

Tony turned to Danny and said "I'm coming back. She's not getting away with that."

Danny smiled and said, "I hear you bud."

Tony walked over to Simon and Chis. This is awkward for them both.

"This is how they are together."

Alan was close by and added,"Tony's right... this is how they are together"

"They're right, Chris."

Danny, Deb and Sue were still in the pool fooling around. Tony and Sue really liked each other and Tony decided to get back in and fool around with them. Besides he had to back up his words from earlier. Danny kept grabbing Deb at every opportunity. She decided it was her turned to grab Danny. She swam under the water and grabbed hold of Danny from behind as she moved he hands round him. He turned round suddenly. They were so close, he looked at her and getting hold of her, he wrapped his legs round pulling her even closer to him. They stared at each other for what seemed forever and the atmosphere was electric between them.

Tony had got back in the pool and was underwater, swimming towards Sue. He grabbed her legs and pulled her under the water as his hands moved around her waist and he pulled her close to him.

"Ahh...See? What you gonna do now?" he laughed.

"Hmm," Sue laughed throatily. "I think that's what are *you* going to do now, Tony? You've got me."

Tony looked at her shaking his head, "Woman. Don't try to confuse me."

She put her arms round his neck

"Me confuse you?" she said so innocently. They smiled at each other knowingly...

Simon appeared with a ball and jumping in they started to play water ball. Reluctantly Danny let Deb go but only because he had to. He shouted to Chris to get in and they played with the ball for a while. Chris swam towards Danny, she put her arms round him and kissed him.

Deb felt an overwhelming jealousy and decided to play the same game. Simon was talking to Sue and Tony when she swam over and grabbed him from behind. He turned round and put his arms round her and kissed her neck. Deb kissed him back seductively. It was Danny's turn to be jealous and jealous he was. He swam over to Simon and pulled him under the water. They started to play rough, chucking each other around in the water.

Alan had been sat drinking, happily watching everyone, particularly Danny and Deb, having fun. Dave went over and joined him.

"Hey, Buddy"

"He's never got over her." Alan was looking over at Danny and Deb.

"What… what ya talkin about?"

"Dan and Deb…They're playing each other."

Dave looked over, "No you're wrong, they're just fuckin about."

"They're still in love with each other Dave… I've been watching them."

Dave looked at Alan with a taut expression. Alan went on.

"Dan has touched her… had his legs wrapped around her… the only thing he ain't done is banged her."

"Fuckin hell, Al."

Just at that moment Danny walked over.

"Hi guys"

"Dan…." They said together

"Al are you OK, bud?"

"Sure Dan"

Danny knew there was something. They had been talking about something as he was walking over and they had gone quiet as soon as he'd approached them. Alan quickly spoke up.

"Tony seems to dig Sue – she's does look pretty hot, though."

"Yeah I think somethin's gonna happen there."

"Yep, think ya right." Dave chirps in.

Alan being Alan mentioned that Deb looked pretty hot too.

Danny looked at Alan and smiled.

"Yep"

"Must be weird seeing her with Si."

"Yeah it is a bit." trying not to show that he was jealous.

Everyone in the pool shouted to Danny.

"Yeah coming – are you guys getting in?"

"Yeah we'll be right with you"

Danny smiled and gave them the thumbs up. As he jumped back in the pool the water splashed up, hitting Simon right in the face.

Alan turned his head looking over his sunglasses at Dave, "Just fuckin about eh?" Dave nodded his head knowingly.

Sue and Tony were getting on really well. They really liked each other and there was a lot of chemistry between them. Tony kept getting hold of her at every opportunity and Sue did the same. He asked her for her number so he could call her after he back from the tour.

All too soon it was time to go but when Simon, Deb and Sue got back to Simon's place, Simon was a bit quiet, mulling things over in his mind. Deborah asked if he was alright.

"I know I haven't got the right to be the jealous boyfriend because we haven't been together long but I was really jealous today. Danny was all over you."

"Oh, Simon, there's nothing to be jealous about. Danny and me are just friends now... That's all. We were just having a laugh."

"You just got so close to each other."

Deborah went over to Simon and kissed him.

"It's me and you now babe, now come on lets go to bed. I have plans for you."

Simon smiled, "Be gentle with me."

Sue had gone straight to bed. Deb grabbed Simon's hand and led him up the stairs. As they reached the middle step. She turned to face him – her big green eyes widening, enticing him with her sexy smile.

"Oh... Baby" as he stumbled up the stair to get closer to her.

When they reached the bed room, she pushed him on the bed and he fell back, breathing heavily. She moved her hands down his body removing his clothes. He started to breath even heavier. He reached out to her as she lowered her head to his, kissing him slowly, biting his lip. "Hmmm ohhhh Deb ohhhh hmmm". They made love passionately, hot and intense.

The next morning they went down for breakfast. Sue was sat at the table eating her toast and smiled at them both. Simon asked why she was smiling.

"Nothing"

"What, Sue?" Deb grinned back.

"Hmm...nothing." she giggled.

"Sue."

"Deborah."

Simon looked at them both quizzically

"I think you're both being dirty girls aren't you? I'm going see you girls when we get back."

Simon went to meet the guys as they were setting off on a tour of Japan for three months.

Deb and Sue flew back to New York as they had work on the Monday. Deb was sat in her office deep in thought when her secretary Trish buzzed her.

"Deborah, there is someone to see you."

"I'm not expecting anyone. Who is it?"

"Mrs. Brooks. She's not on your list of appointments." Trish said.

"I have no…" She stopped as she realised who Mrs. Brooks was. "Erm… Send Mrs. Brooks in."

Chris walked in sheepishly

"Hi" She said, peeking her head round the door. "I've come to ask you to lunch but I just feel stupid now."

"Long way to come for lunch…" Deb said.

She grabbed her purse and told Trish she was having an early lunch. They went to the little diner on the corner and sat down and ordered.

"I know why you have come to see me. You want to know if I'm back to try and mess things up between you and Danny."

Chris looked at Deb.

"Yeah, it's stupid. Saturday, Danny was very…shall we say *friendly* with you."

"No, it's not stupid… I would be the same."

"Would you?"

"Yes I would. Well there is no going back. Danny must love you otherwise he wouldn't have married you and I'm with Simon now… Danny and I are friends and that's all – I hope that doesn't change."

Chris got hold of Deb's hands. "I don't want to stop you being friends. I'm hoping we can *all* be friends?"

Deb smiled and said, "Yeah, that would be good."

They finished their lunch and Deb went back to work. Later she met Sue and told her all about Chris coming to see her.

"Why?"

Deb explained that she was really worried about her and Danny.

"I suppose it was to be expected. Danny was pretty full on with you in the pool"

"Was he? We were just messing about." Deborah said, surprised.

"Yeah…he was. At one point I thought you were gonna eat each other."

Deb just laughed.

Simon rang Deb to tell her the first gig had gone great, the fans were awesome.

There were girls everywhere. Two girls grabbed Danny and pulled him in to the bedroom, ripping his clothes off. Their hands were all over him, kissing every inch of his body. His eyes widened with excitement – 'some girl on girl action, a threesome.' he thought. They blew his mind with the stuff they did to him. They were in there all night with him. There was a lot moaning and that was just Danny. Dave and Alan were also having fun with the other girls. Simon handed the telephone over to Tony so he could talk to Sue.

After she had spoken to Simon, Deb put on her leather miniskirt and crop top T-shirt then slipped her shoes on, grabbed her purse and got in a cab and headed to the club.

The cab pulled up outside the club. They pushed their way through the crowd and finally got to the bar where they ordered two vodkas and coke.

While they were waiting for their drinks Deb noticed a very attractive man looking at her. He looked really familiar, as if she had seen him before although she couldn't think where she might have seen him. She smiled at him he smiled back at her.

"Who are you smiling at?" Sue asked.

"Him…There…he is gorgeous…Don't you think he is gorgeous?"

Sue looked at Deb, "Hmm he sure is." She looked at him more closely, "I've seen him before"

"Yeah, I know I have.

"Oh my, he looks like… Oh God."

"Who … who?" Deb said, pushing her for an answer

"Oh shit – I can't remember his name."

"Oh Sue, you had me all excited then."

Deb pulled out a $10 bill out of her purse to pay for the drinks. The bar tender told her that the young man had paid her bill.

Deb smiled over and mouthed, "Thank you."

He mouthed, "It's my pleasure. See you later perhaps?" back at her as he went over to a group of men. They looked familiar too.

The young man was still in the nightclub and he watched Deb all night. He seemed to have his eyes fixed on her but he never made a move on her.

He was a very good looking man, tall with blue eyes, long shaggy blonde hair and a nicely toned body – he obviously worked out. At the end of the night he made a move. He asked her to dance to a slow song and he put his arms around her waist and they swayed rhythmically. She was still trying to figure out where she had seen him. She was clearly attracted to him and he was to her. At the end of the song he simply kissed her hand, gazed up at her with his big sky blue eyes and left.

Chapter 17

The following Morning Deb got up, got ready and went to work. She was still thinking about the young man she had met in the club. As she flicked through her paperwork she got a call from Chris.

"I'm in new York"

"Great we can meet up tonight"

She headed down to Sue to make sure that everything was ready for the wedding party that was booked in for the afternoon.

"Yeah everything is ready…

"What are you doing tonight? Chris is here."

"Why don't we go for dinner?" suggested Sue.

"Yeah great…I'll meet you here at 12 for lunch… I'll ring Chris back"

Deb called Chris and arranged to meet her at her hotel. At lunch time she met Sue and they went to the diner round the corner. They were sat eating their sandwiches and Deb was talking about the young man from the night before.

"You liked him didn't you?"

"Yeah, Sue – it's odd, he has been on my mind all morning… I know I've seen him before, though – its driving me crazy."

They went back to work and the wedding party that was booked arrived. Sue and Deb made sure it ran smoothly and the bride and groom, all the guests were happy. Deb and Sue had this natural way of impressing the guests. The hotel always got good reviews.

After work Deb went home and got ready, jumped in a cab and headed off to meet Sue and Chris… They talked and talked. Suddenly a man with a camera rushed up and took their photograph, flash bulbs going off everywhere.

"You're Simon Richards new girlfriend," he shot at her

This was hot news. He had got a picture of Decade's wife and girlfriends. Their main interest was Deb… She had made Simon settle down. Gone were the days of seeing Simon Richards with different woman every night. What a scoop this was. This was going to hit the headlines.

Nick, an English rock star in the band *Rona* had met up with Decade. He was telling Danny and Simon that he'd met a girl in a night club the other night. She was beautiful and he was in love.

"Did you get laid?" Danny asked

"No…She was perfect. She had great legs."

"Call yourself a rock star and you didn't get between the great legs" Simon said.

"No – I don't think she even knew who I was, which was nice because when they know you're a star that's all they are interested in."

"Yeah… but chicks love all that shit." Simon said.

Simon went to the bar, leaving Danny and Nick still talking.

"If I meet that girl again I think I'll ask her to marry me. I can't get her out of my head."

"She's really got to you buddy."

"Yeah…You should have seen her…? Well you must have felt like that … you're married."

"Yeah I did… but not about Chris. There was this one girl…"

Nick sat back while Danny told him all about Deb. Nick couldn't believe what Danny had told him

"Well if I see my girl again she is mine. She's not getting away."

"Go for it my friend."

When Deborah got home from work she got a big surprise. Simon was hiding in the lobby when she walked in. As he grabbed her she turned round quickly and he gave her a fright. She slapped him playfully.

"I'm sorry Deb" he laughed.

He felt that she could be falling in love with him. She had told him she was missing him whilst he was away…These were all good signs. He told her he had a surprise for her.

"What?" she asked.

"I can't tell you yet," he teased her.

"Oh yes you can." she said, pushing him into the apartment.

"No… no… I can't."

"Oh yes." she laughed.

She pushed him on the sofa sitting on top of him she started to tickle him. He was very ticklish and couldn't say anything for laughing.

"OK…OK … Deb… Deb, stop tickling please…I'll tell you…" He took a deep breath after laughing so much.

"I'm taking you away. We're going to Hawaii."

She had always wanted to go to Hawaii. She was so excited she jumped up and started jumping up and down.

"Oh… oh…Hawaii …Hawaii." she shouted with excitement. She grabbed Simon and kissed him.

"I need new clothes." she exclaimed.

"Deb… slow down." Si laughed. He took hold of her tenderly.

"I love you so much"

She kissed him slowly. "Thank you" she breathed.

"I love doing things for you. I get a real buzz from it…and you make me happy."

"Do you know you are one of the sweetest men I know?"

She grabbed a bottle of wine out the refrigerator and two glasses.

"Come on …"

She took his hand and led him to the bedroom. Pushing him on the bed she gently fell on to him kissing him slowly. He responded, kissing her back.

"Don't you want to get something to eat first?"

"No I just want you, Simon, just like that." That's what he wanted to hear.

"I've missed you and I feel very horny."

She looked down at him and bent forward kissing him. He pulled her firmly towards him, taking her clothes off bit by bit, unhooking her bra with one hand, his other hand moving slowly up and down her back, pulling her closer to him following the curves of her body. Trembling from his touch she sighed, "Ahhhhhhhh…"

He eased himself between her thighs and made love to her slowly and passionately. Her thighs tightened up around his hips as they moved together and she groaned with delight. She ran her tongue over his lips, moving her hands over her breasts, down her body, driving him wild.

He couldn't hold on any longer, he had to come. As they climaxed his eyes rolled to the back of his head.

Chapter 18

Tony called Sue and asked her out on a date. Sue jumped at the chance, she really liked Tony. He told her he would pick her up at eight and, at eight on the dot, there he was on the doorstep. They went to a little exclusive restaurant that all the guys used when they were in new York. The waiter showed them to their table and Tony ordered drinks.

"This is nice," Sue said looking round the room.

"Yeah, we all use this place when we're here."

They sat and looked at the menu and Tony asked Sue what she would like.

"Hmm, Chicken salad...I think"

Tony looked at her scathingly, "Chicken salad?"

"Yeah I have to watch my figure," she grinned.

"Why?" Tony laughed

"I have to work at this figure...

"I don't think you realise how beautiful you are."

"Thank you, that's a really nice thing to say," she said, feeling embarrassed, and blushed.

"It's true." he said, winking at her

"It's funny how things turn out… I still can't believe that Simon is with Deb."

"No, me neither. I thought Dan and Deb were forever…he was never like that over any woman before…"

"No, he really loved her…he still does…"

"Why are we talking about Dan and Deb? It's our first date we should be talking about us." Sue laughed.

"Yeah, you're right…We should".

Tony asked Sue about her family. "The only family I have is Deb."

"What about your mom and dad?"

"My dad… whoever he is… left when my mom got pregnant. And then my mom gave me up so I don't know who she is… "

"Oh?"

"Deb changed my life… What about you?"

"Me and my sister grew up with our mom. Our dad left just after my sister was born and we haven't seen him since…he was a drunk… he could be dead for all we know…My mom worked all hours to keep us. So I look after her now."

"That's nice."

Sue and Tony talked for hours… in fact they were the last ones in the restaurant. When they left, Tony took her home and asked if he could see her again. Sue said she would love to. He confessed that he had liked her since the night that Danny met Deb.

"Oh My God?" Sue laughed, "Me too."

"You're joking right? We could have done this sooner."

As they stood outside Sue's apartment building, Tony pulled Sue towards him and kissed her.

"Do you want to come in?"

"Yeah"

Sue took his hand and led him in. She opened the door, turned and kissed him. He kissed her back very passionately and moved her backwards, shutting the door behind him. They talked and talked. He didn't know how he kept his hands off her but he did. From there they saw each other every night.

Sue really liked Tony…he was just her type, wavy, longish dark hair, brown eyes and a muscular, tanned body.

A couple of weeks later, Deb and Simon went to Hawaii. It was beautiful... The suite they had was gorgeous and had a four poster bed. Deb loved it in Hawaii. They spent a lot of time on the beach.

She enjoyed being with Simon...he made everything perfectly romantic...he was a very romantic and loving man. She thought she was falling in love with him. Maybe this was going to work. Simon wasn't the love of her life, she was never going to feel like again but she really wanted this to work.

She got up and ordered some coffee as Simon was still asleep. She poured it and went on the balcony gazing at the glittering water of the ocean. It was so beautiful... such a romantic setting. Simon woke up and stood behind her

"What are you doing?"

"I'm looking at the ocean and thinking how perfect everything is."

He put his arms around her waist kissed the side of her neck.

"You are so beautiful and I love you so much."

She turned round and kissed him. Swiftly he picked her up into his arms and took her back to the bedroom. Laying her on the bed he touched her face and put his fingers though her hair. He kissed her again and taken away with the romance of it all, he made love to her again and again... Later they went to the beach and talked. Simon suggested she gave up her job.

"Yeah Si, that's going to pay my rent."

Simon suggested she did something else.

"What?"

"Move in with me."

"Simon, I can't do that"

"So...what do you want to do?"

She told him she wanted to own her own restaurant one day.

"So why don't you?"

"Money... I have what my mum and dad left me but that is not enough,"she explained.

"You need a partner," he said smiling.

"Yeah that's great... but Sue hasn't got that kind of money..."

"What about me?"

"Why would you want a restaurant?"

"I love you" he said simply.

"That's not a good enough reason."

"OK… Then it would be a good investment."

She laughed. "You're joking right?"

"No – I'm serious Deb… So what do you say, Partner?"

Deb looked at him and said, "Really?"

Simon smiled and said, "Really… Think about it Deb – I've got contacts to the rich and famous… That would be my part… and you do what you do best."

Deb flung her arms around him.

"I absolutely adore you…I'll start looking when we get back." She was so excited.

They had a wonderful holiday – they did everything together: paragliding, water skiing, he even sang to her under the moonlight. They a great time and Simon thought he had won her heart at last. They flew home and Simon stayed at Deb's.

In the morning Sue turned up with Tony. They had been seeing a lot of each other and were enjoying each other's company. Simon was still in bed but Deb was bursting at the seams and she couldn't wait to tell Sue all about the restaurant. She wanted her to run it with her. Sue got so excited.

"Oh God… Yeah." She said jumping up and down. With all the noise they woke Simon who appeared looking as if he was still half asleep.

"What's all the excitement about?"

Tony explained that the girls were excited about the restaurant. Deb turned round quickly to face him.

"You haven't changed your mind have you?"

"Nooooo…. But can someone make some coffee please?" Simon laughed.

Simon disappeared, had a quick shower, got dressed and had his coffee. They were all sat round the table when Tony chirped up:

"So where's this restaurant going to be? Here or Beverly Hills?" He asked, swept up in the excitement of it all.

"Oh yeah…never thought of that…Deb…how do you feel about moving to Beverly Hills?" Simon asked casually.

"I don't mind… But only if Sue moves too"

"Yeah Deb...I'll move to Beverly Hills." she said extremely excited.

"Beverly Hills it is then." Deb said as they all high fived each other.

Simon and Tony flew back to Beverly Hills to meet up with the rest of the guys. They had to go over some new songs.

"Was Hawaii nice then Si?" Danny asked.

"Great...You should take Chris...Very romantic...."

"Yeah... maybe. Did Deb find it romantic?"

"Yeah...She loved it"

"You sound as if you're getting on well together."

"Yeah Dan, we are. She and Sue are moving here. We're going to be partners."

"She's moving here...Partners...What do you mean?"

Danny's heart was racing. He thought Simon meant he was marrying her. He didn't want that to happen. That was the last thing he wanted.

"We're going to be partners in a restaurant."

"Oh right...Great." He was so relieved.

Simon started looking around and he found the perfect place. Deb would love this place he thought and called her.

"You need to see this place, Deb."

She and Sue arranged to fly to Beverly Hills and see the restaurant he had found. He took her and Sue to see it. Deb fell in love with it as soon as she saw it. It was just what she was looking for – the location the size and with some imagination and some redesign this place would be perfect. They told the owner they would contact their lawyer to prepare contracts as soon as possible.

After they had signed the contract, Simon introduced her to a designer and she explained what she was looking for. After a number of sketches they had the dream restaurant that made her so excited. She wanted to get the builders in yesterday but had to make sure she got the ones who could make the design come to life. After a few weeks the builders started work ripping walls out and old furnishing.

Whilst the builders restructured the place, Deb met with the interior designers who would be responsible for the decoration of the restaurant. It was going to be a luxurious ivory and pearl backdrop with pine floors and a solid oak bar. There would be cream leather settees whilst guest wait to be seated.

On walking through the arched entrance to the restaurant your eyes would be drawn to the chandeliers, in chrome with stunning pendants dropping down, sparkling and shining when illuminated. The tables were dressed in white linen table cloth, each with fresh flowers in pearl encrusted vases. The chairs were deep cushioned and elegantly shaped.

Next on the to-do list was moving to Beverly Hills. They found apartments near each other. They packed up everything and set out.

Simon wanted to make sure that when the restaurant was running that it had the best chef and started looking and taking guidance. Now everything was ready. Simon came round to check the place over, bringing the rest of the guys with him.

"This place is awesome…Are you ready for the grand opening?" Danny commented.

"Yeah I think so," Deb said smiling at him

"Is there anything we can do to help?" he asked.

Deb looked at him and smiled."Well now you mention it if a certain band was to open the restaurant that would be really good…"

Danny smiled. "She's not just a pretty face is she? Yes…I suppose we can do that for you."

Putting her hands together and grinning, "Thank you, Guys."

Danny asked her if she was going to show him round… She took his hand.

"Yeah come on."

She took him into the kitchen and started to tell him what she had planned. Danny just stared at her… she stopped talking and looked at him.

"Danny," she said.

"Sorry… You got what you wanted…Your own business…You are so fucking beautiful." He reached to touch her face and gently ran his finger over her cheek.

She looked at him wide-eyed. "Not *everything* I wanted Danny."

"Deb I… I…."

"Yeah?…" waiting eagerly for what he was about say.

Just then Simon came in and put his arms around her waist.

"I was just telling her what a good job she's done with this place." Danny said walking away.

He couldn't stand it when Simon touched her… he just had to get away. Tony went to look for Sue. She was at the delivery door taking a food order.

"Hi Tony…I'll be with you in one second."

"Hey"

When she had finished the order he asked if she wanted to go out that evening and she said she would like nothing better.

"Great." he said as he moved closer to her and kissed her. "I want us to become an item."

Sue looked thoughtful for a moment as though she was mulling it over.

"I thought you were never going to ask" she laughed.

Tony smiled. "So… now we are an item does that mean you'll be using my body for lots of sex?" he grinned.

"Hmm…Yeah……Is this going to be a problem?" she smiled back.

"Ahh… Um…no…I shouldn't think so."

"Well that's good to know."

"Well, you have needs, I know that." he laughed and then kissed her again.

Deb came in and caught them.

"Oh…What is this then? Tony…Are you taking advantage of the management?"

Tony turned round with a wide grin on his face.

"Oh yes I am," Tony turned back to Sue. "She's so kooky."

"Yeah… But you've gotta love her."

Chapter 19

The following week, the band opened the restaurant. The press was all over it. Lots of rich and famous people arrived for the biggest thing happening this month. The media wanted Deb and the band to pose for photographs. The band was used to all the publicity and flashing bulbs but Deb wasn't. She was a bit reluctant to be in the pictures so Simon and Danny grabbed her. They both put their arms round her waist and told her this was her big night. She wanted Sue in the picture with her so Tony grabbed Sue's hand and pulled her to him. Deb wanted to share this with her. She and the rest of the staff had worked so hard to get everything right.

"This place is great Deb" Chris said.

"Thanks Chris…You look fantastic by the way."

The party was in full swing when Simon came over.

"I want you to meet a friend of mine – Meet Nick"

Deb turned round smiled and said, surprised, "Oh … Hello…". 'Oh my God, my mystery Englishman,' she thought.

"Hello" said Nick. His mind was doing somersaults as he thought, 'Oh no… My perfect girl is Simon's girlfriend. '

Sue had been trying to tell her all night that the young man she met in the club was here.

"You know each other?" Simon asked.

"We met months ago…Remember I told you all about the girl I'd met at the club?"

Simon laughed nervously.

"Oh yeah, and what you were saying?" Deb asked curiously.

"I told Simon and Danny I'd met the most beautiful woman I had ever laid my eyes on and that I was in love with her and that I had frozen."

Deb laughed."Thank you"

"I meant every word… I couldn't believe I froze. You must have thought I was nuts."

Danny noticed how Deborah was looking at Nick and went over.

"Hi Nick"

"Hi Dan"

"You've met Nick then, Deb?"

"Yeah… We met months ago."

"Nick is the singer in *Roma*" Danny explained.

"Oh yes, of course. I thought you looked familiar."

It was obvious that Deb and Nick were really attracted to each other. Danny was quite jealous but his mind was working overtime. This could be handy he thought. Danny left Nick and Deb talking and went over to Simon.

"Did you know that it was Deb that Nick met that night?"

"Yeah I've just found that out."

"He likes her doesn't he? Of all the girls he could have met… and he meets Deb."

"Yeah that's weird isn't it."

"Yeah it is… and we asked if he'd got laid, Si."

"Shit yeah…Fucking hell."

Deb and Nick talked for ages, reminiscing about England and chatting about their likes and dislikes. They had a lot in common and they got on really well. Simon thought they got on a little too well.

The year 1990

Simon had been thinking about asking Deb to marry him…he'd even bought a ring. He had arranged a dinner for two. The room was surrounded in candlelight, romantic music was playing in the background, he had champagne on ice and the ring in his pocket

After the meal, he leant over the table and took Deb's hand. He pulled out the box with the ring in it and placed it in her hand. She opened it and gasped. It was beautiful. It had one big diamond, surrounded with six little ones…

"Will you marry me Deb?"

Deb looked at him a little stunned and hesitated.

"I need to think about this Simon," she replied.

"Well… That's OK – as long as it's Yes." he smiled confidently.

Deb needed time to think about her answer. She only wanted to do this once and it had to be right for both of them.

A few weeks later at the Awards Night. Deb had bought a white, figure hugging floor length dress, with a plunging halter neck, trimmed with gold and she had scooped up her hair to reveal the back of the dress.

The band won best band and Danny won Sexiest Male. Deb could see why he'd got that. He'd always been sexy. The girls were deep in conversation when Deb felt a tap on her shoulder. It was Nick, looking very handsome.

"Nick… Hello you," she said, sounding pleased to see him.

"Hi beautiful. …Come on I'll buy you a drink," he said as he turned to Chris. "See your husband has done it again …Sexiest male."

"Well…he is." Chris grinned at her husband lovingly. Danny smiled coyly.

"Oh I don't know Nick… I think you're very sexy. You must have come a close second." Deb teased.

Nick smiled at her, "Oh yeah babe, you're very sexy too."

Sue laughed as Deb blew him a kiss. Nick grinned at them, shaking his head.

"You're just after my body. Come on you…" he said, crooking his finger

Deb raised an eyebrow,"Wow isn't he the masterful one?"

Sue and Chris smiled at her.

"She is so attractive" Chris said.

"Yeah she is… I love Deb…She's like a sister to me."

Danny sat back in his chair smugly and waited for Simon to come back. When Simon did come back he asked where Deb had gone. Danny saw his opportunity and was quick to tell him she'd gone off with Nick. Tony came back and took Sue by the hand.

"Come on babe," he said leading her away.

She asked where they were going. Tony told her they were going to the dance floor to do a little boogie woogie.

"Yeah babe… I'll show you my rockstar moves."

Sue screamed with laughter.

"What ya laughing at?"

"You baby, you."

On the way to the dance floor they passed Deb on her way back to the table. Danny was all alone at the table. He looked straight at her.

"I believe Si has asked you to marry him?"

"Yeah he did…"

Danny flinched. "Are you going to say Yes?"

"I don't know?"

"May be we weren't meant to be together after all Deb." Danny said.

With jealousy oozing from every pore, he tried to hurt her some more.

"I guess we were just having fun, uh?"

Danny had just hurt Deborah more deeply than he could ever imagine those words cut like a knife. He had just made her mind up for her without even knowing it.

"Maybe you're right… Maybe Simon *is* the man for me." Deb hurtfully threw back.

Dave and Alan came back to the table. They'd been with Nick and the other guys.

"Where is everyone?"

"Oh they're all on the dance floor" Deb told them

"Are you OK?" Alan asked questioningly.

She nodded at him and smiled. She was fighting back the tears as Sue, Tony, Chris and Simon came back.

Simon sat down and smiled lovingly at Deb. She smiled back

"I'll be right back, Simon"

Deb made her way to the restroom tears rolling down her face. She couldn't hold them back any longer. Yes, she was going to tell Simon she would marry him. When she came back, she moved closer to Simon.

She whispered, "Do you still want to marry me?"

Simon turned to look at her intensely.

"Do I still want to marry you… Does a bear shit in the woods?"

Deb laughed. "Ask me again"

"Deborah… Will you marry me?"

"Yes…"

Simon jumped up waving his arms.

"I so love this woman. … She has just agreed to marry me."

Danny's eyes darted to Deb's face and then looked away quickly. He didn't want her to see the despair and longing that he must have been showing on his face.

Chris looked at Danny… Sadly she had seen the look on his face. She was upset but she managed to congratulate Simon and Deb

Deborah looked at her closely"Are you OK? You look upset."

"No…I'm OK" she managed to smile.

"Are you sure?

"Yeah…I'm fine."

Everyone started coming up and congratulating them. Simon must have told everybody in the building. Sue got hold of Deb and gave her a hug, "Be happy Deb."

Simon and Tony went off to get champagne but Danny just sat looking intently at Deb. He took hold of her hands firmly.

"Are you happy Deb? I mean really happy?"

"Yeah I am Danny… Really happy…."

"That's all I want for you, Deb." He said, looking straight into her eyes.

Chrissie watched Danny closely and Sue took her hand. Chrissie smiled at Sue. Sue could tell she was concerned and reassured her. Nick came over, and gave Deb a great big hug.

He asked, "What's this I hear? You're getting married? I thought we were going to have a big affair."

Deb laughed, "Nick...You never made your move."

"I was getting round to it" he said

She kissed him as he said, "Congrats... I hope you will be very happy."

Nick headed back over to the bar and the rest of his band. Danny looked straight at Deb giving her a sorrowful look. Then he got up and walked over to the bar with Nick.

"Are you OK mate?" Nick asked.

"Don't ask, Nick... This is a fucking nightmare I'm in."

"I know Dan. She's a beautiful woman. When I first saw her in that nightclub I just stared at her... I couldn't keep my eyes off her."

Danny smiled remembering, "Yeah... I know... I was the same... She was the one for me... She still is."

"I'm sorry mate... Here...have a drink."

"No, I'd better go back... Oh fuck it... Yeah give me drink... I've got nothing to celebrate over there."

When he did get back to the table the bubbly was going round and there was an air of excitement. Danny was quiet for the rest of the night and it was noticeable. When Simon and Deb got back to her apartment Simon took hold of her and kissed her very passionately. He told her he loved her very much and she had made him the happiest man alive.

"Oh Simon you are so sweet."

He took hold of her hands and led her into the bedroom.

"Do you know what I'm going to do to you baby"

"Why don't you show me"

He started to kiss her slowly, biting her bottom lip. Caressing her body, slowly he started to take her clothes off. He moved his hands over her body, moving down to the inside of her thighs. His kisses were slow and devilish, his lips firm and carnal.

She swallowed fast, aching to feel him, desperate to respond. His lips roved over her body. He eased between her shapely legs and made love to her. He was always gentle and took his time and he always made her feel special.

She knew he loved her. She never doubted that for a minute... however, she doubted herself.

When Danny and Chris got home. Danny was still being quiet and moody. Chris asked him what was wrong, even though she knew.

"Nothing," he said abruptly.

"There is something." She insisted

"Nothing… now go to bed"

"It's Simon, isn't it?"

"What?"

"It's Simon asking Deb to marry him."

"NO"

"Yes… Danny… I saw your face when he announced it."

"GO TO FUCKIN BED" he shouted, jumping down her throat.

"Danny."

"For fucks sake go to bed woman…"

"Danny."

Danny turned, grabbed the lamp from the table next to him and threw it across the room. He made Chris jump – she'd never seen him lose it like that before.

"Go to bed Chris, just go to bed" he then said quietly.

Chris went to bed… She knew exactly what was wrong with Danny and cried herself to sleep.

Danny sat downstairs drinking… This wedding proposal had created a big problem for him.

Chapter 20

Deb awoke next morning bright and early. She made some coffee and woke Simon up

"Come on sleepy head," she teased ruffling his hair.

"Hey...You wore me out last night," he accused.

"Do I need a younger man then?" she laughed.

He looked at her, insulted. "Come here you... I'll show you if you need a younger man or not."

He laughed as he grabbed her hand and pulled her back into bed. He kissed her passionately , slamming his body into hers, pushing his hips between her legs, levering her over until she straddled him. Their breathing was muffled and ragged as they moved in rhythm, until they orgasmed together.

Deborah showered, got dressed and went to the restaurant. Later that day Simon appeared looking smug.

"What are you doing here?" she said as she kissed him.

"I have something for you," he said as he gave her the box with the ring in it. She opened the box and put it on.

"You do like it right, don't you?"

"It's a beautiful engagement ring"

She shouted to Sue and held out her hand showing her ring off.

"It's beautiful, Deb"

"You and Tony's turn next?"

"Maybe…We'll see…"

Deb suggested that they all had a meal together later on.

"Great I'll tell the guys… Will you ring Chris?" Simon asked kissing her.

"Yeah … I'll see you later," kissing him back lovingly

Later that evening the guys and Chris went to the restaurant after the restaurant had closed. Deb had arranged a meal for them and they were all sat talking.

"It's your wedding anniversary soon Dan" Simon reminded him

"Yeah I know. What you giving us Si?"

"I don't know…What do you want Dan?"

Danny just smiled…

"I'll think of something." he said, looking at Deb with a gleam in his eyes.

"He is so cheeky," Chris said thumping him in the arm.

Deb and Sue laughed.

"Yes he is, but this is why we love him." Sue said. Danny looked at them both

"So you love me do you?"

"Yeah" Sue replied smiling at him – 'mwah' – blowing him a kiss. Danny blew a kiss back at her.

"So when are you guys getting married" Alan asked Deb and Simon.

"Sooner the better for me," said Si

"We haven't set a date yet… We'll have to think about that one." Deb said.

Every time the wedding was mentioned Danny cringed. He just hated the thought it.

At the end of the evening Alan and Dave gave Deb a kiss and thanked her for a great evening.

"After meal like that, I'll marry you Deb!" Alan said.

"Sorry Alan, I'm taken now."

"Oh Shit... Too freakin slow again."

"Awww babe" Deb laughed.

Chris and Danny thanked her for a lovely meal.

"It was great night we must do it again soon."

"Yeah...We must." Deb said.

Danny leaned in close to Deb and kissed her cheek. She could feel the warmth of his breath on her neck.

Everyone had left apart from Sue and Tony. Deb scanned the mess left over.

"You go...All this can wait till tomorrow." She said sleepily.

Sue coughed nervously.

"We've got something to tell you."

"What?"

"We are pregnant."

"Oh Sue, Tony that's great"

"Yeah... We are pleased"

Deb shouted to Simon who came out of the kitchen"

Yeah?"

"Tony and Sue are having a baby."

"Awesome bud... Sue...plant a kiss here." he said pointing to his cheek.

"We wanted to tell you first."

"I love you both... And you... no more work."

"Oh Deb, No...Just let me come in and do paper work."

"That's all you do then. No lifting... no carrying."

Sue nodded in agreement.

A few weeks later Danny and Chris's wedding anniversary was coming up. Simon thought it would be a great idea if they had a surprise party.

Deborah was very reluctant about throwing the party, she didn't want to celebrate their anniversary. However, she went ahead with it. They had to close the restaurant for the night but Deb and Sue arranged it all – Sue wasn't allowed to do much, though.

Simon asked Danny and Chris to meet him at the restaurant. Everyone hid and as they came through the door and then they jumped out at them.

Chris was delighted. Danny wasn't… but he didn't want to spoil it for Chris.

The party was in full swing when Simon banged on the table.

"Can I have your attention, please. I think, we would all like to wish Chris and Danny a happy anniversary."

Deborah and Sue brought the cake out. It was beautiful with *Happy Anniversary* decorated on it. Everyone cheered and shouted.

"Come on Dan… Kiss the lady."

Danny gave Chris a long lingering kiss. Deb lowered her eyes and walked away. She felt an overwhelming jealousy. Her eyes started to fill up and tears started rolling down her face as she rushed into the kitchen to wipe them. Danny had noticed how she'd reacted to the kiss and sneaked off in to the kitchen when no-one was looking. He asked her why she was in there."

Oh Danny…Do you like your party?" She said trying desperately to change the subject.

Danny asked again."Why are you in here?"

He walked over to her.

"Look at me" lifting her chin up tracing her lips with his fingers…

"Deb…" He moved closer to her and was just about to kiss her when Sue came in

"Ohh…Erm…Sorry…I've come to get more champagne." There was an awkward purse

Deb took a deep breath, sighed and moved away from Danny. Danny looked at her and went back to the party… back to Chris… Sue was annoyed…

"What are you thinking of ? What if I'd been Simon?"

"I don't know Sue" Deb spluttered, close to tears again.

Sue suddenly felt sorry for her. "Oh Deb… Oh babe… Don't."

"I didn't want this bloody party… Why would I want to celebrate their anniversary?"

Sue gave her a hug. "Are you OK? Don't do this"

"I will be…I just need a minute."

She wiped her eyes and sighed deeply.

"Why are you getting champagne?"

"We need it"

"No Sue... Were you going to carry it?"

"Hmm... Yeah."

"Hmm...Baby, Sue...What did I say?"

"Oops...no carrying."

"Hmm Yeah..."

As Simon walked in he said, "Why are you both hiding in here?"

"We're getting some more champagne" Sue replied

Simon looked at Deborah and asked if she was OK. Her eyes were a bit red

"Yeah I'm fine...Will you take this champagne in?"

He kissed her, "Yeah anything for you." Deborah smiled at him.

She tried to keep away from Danny for the rest of the night, which wasn't easy. Chris went over to and thanked her for the surprise.

"It was a pleasure. Enjoying yourself ?" she asked, trying to sound happy.

"Yeah, It's awesome... We had no idea. You and Simon sure kept this well-hidden."

"Good... That was the plan."

Deborah noticed Danny's parents and excused herself and made her way over. Danny watched her go... he'd watched her most of the night.

"Hi Dan," Sue said creeping up on him.

"Sue." he said startled. "How are you and Tony doin?"

"We're fine... What about you and Chris?" Danny looked at her searchingly.

"Is this question to do with what you saw in the kitchen earlier?"

"I never saw anything in the kitchen."

"Very good Sue, but I know you did."

"Danny I love Deb... And you too... I want you both to be happy but..."

"I know what the but means...But she would be happier if..."

Sue interrupted him.

"She can't...And you can't Danny...It's just impossible."

They both looked over to where Deborah was having a good catch up with Danny's parents. She had been talking with them for ages. There was a lot to catch up on.

Danny made his way over.

"This is cosy. What we talking about?"

"We were talking about Deb's wedding." Marie said.

"Oh yeah…The wedding…That's another party." He said sarcastically.

"Danny…" Marie said warningly.

"Mom…Don't…Really…Don't."

He gave Deb a cutting look then walked away. Deb put her head down. Danny's parents noticed the tension between them, it was electric.

"Excuse me a minute." Deb said stunned.

Marie and Pete looked at each other.

"Oh no…There's a big problem."

"Yeah… and it shows." Pete said.

"I know my son and he's not over her. I have a bad feeling about all this." Marie said with concern in her voice.

The night came to a close and everyone started to go. Pete and Marie said they were going too. Marie took Deb to one side and told her that she must come and visit them. They did like Chris but always thought that Deb was the girl for Danny.

"Oh Marie course I will come and see you but you must come and see me first. Come and have a meal at the restaurant on me."

Deb gave Marie her phone number and kissed them goodnight. Chris and Danny said they were going. Chris thanked Deb again for the party.

"It was my pleasure. Call me in the week, Chris, and we can go for lunch."

"Yeah, That would be great"

Danny kissed her the cheek. "I'll see you Deb."

"Yeah… See ya Danny." Her stomach was churning.

Sue looked at Deb closely, "Are you OK?"

"Yep…"

But she wasn't. She was very weepy and was holding it all in. Danny had made her really uncomfortable.

"Why, what's wrong?" Simon asked appearing from nowhere.

"Oh, Simon!" Sue nearly jumped out of her skin. "She just looks tired… That's all."

Tony came out of the kitchen and put arms around Sue's waist.

"That went well."

"Yeah – Chris loved it but Danny was in a bit of an odd mood." Simon said.

Tony shook his head. "I never noticed"

Sue interrupted their conversation. "No…no – he was fine."

Tony got their coats.

"So you didn't think he was in an odd mood then?"

"No." Sue said

Simon turned to Deb. "Are you alright? Is there something bothering you?"

She shook her head. "Why do you think there's something wrong?"

"I don't know… I've just got this shitty feeling."

"There's nothing to worry about."

They locked up and went home. The next morning Simon made breakfast. He said 'morning' but he was a bit quiet. Deborah asked if he was alright.

"You're not still thinking there's something to worry about, are you?"

"No," he said sulkily. But he'd been thinking and it had occurred to him that she had never told him that she loved him so he asked her.

Deborah looked at him. "Yes, of course I do."

"Really?"

"Yes"

But she still hadn't actually said 'I love you.'

"Simon look… You know, what we need is to set a date for our wedding."

Simon smiled.

"Yeah we should… When?"

Deb breathed a sigh of relief, she'd taken Simon's mind off the love question."

"What about December this year… the 12th?"

"Yeah…The sooner the better for me now…You have made me so happy. I'm going to meet the guys so I'll see you later."

He kissed her and left. She gave Chris a call and asked if she wanted to have lunch with her and Sue at the restaurant. Chris said she would love to and arranged to meet them there. Sue was already there when Deb arrived. She asked her chef to prepare lunch for three.

He prepared a delightful lunch and when Chris arrived they all sat down to eat. Deb told the girls that she and Simon had set the date for the wedding and they were ecstatic.

"When…?" Sue asked.

"We're getting married on 12th of December." Deb squealed.

"That's great." Chris said.

Deb mentioned that she was going to need help with organising and both girls were very eager to volunteer even though Sue's baby was due in October.

"Do you know how much working out I'm going to have to do to get back in to shape?"

"Yeah… but I know you can do it." Deb said grinning at her.

"We'll do it with you… Won't we, Deb?" Chris said.

"We'll be there with you…." Deb started grinning at her again with hint of a giggle coming on.

"Yeah…You'll be there, but not doing anything."

"Oh Sue…That really hurts."

"Yeah… yadda… yadda… yadda. Bull shit."

"Bullshit?… Oh Sue babe…That really, really hurts."

Sue looked at her laughed putting her middle finger up at her. Deb laughed and rolled her eyes. They finished their lunch and talked about the wedding and the baby.

Deborah asked Chris about her wedding.

"We went to Vegas to the 'Little White Chapel'…That was it."

"Did you not want the white wedding?"

"Yeah…But Danny didn't."

There was an awkward pause and Deb managed to say, "Oh…Right."

Chapter 21

Simon and Deb started plans for their wedding and both Sue and Chris got really involved. They went with her dress shopping and eventually she picked a slimline chiffon gown. It was scooped at the neck line with crystal beaded straps. It was gently ruched asymmetrically around the waist and it gathered at the back of the gown to create an alluring train. She'd decided to wear her hair up and curled into ringlets, dropping down subtly so she could have the tiara and veil with the crystal beading to match. Sue and Chris had picked their dresses. They were a very deep red and they had picked little crystal rosebuds for their hair. Sue was going to have to wait to have her dress fitted until after the baby had arrived.

They had booked a big hotel for their reception and their wedding cake was in five tiers with red roses on it. Their wedding list was getting bigger by the day and Deb had asked Tony to give her away. He said it would be an honour.

Simon asked Danny to be best man but he said that he would understand if he didn't want to… Danny said he would.

The wedding had put Chris in a sentimental mood. It was all the talk of the wedding that had started her off and she asked Danny if he wanted to renew their vows but Danny was not interested and said so, very abruptly.

"Why not?"

"No."

"At least give me a reason…?"

"No… We are already married."

"Yeah… But we got married at the chapel in Vegas."

"I told you at the time I didn't want all that big white wedding shit."

"But I……"

"Don't bang on. Fucking weddings do my fucking head in."

Danny totally dismissed the idea. He was more concerned how he could stop Deb's wedding. It hadn't occurred to Chris that Danny was so against the wedding. She knew it had bothered him but not as much as this.

The months passed by. Sue gave birth to a beautiful baby boy. They called him Daniel after Danny. He was a beautiful 7lbs 3ozs. Deb just doted on him and took him off Sue's hands every opportunity she had.

The wedding was getting closer and Sue started working out to get back in shape. Deb and Chris went with her and soon she was looking really good. She had lost the baby weight in no time and she and Chris had sorted out Deb's hen night. They had arranged a bachelorette party and all the girls gave her a night to remember.

They arranged wine tasting and used this as their excuse for blindfolding Deb so they could sneak a male erotic dancer in without her knowing. The music started playing and Deb asked what was happening. Sue told her she would soon find out. The guy walked toward her, took hold of her hands and moved them down his body She wanted to take the blindfold off but the girls wouldn't let her. He pressed his body into her and moved provocatively against her. The girls all shouted.

"Take your blindfold off now, Deb."

She peeled the blindfold off and screamed, "Ohhh… my God… he's… so…"

He was gorgeous. Tall, dark, tanned with a muscular body and dressed as a police officer. Deb helped him take his uniform off and moved her hands up and down his body massaging him with lotion. She had a great night.

Simon was having his bachelor night the night before the wedding. Deb said he was brave because he would suffer the next day. There were only days to go and Deb and Simon were finishing the last-minute things off.

Danny was stressed and very bad tempered. He couldn't handle this situation and he was running out of time. He needed to think of something quickly. Simon on the other hand was very excited and had sorted out their honeymoon. He had chosen to go to Hawaii again... Deb loved Hawaii.

Nick went to see Deb at the restaurant and she asked if he was coming to the wedding.

"Wouldn't miss it for the world... Besides I'll be the one shouting 'No –she should be married to me!'"

"No Nick...You wouldn't," she said, with hint of a giggle. "Would you?"

"I might." he shrugged.

"No...You wouldn't."

"Oh Deb... Wouldn't I." he said with a naughty laugh.

"Nick...Stop teasing me." she said smiling at him..."anyway what can I do for you ?"

Nick smile and raised his eyebrows and told her she didn't want to know what he was thinking. She gave a giggle and told him to behave.

10ᵗʰ of December

Deb and Sue had just closed the restaurant and were closing all the blinds when there was a bang on the door. BANG... BANG...BANG... It was really loud, so that loud it made them jump out of their wits. Sue looked through the blinds It was Danny so she let him in. He seemed very agitated.

"I need to talk to you," he said pointing to Deb.

Sue went in the kitchen to get her coat. She thought it would be better if she got out of the way.

"I'll see you tomorrow Deb... See you Danny."

"Yeah...See ya Sue.". he kissed her on the cheek.

"What's wrong, Danny? What do you need to say?"

He took hold of her hands and looked her straight in the eyes

"You can't marry Simon."

"What...? No Danny..." she cried. She couldn't believe what she was hearing.

"You heard me."

"Oh Danny I heard you… I don't believe this… We have been here before."

"You don't love him. It's me you love," he said confidently.

"Danny. You are married. You can't do this…. You must love her." she said in despair.

Danny looked at her longingly.

"I love you… I never stopped." he whispered.

Deborah put her hands to her head, shaking,"No…no…no…."

He moved closer to her.

"I saw how upset you were at the anniversary party. So tell me you don't love me… tell me you don't want me…"

Deborah put her head down.

"No… No… No… Danny."

"Tell me."

"Please… Don't Danny."

"Tell me Deb. I know you can't…Can you?"

She couldn't tell him. She did love him. Danny moved closer and touched her face tenderly.

"Kiss me."

"Danny please…Don't."

Deb went to move away and he pulled her back and kissed her.

"I know you want me, Deb," he said, looking straight into her eyes.

He moved his head closer to hers. He looked deeper into her eyes. She couldn't stop herself. They kissed with some urgency. She gently reached up and touched his face. She moved her hand to the nape of his neck. Their bodies seemed to gel as he started to unbutton her blouse and, moving his hand over her breasts, he began to explore her body.

She could feel herself getting turned on as his touch sent shivers through her body. Her body went into spasm. She couldn't stop herself. her self-control slipped away. He felt so good… She pressed herself against him. She could feel how hard he was. He moved his hands to her waist and unzipped her skirt; it dropped like a pool round her. They kissed passionately as he undressed her slowly. He pulled her gently down to the floor and laid her down, moving his hands over her body. He could feel her body rise to his touch. She clasped him to her… He excited her with his fingertips.

He moved his mouth down her body trailing his tongue back up the inside of her thighs. She gasped he took her breath away. He looked at her, his eyes full of desire. He wanted her so much

Slowly, he unbuttoned his shirt and threw it on the floor. She moved her hands over his bare chest. She began to moved her hands further down his body moving them to his waist round to his back, digging her nails in as she moaned softly.

Unzipping his jeans he pulled them off and threw them across the room. He looked down at her with his smouldering eyes, his hands slowly making their way up her legs. He stopped at her knees, pushing them apart bringing her thighs up. She wrapped her legs round him, gripping him like she was never going to let go. He teased her with his manhood making her want him more.

He made love to her right there on the floor of the restaurant. The sex was hot, frenzied and carnal and went on for some time before they reached a crushing climax together.

She had missed him so much…. She couldn't believe that she was doing this. He had wanted her so much and now he thought he had changed her mind. They lay naked in each other's arms, their legs still entwined.

Deb suddenly felt an overwhelming guilt and jumped up.

"Danny… This should not have happened."

"Deb…no… no…Please don't do this to me."

"You're married"

"Deb please…I beg you…Don't marry him."

"Danny…This was so wrong."

"No it isn't… this is how it's meant to be. I've got to go… But this is not finished."

Danny left and went home. Chris was in bed asleep and he crept in and slid in at the side of her, desperately trying not to wake her. Dawn was just appearing, breaking through the drapes. She looked so still …, so content … he felt really bad.

But being with Deb in the restaurant tonight. The way she made him feel… the way he felt every time he touched her. He wanted her back. He was determined, this night had just made him want Deb more.

Deb was still at the restaurant. Danny had been gone a few hours and she had been feeling so guilty she didn't know what to do. Eventually, Sue arrived.

"Hi Deb…You're early."

"I haven't been home," she said glumly.

"Why? …Oh no. What time did Danny go?"

"A few hours ago."

"Oh Deb…You didn't?" Deb could only look at Sue."You did…Didn't you…."

"I don't know what to do." Tears started to flow down her cheeks

"You forget it… That's what you do."

"How?" she spluttered

Just then Simon walked in with the rest of the guys. She wiped her eyes quickly. Sue looked at Deb and whispered.

"It will be OK, Deb…Last night didn't happen…You're getting married tomorrow."

Simon walked over to Deborah and kissed her. "I tried to call you last night."

"Did you? I err…unplugged the phone and went to bed."

"Why? Are you ill? You don't look so good, your eyes are all red and puffy like you've been crying."

"No, I'm fine – I just had something in my eye."

"Here let me look"

He took hold of her face gently and proceeded to look in her eyes. The door swung open just at that point.

"Good morning Deb…You look tired." Danny said knowingly.

"Didn't sleep that well." She said looking at him darkly from under her eyelashes. He just threw her a cheeky grin.

Sue came out with coffee. "Come on guys… Coffee's ready."

They made their way over to the table but Danny pulled Deb back.

"I want to see you." he whispered.

"No…That's not a good idea Danny." she said, trying to control her voice.

"Please Deb…I need to see you about last night."

Deborah looked searchingly at him.

"My place – 7 tonight…" she said, feeling she had no other choice.

She was worried about seeing Danny again... *'What if it happens again? It will happen again. No... No. It can't...'* All these thoughts were running round inside her head.

The guys sat and had their coffee. Sue even threw in some breakfast muffins filled with bacon, eggs and hash browns. Alan told Tony if he didn't marry this women he sure as hell would. After breakfast they left for the studio. Deborah was very distant all day and Sue asked what she was thinking about.

"I've got allsorts going round my head." Deb admitted.

"It's all going to be fine."

"How can it be fine? I've just cheated on Simon"

Chapter 22

That evening, Danny went round to Deb's before he going on to Simon's bachelor night. She asked him if he wanted a drink and poured them both a vodka and coke. Danny came behind her and put his arms round her waist. She felt his warm breath on the back of her neck as he moved her hair to one side and started to kiss her.

"Danny" she warned.

"Yep?" kissing her neck gently.

"Danny, No..."

She could feel herself weakening and turned round. He looked at her and smiled. She knew she wanted him. She kissed him passionately. Their arousal was immediate. Stumbling and fumbling they ripped at each other's clothes, dropping each item. There was an urgency to get to the bedroom. They just couldn't keep their hands off each other. His lips came crushing down on hers.

"You feel so good baby," he muttered against her mouth.

Their emotions were running high. She trembled from his touch as he pressed his erection against her, he was so hard. He eased himself between her thighs making her legs open wider. He pressed down on her. She let out a long groan as they began to make love. It was hot, and frenzied.

In the past two days she'd had the best sex she'd had for such a long time. Danny really knew how to turn her on and she was never disappointed. Afterwards, they lay silently in her bed, tangled between the sheets...Danny softly trailed his fingers through her hair.

"What's wrong?" he asked, concerned.

"Danny... This is..."

"No Deb. Do you know how long I have waited for you to come back?"

"You're married now Danny and I am getting married tomorrow. This can't happen again. This shouldn't have happened again."

Danny looked at her, puzzled.

"What?" he said disbelievingly

"This is not going to happen again."

"But we have just made love yet again. Doesn't that tell you something?"

"Yeah it tells me it was wrong and it shouldn't have happened."

He sat up and stared at her disbelievingly.

"You said this last night but here we are again. You don't even love Simon."

"Yes I do." she shot back at him

"If you loved Simon why am I in your bed? Why have we just had amazingly hot sex and why is it so amazing? Don't do this Deb."

She looked at him sadly.

"We have got to forget this ever happened."

Danny jumped out of bed and started to get dressed. He turned to Deb, his eyes level with hers

"Why the fuck are you doing this. And whatever you say, it *did* happen!"

He was so angry.

"This is not over" he shouted. His eyes were cold and hurtful. He put one knee back on the bed, leaning over her

"It will *never* be over baby" he scoffed at her. He stormed out slamming the door behind him.

Deb buried her face in the pillow and burst into tears. Salty tears drenched her pillow as she cried uncontrollably. She was so confused – not only did she feel so guilty but, deep inside, she knew that Danny was right. She cried and cried the whole night. She didn't sleep and she really doubted things even more.

Danny finally arrived at Simon's bachelor night but he was so angry, so hurt.

"And where have you been" Tony asked.

"Why is she doing this? Is she trying to do my fucking head in?"

"Are we talking about Deb by any chance?"

"Yeah," Dan said sulkily.

"She loves him, why else?"

"Well, if she loves him so fucking much why have I just left her bed after we've just had amazingly hot sex? And man it was hot"

"What…? Dan… What the fuck are you doing?"

"I love her and I want her to change her mind." Danny looked at Simon with contempt.

"Look at him the fuckin asshole… he has got the one thing I want – She can't do this." he said through gritted teeth.

"I think you might have to let her go Dan…I'm sorry buddy."

"I don't fucking think so. Sooner or later he'll fuck up."

Just then Alan came over.

"Hey guys – just look at him…" he said laughing and pointing at Simon.
"He's having an awesome night. He's absolutely hammered."

Nick came over in fit of laughter

"Look at him … what a prick he's so fucking wasted."

Dave was behind Simon and yanked his pants down. Simon was so drunk he fell over trying to pull them back up. The guys just laughed and made fun of him – going back over to him and pulling them down again.

Tony looked over and laughed… He knew, however, that he really needed to talk Danny out of whatever he was planning.

"He loves her, my friend. You are just going to have to accept that they are together."

"Fuck that …Maybe I should tell him that I have just come from her bed."

"No Dan… Don't."

"What about if I tell him how I touched her and where I touched her

"Dan…he'd be fuckin devastated"

"You mean like I was, when he fucked it all up for me"

"Dan you can't"

Simon saw Dan and staggered over to him.

"Dan my bud… I love you…Where've you been?"

"I've been…" he hesitated for a moment."Here, buddy."

"Have you? I'm hammered – my fuckin pants keep falling down."

"Yeah… I know."

Nick, Dave and Alan grabbed Simon and sat him in the middle of the dance floor. A beautiful, dark haired exotic dancer came on. She was stunning. She had long, dark glossy hair, long shapely legs and one hell of a figure, just Simon's type. She danced around him, touching him. She placed herself over one of his knees and lowered herself on it, moving seductively, removing her clothes. She pushed her infeasibly large breasts in his face. Simon was so hammered all he could do was raise a smile, never mind anything else. The guys egged him on with cries of drunken encouragement.

There were lots of girls at this bachelor night and they were all over the guys. Danny, however, wasn't interested in any of them. Simon staggered back over to Danny after the dancer had finished.

"Danny you are so faithful… I'm going to be faithful too." Simon said drunkenly.

"Faithful? What the fuck are you banging on about?"

"Well you're not interested in any of these girlzzzz." he said as he hiccoughed.

"No… I've just been with a beautiful woman… I have just left her in bed."

"Ahhhh…Luckyyyy Chris."

"No, Si… you've no idea"

"Ohhh Dan… You fuckin bad, bad boy. Have you been fuckin about I won't tell……Was it great sex?"

"Oh yeah … the hottest sex ever Simon… do you want to know who with? Danny said goading him.

"Ohhhh fuckin hell Dan, Yeah…" then Simon fell over.

Tony looked at Danny, shaking his head. Danny looked back at him and smiled. Tony was really worried about Danny and what he might say… being filled with jealousy and he was crazy about Deb. He wasn't going to let go easily. Nick came over to Danny

"Hi mate… You're late."

"Yeah… had someone to see."

"Oh right… Dare I ask who?

""No… I wouldn't."

"OK I won't." He laughed – but he had a fair idea who Dan had been to see.

A beautiful strawberry blonde girl wandered over to Nick. She was all over him, touching him, moving her hands to his jeans and unzipping them.

"Enjoy, bud." Danny laughed, nodding at him.

"Oh I will!" Nick grinned. He grabbed her hand and disappeared with her.

Simon had a truly great bachelor night. He had had lots to drink and the next morning he had one hell of a hangover.

Chapter 23

Next morning, Sue arrived early at Deb's. She was really excited about the coming day.

"Good morning" she said with a cheery tone.

"Is it?" Deborah said abruptly. She'd had a bad night… She'd tossed, turned and cried most of the night.

"Are you OK?"

"No."

"OK Deb… What's wrong? You should be happy… It's your wedding day."

"Why am I doing this? I don't love Simon…."

"It's just jitters… with what happened with Dan."

Deborah laughed sarcastically looking up at the ceiling as tears start again rolling down her cheeks

"Where do you think Danny was last night?"

"He was at Simon's bachelor night, wasn't he?"

"Uh huh… he was with me most of the evening. In my bed…. We made love…. Why did he have to get married?"

She burst in to tears again. Sue went over to her and put her arms round her and hugged her.

"Oh babes don't," She said, rocking from side to side stroking her hair and wiping her tears from her face. "Don't do this Deb… Dan is married… Just forget it and be happy with Simon. Simon never needs to know about any of this…It would hurt him and Chris so much"

"Oh Shit – Chris is going to be here soon."

Deborah put her hands to her head.

"What I'm I going to do? Oh shit…how do I face her?"

"You are going to be a real hard-faced bitch and just forget it. This… It didn't happen."

Deborah shook her head.

"I can't do this… I can't do any of this…."

"Go and get in the bath and have a long soak…I'll make some coffee."

Sue could hear her crying in the bath when Tony arrived and asked how the bride was.

"I know what happened last night."

"Do you?" Sue said looking unsure.

She wanted to make sure they knew the same thing before she said anything.

"Yeah…I know that Dan was with Deb last night…he was trying to change her mind and I know that they ended up in bed."

"Well…he's done an excellent job… She doubts everything."

"It's a mess Sue…Dan is so miserable, so stressed he can't handle this

There was knock on the door

"Oh shit… that must be Chris"

Sue let her in and tried to smile cheerfully.

"Good morning. Where's the blushing bride."

"Ohh…She's in the tub."

Deborah came out of the bathroom took one look at Chris, burst out in to tears and ran back into the bedroom. Chris looked at Sue helplessly.

"What's wrong?"

Tony tried rather nervously to explain.

"She's just really emotional this morning."

"Oh...Is she nervous?"

Deborah took a deep gulp of breath, went back into the lounge and poured herself a large drink.

"Does anyone else want a one?" she spluttered.

"I will." Tony said.

"I've made you coffee Deb." Sue said sensibly.

"Don't want coffee."

Chris looked at her quizzically...

"We are going to get ready."

"Is she OK?" she asked Sue.

"Yeah...She's fine."

As Deb poured Tony a drink she looked at him closely.

"You know... Don't you?"

Tony nodded his head.

"Tony... Am I doing the right thing?"

"Only you can answer that, babe."

"No Tony...I can't answer that... I simply don't know."

Sue and Chris were ready. They came out of the bedroom and Deborah took a quick intake of breath.

"You both look so beautiful... Don't they Tony?"

"Yeah you do."

"This is supposed to be the happiest day of my life"

Chris asked what she meant by that and Sue told her that she was so nervous she'd got an attack of the jitters. Chris was concerned – Deb had been so excited about the wedding. What could have made her feel like this. She'd had not felt like this when she married Danny.

She asked if something had happened and Deb looked at her with her big sad eyes and told her she was sorry. Chris wanted to know what she was apologizing for.

Tony interrupted and told Deb that she really needed to get ready now. She trekked to the bedroom. She turned back and sighed heavily. Her eyes were red from all the crying she had done. She looked so unhappy. The car arrived and was outside waiting for Chris and Sue.

They got in and Chris turned ask if Deb was alright. Sue reassured her that it was just pre-wedding jitters and she would be fine.

Deb put her make up on. Staring at herself in the mirror…she quietly said 'pull yourself together!'. She put her dress on then her veil. 'Come on … come on …' she murmured to herself. She appeared from the bedroom and Tony gasped. She was stunning.

"You're beautiful… Are you ready?"

"Yeah… Come on…Let's do this."

She certainly didn't sounded like the happy bride she should be

The bride's car arrived and Tony helped her in. She asked the driver to take the longest way. Tony held her hand she smiled. As they pulled into the church grounds Deb whispered, *"Tony… I can't."* She just wanted to run away

"OK Deb… We'll just sit here a minute."

Tony got out of the car and spoke to Dave and Alan. They looked at Tony with concern and Alan asked if everything was OK.

"Just nerves… that all." Tony said

"Not Danny then?" Dave asked.

Tony looked at them both and shook his head.

"Don't even go there."

Alan mentioned that Danny looked so unhappy. Tony sighed, shaking his head, not quite believing this was happening. He went back to the car and sat down next at the side of Deb.

"I know Dan has put doubts in your head."

"Yeah but if I really loved Simon, none of this would be happening… Last night… This feeling … any of it."

Simon looked down at his watch and then at Danny with trepidation. She was late. Danny was hoping she had changed her mind.

Sue asked Alan what was happening. Why was she not coming in? Sue had seen the state she was in that morning and was really worried. Chris made her way over to them. When Alan saw Chris heading their way he told Sue that she was just making some last minute touch ups to her make-up – he didn't know what else to say.

"Deb…I don't know what to say apart from…how do you feel right now?"

"I don't know…" She pulled herself together, desperately.

She looked at Tony hard for a minute.

"OK... Let's get this over with."

Tony winked at her and breathed a sigh of relief. He'd been thinking he might just have to go in and explain why the bride had taken off.

"Come on."

He took her hand and helped out of the car. He knew she didn't love Simon, at least, not the way she should...It was always going to be Danny. He just hoped everything would work out alright in the end.

Simon and Danny both turned and watched her walk down the aisle towards them.

"Si...She's beautiful"

Danny swallowed hard and his eyes scanned her as she approached. His stomach turned over as he realised that she was really doing this...But why?

"Yeah...She is Dan"

When Deborah got to the alter Simon smiled at her...Danny dropped his head despairingly. Chris was watching him. She knew... she knew it was Deb and it was always going to be her but did she feel the same way as Danny? Is that what this morning was about and if so she, why was she marrying Simon? All these crazy thoughts were running round Chris's head. Sue was watching Chris and could see that Chris knew.

After the ceremony they went to sign the register and have their photographs taken. The press got to take lots of pictures for the papers the next day. Simon looking lovingly at his bride. He took her hand and led her to the car and then they headed off to the reception where they greeted their guests and had more photos taken cutting the cake. Simon just wanted to get Deb to himself so he asked her if they could go.

"No Simon...We can't."

"You look beautiful, Mrs. Richards," he said kissing her.

"You don't look so bad yourself, Mr. Richards," she managed to say, just before someone came and grabbed him and dragged him over to a crowd.

Danny went over to Deborah and whispered in her ear

"I didn't think you would do it... not after the last two nights we have spent together."

"Danny... We need to put this behind us and move on."

He pulled her closer to him.

"You are so beautiful…I love you so much…do you really think you can forget what happened…"

Simon saw them talking to each other and went over. He was intrigued to what they were talking about.

"Hey Dan… thanks for today."

"Si …I was just telling Deb want a beautiful bride she is."

Danny made his way back over to Chris. She'd been watching them and asked what they had been talking about.

"Oh… I was just congratulating them… You look beautiful …" he complimented her as he leaned over and kissed her.

He kissed her very passionately, all the time knowing that Deb could see him, he was directly in her line of sight. Deb felt her skin prickle when she saw Danny kiss Chrissie. Simon and Deborah went over to sit with Gary. He was so proud of his son – and now he had a beautiful daughter in law as well. He took Deb by the hand.

"Come on, I want to dance with my beautiful daughter in law" As he gave her a soft smile

So Deborah went off to the dance floor with Gary. Nick had gone over to Simon and wished him well and told him he was a lucky bastard.

"Yeah…I am."

"I would love to be in your place tonight, Si."

"Yeah I bet you would… not happening though, my friend."

Deb and Gary came back laughing. Nick moved over to Deb and kissed her.

"You surely are a beautiful bride."

"Thank you…"

Simon looked at his watch.

"Deb we need to be going."

They got changed and everyone waved them off. Deb threw her bouquet, aiming it at Sue and, of course, Sue caught it. She blew a kiss at her friend and winked. The press took some more photographs of them leaving. They wanted to know where the happy couple were jetting off to for their honeymoon. Simon refused to comment, it was to be a surprise for Deb. She had no idea where they were going.

They left everyone at reception to carry on partying the night away. The press had been told to leave at this point but they still congregated outside, waiting for that extra picture there were a lot of celebrities in the building and they weren't going to miss that chance.

Chapter 24

When they arrived in Hawaii they were shown to their hotel room. There was a beautiful bouquet of flowers, a bottle of chilled champagne and a basket of tropical fruit on the table. Simon wanted everything to be perfect for Deb.

"Simon." she sighed. "This is all so beautiful…Thank you"

She kissed him lovingly but still she felt so guilty about Danny. She had to put the nights she and Danny had spent together behind her. She wondered whether she should tell Simon or not but when she thought of the hurt it would cause him she decided not to.

He moved towards her and told her he loved her so much. He pulled her close and kissed her tenderly, scooping her up in his muscular arms. He took her to the bedroom and placed her on the bed, his eyes wild, his voice soft, almost a whisper, *'I love you'*.

He kissed her tenderly, his hands moved over her body, undressing until she was naked. She responded to his touch. His lips trailed down her body and he caressed her skin. Her guilty feelings slipped away. She didn't want them. She'd decided Danny was in the past – it was her and Simon now.

She started to undress him, caressing his beautifully tanned, muscular body with her fingertips.

Moving her hands down his body she felt his thighs press against her. He was so turned on … he could hardly contain himself, he wanted her so badly the desire in his eyes was like fire. Her hands slid over his shoulders encouraging him to deeper intimacy. He pulled her body closer to him and trailed his hot breath to her breasts, wrapping his mouth round her nipples. Leisurely he made his way to her stomach down to her thighs, making her arch her back and moan with desire. He moved between her thighs and made love to her passionately.

It lasted for some time. They collapsed in the rumpled sheets breathing heavily. They were silent for a few seconds lying in each other's arms. Simon reached over for the champagne and pouring two glasses, handed one to Deb. He traced his fingers over the curves her naked body, telling her how much he loved her.

Next day, Simon ordered breakfast as Deb stood on the balcony watching the waves crash onto the sand. He put his arms around her.

"It's so beautiful here…I so love it," he murmured.

They sat and read the papers to discover they had made the headlines. The press had done some digging and they had found out that Deb was Danny's former girlfriend and he had been set to marry her.

The story suggested that Deborah had left Danny just before they were to marry leaving him devastated.

ROCKER SIMON RICHARDS MARRIES
HIS GIRLFRIEND DEBORAH CARNELL YESTERDAY
FORMER LOVE
OF BAND MEMBER DANNY BROOKS

Later they hired a car and drove to Kauai. They went to a beautiful secluded waterfall with a 113ft drop. They made their way down the path so they could go for a swim. It was beautiful and refreshing as they went into the waterfall its self. The water running over their bodies aroused Simon.

"I want to make love to you, right here… right now…" he murmured.

As he pulled her closer she could feel how hard he was. She wrapped her legs around him, kissing him seductively. He tugged at his shorts, pulling them down and quickly moved her bikini bottoms to the side, pushing himself in to her. They made hot passionate love under the waterfall. They were lucky that they weren't caught by the press as the paparazzi were on the hunt for them. They wanted to get as many snaps of the happy couple as possible

They stayed there all-day. Soaking up the sun as the sun beat sensually down on their bodies. The paparazzi soon found where they were staying and managed to get lots of photographs of them kissing and fooling around. They showed them really having fun, loving each other.

Danny just couldn't hack it. It was driving him crazy and he knew he had to come up with something that was going to make her jealous and reveal her true feelings.

Deb and Simon had a fabulous honeymoon but all too soon it was over and they had to go back home. They both had to get back to work... The band started work on some new songs in preparation for their tour dates. Deb was back in full swing in the restaurant.

Deb was enjoying being married – she really wanted their marriage to work. She was trying so hard. They had even talked about having children. Simon wanted to have four, Deb wanted two. But they would wait a couple of years, there were things that she wanted to do first.

A couple of months later Tony told Deb that he was going to ask Sue to marry him and wanted to know if he could have the restaurant after it closed

"Yeah…Which night do you want?"

Tony asked if he could have it on Sue's night off as he was going to cook.

"Yes, of course…I am so happy for you."

So Tony arranged everything and had asked Deb if they would have Daniel overnight. He had got the ring, he had got the roses and he had arranged the meal. He had made everything really romantic.

When Sue arrived Deborah said, "See ya later."

Sue looked at her, puzzled, "Why, where are you going?"

"Home."

Sue looked at Deb closely.

"But you called and asked me to meet you here."

"Yeah…I know… Daniel is with Simon. … Enjoy your evening."

Silently Tony came out of the kitchen, Deb nodded, said goodbye and left. Tony took hold of Sue's hand, led her to the table and swiftly got down on one knee. She smiled excitedly, her eyes widened and was as bright as the moon. Tony told her he had loved her since the first day he'd seen her then asked her to marry him. Her answer was to kiss him seductively.

"Yes…Yes…Yes – I love you so much."

Tony pulled out the ring and put it on her finger. She kissed him again.

"It's beautiful." she sighed as she looked at the large solitaire on her finger.

Tony had spoilt her with the meal the champagne and the romantic setting. she was overwhelmed by it all not to mention impressed. She hadn't realised that Tony could cook.

"I hope Deb is as happy as me."

"I hope so too but I don't think she is… not really and Dan certainly isn't."

"What do you think will happen?"

"I don't know… but Dan is devastated that Deb married Si and I'm afraid we are going to see a very different Danny."

"What do you mean?" she asked curiously.

"Well, when Deb left and went back to England, Danny was really bad… he didn't give a shit about anything or anyone. Well, I think that Danny will be coming back."

The next day Tony and Sue announced their engagement. Deb wanted to get the caterers to do Sue's engagement party. She wanted her to have the biggest and the best engagement party ever. Sue had no family and she'd never had anyone to do anything for her. Deb so wanted her to have a special day.

"You don't have to do this Deb"

"Yes I do… You are my best friend…You are the only family I've got so please don't stop me from doing this for you."

Sue hugged Deb tight.

"Yes…We are family and love you." she said as tears rolled down her face.

"Yeah…I love you too you sentimental woman." Deb grinned.

Sue half laughed between the tears.

"Really Deb…When I met you, you changed my life."

"Yeah, yeah…. now come on, we need to sort out this engagement party."

They sat down and discussed what Sue wanted for her engagement and made a list of guests. They sorted out the invitations and sent them all out… Tony knew his place and just left the girls to it.

The night of the party Danny was on fine form, he had been drinking heavily before he and Chris got to the party.

He had been out for a meal with the actor Marshall Rogers, a new, up and coming actor. He had made two previous films and was very good looking. Tall, dark and handsome, he was a babe magnet and he was currently dating Alison Young from the girl band, *Ziggy's*. Danny invited them to Tony and Sue's engagement.

Sue and Tony greeted their guests. Danny introduced Marshall and Alison. Sue had noticed how good looking Marshall was and said so to Chris.

"He is absolutely gorgeous"

"Yeah, he is… but you should not be drooling," Chris laughed.

"A girl can look… that's what Deb said when she met Nick."

Talking of Nick, there he was with a lot of other stars. Deb went over to Sue and put her arms around her.

"Are you enjoying yourself?" she asked.

"Oh… yeah Deb. This is awesome." Sue replied, as Nick came up behind Deb and put his arms round her.

"Guess who."

Deb turned round. "Nick," she cried sounding really pleased to see him.

Sue and Tony went to mingle with their guests leaving Nick and Deb talking. Danny noticed Deb and went over…

"Hi Nick and Hi Babe," he slurred as he turned to Nick. "This woman is hot don't you think?"

"Very." Nick replied as he smiled at her

"Did you know that she was mine first? Simon stole her." Danny said

"Danny." Deb cried, worried what he was going to say next.

"What? You are so fuckin sexy…Do you know that?"

"You're drunk," she accused.

Nick looked from one to the other and shook his head.

"I'll catch you later" he said, feeling a little awkward.

Deb managed a smile."Yeah" she murmured.

Danny looked at her longingly and took hold of her hand.

"Come with me some where we can be alone."

"Danny stop it."

"Why Deb…? Why did you do it?"

"We agreed Danny," she whispered.

"No Deb...no...no...You... *You* agreed baby." He was so drunk he couldn't get his words out

"Please Danny."

"OK Deb...If this is it...You got it.... I'll show you baby."

He went over to Chris and was all over her. He knew Deb was watching. She was jealous... he knew she was.

Deb went over to Simon. He put his arms around her and kissing her he asked where she'd been.

"Just talking to Danny and Nick"

Simon started telling Deb that he had been discussing a deal for the band and that he had to talk to the rest of the guys.

"That's great Simon...But what deal?"

"A tour of Australia!" he enthused.

Before he had chance to say anymore Sue appeared.

"Hey, are you having a good night?" Si asked, as he put his arm round her, giving her a kiss.

"Oh yeah, Si"

Tony came over to the group and demanded, laughingly,"Where is the woman I love?" He took hold of her sensuously.

"I saw you drooling over that Marshall dude," he laughed.

"Yeah...Only looking though...I've only really got eyes for you babe."

"Sorry Sue, but can I just have Tony for a sec?" Simon asked.

"Yeah sure" she answered as Tony and Simon went off to talk.

Sue looked at Deb and then waved her hands in the direction of Danny.

"Is all that for your benefit?"

"He's drunk. He was so embarrassing before...Poor Nick, he didn't know where to put himself."

"Oh...Poor Nick..."

Deb had been scanning the room and she had noticed Marshall Rogers' girlfriend watching Danny. She seemed to staring at a lot. Chris was oblivious, she was too busy soaking up all the attention she was getting from Danny.

Deb, however, had noticed and thought she could be a problem

"Who is she?"

"She's out of that girl group, Ziggy's – Why?"

"Well she seems to like Danny, she's been watching him all night"

"Seriously?"

"Yep"

They both looked over at Alison. She was still eyeing up Danny and he had noticed it too. Sue changed the conversation to something else. She started telling Deb about Marshall and the two films he had starred in. He played small parts before that then he got his big break with a starring role in the romantic comedy *'You can't tie me down'*. Women go crazy over his muscular body and stunning looks.

"Have you met Marshall yet?"

"No…Who's Marshall?" Deb asked curiously.

"Marshall Rogers. You know…The actor… Wait till you see him, he's a heartthrob."

"Lead the way."

"Come on…I'll introduce you to him…."

Grabbing her hand, Sue took Deb to meet Marshall and when she saw him her jaw dropped and her eyes widened. "Wow!"

"Pleased to meet you, Mr. Rogers"

"Oh please call me Marshall"

"Marshall"

"You are Simon's wife aren't you?"

"Yes"

"It's lovely to meet you"

They chatted a while then Alison came over and took him away.

"I told you he was a heartthrob," Sue casually dropped in.

"Bloody hell…You're telling me, but he isn't a Brad Cannon, is he?"

"Oh God…Oh Deb, you're obsessed with Brad Cannon." Sue laughed.

CHAPTER 25

Next morning saw Simon and Deb in the garden., Deb was gardening and Simon was in the pool when Danny arrived to pick Simon up. Deb was still horrified from the night before as she had never seen this side to Danny. Simon went inside and came back carrying a beer for Danny.

"I won't be long I'll go and get changed."

"You're looking good this morning Deb. Married life must really suit you though it would suit you even better if you had married the right man."

Deborah looked at him coldly.

"Just stop it."

"Oh I know what that look means… You're angry with me…Right? OK… OK." he said, smirking at her.

"Did you have good night, last night?" she asked."Was that little display with Chris for my benefit?"

Danny smiled sarcastically.

"I don't know what you're talking about. You told me to get on with it…So I did just that."

Simon came back.

"Are you ready then, Dan?"

"Yep," he smiled at Deb.

Deb went upstairs and jumped in shower. She changed in to her slacks and T-shirt. She was quite relieved that Simon and Danny had gone. Danny had made her agitated. This was not the Danny she had met and fell in love with.

She got in her car and headed in to the restaurant. Sue was already there. She could see Deb was on edge but she said nothing. They had gone in early to do the stock take. Shortly after Deb had arrived, Chris turned up.

"Hi Chris … what you doing here?" Sue asked

"Oh, I've been shopping and thought I'd come and see you."

"Danny was in a good mood last night, wasn't he?"

"Yeah…he was all over me at the party."

Deb shouted from the kitchen as she came in with the coffee she'd made.

"Yeah we saw."

"Yeah when we got home he fell asleep."

"We thought you were in for a good night." Deb smirked.

"Yeah," Sue said smiling.

"So did I." Chrissie said laughing.

The phone rang and Sue answered it. It was Tony.

"Oh my God!" Sue exclaimed as the colour drained from her face.

"What's wrong?" Deb asked as Sue came off the telephone.

"We need to go to the hospital." Deb looked on, horrified.

Chrissie asked, "What is it is? Is it one of the guys?"

"Yeah… It's Dave and Alan… They've been in a car crash… Alan is in a real bad way but I'm not sure about Dave."

They locked up and Deb drove them to the hospital where they parked up and raced in. They found Danny, Simon and Tony with Dave and Alan's parents, all looking slightly dazed and pacing the floor.

"Alan is in surgery Dave isn't too good neither." Tony exclaimed.

 Everything seemed to be taking forever, so Sue, Deborah and Chris took Dave and Alan's parents for a cup of coffee. As they came back with coffees for the guys a doctor appeared from Dave's room and told his parents they could go in and see him.

It was another hour before anyone came to see Alan's parents. The doctor took them in to a side room. Danny, Simon, Tony and the girls waited impatiently, holding their breath, until they heard Alan's mum scream,"NO!"

They all looked at each other aghast. This just couldn't be happening. Alan's dad came from the room, shaking as he told them that Alan had died on the operating table. The guys were devastated. They told Tom that if there was anything they needed to let them know and they would do it.

"I'm going to take Anna home now... Could you let us know how Dave is?"

The guys told them they would let them know as soon as they knew anything. Tom went back into the room to get Anna. When she appeared, her head was bent and her eyes bright red. Deb put her arms round her.

"I am so sorry Anna..."

Anna put her arms round Deb.

"I've lost my boy," she cried as she burst into tears.

Deborah kissed them both.

"You know where we are if you need us..." she said as they left.

Simon, Danny, Tony and the girls waited to see how Dave was. Des, Dave's dad came out and asked about Alan. Danny told him that Alan had died.

"Oh my god... I'd better tell Myra."

"How's Dave?" Simon asked

Des told them Dave had broken his ribs, his arm and his leg, which they had to put a pin in. He also had a head injury.

The doctors decided that he'd had enough excitement for one day and so they all went home, promising they'd come back tomorrow to see Dave. Simon rang Nick to tell him about Alan and Dave. It was all over the news and the papers the next day.

ALAN WINTERS AND DAVE TURNER
IN CAR CRASH YESTERDAY

ALAN WINTERS DIED SHORTLY AFTER–
DAVE TURNER SERIOUSLY INJURED

Tom and Anna went to see Dave. They needed to know what had happened. Dave told them they had been driving to the studio and Alan had swerved to miss a dog. He said he couldn't remember anything after that. Dave was so upset about Alan, They were best friends, they had all grown up together.

They all had started their band in Danny's garage and they had all stuck together. Dave wanted to get out of hospital for Alan's funeral, he needed to be there.

The funeral was held a week later. Besides his family, lots of famous people attended. A lot of people liked Alan. Danny, Simon, Tony and Nick walked with the casket. Dave couldn't do it as he was still in a wheelchair, so Nick was standing in for him.

Danny's parents and brothers were there, Tony's mom and sister, Simon's dad and Dave's parents as well. Everyone was telling their own stories about Alan. They all had a funny one to tell, Alan had been the band's clown.

The guys hadn't to decide what they were going to do about the band. They had lost one of their best friends. They had all agreed that they should postpone the tour. They didn't want another guitarist. They organised a press conference to let their fans know that the tour was cancelled temporarily, out of respect for Alan.

They had to get used to not having Alan around. It was going to be hard. They took a long break then started working on a new album. One song was dedicated to Alan. They called it *Best Friend'*.

Simon spent some time in the restaurant. It was crammed every night. People were queuing to get in and it got a lot of press coverage because of all the celebrities that Simon was bringing in: the likes of Marshall Rogers, Dendra Pierce (she was the famous actress, one of the most beautiful women in the film industry) and the legendary singer, Melvin Jeffries.

Eventually Dave recovered and they decided to put their tour back on. Their first tour was in Canada and the tickets sold out within hours.

Deb, Sue and Chris spent some nights together. Sue tried to get her wedding organised. She had seen the wedding dress she wanted, it was ivory with a lace bodice and Deb's and Chris's dresses were a very pale lemon. Little Daniel was fixed up with a little suit and lemon cravat.

She had picked her venue and the food while the guys were away. Tony had asked Danny to be his best man and Danny told him he would be honoured. Sue was going to ask Simon to give her away and Dave was going to be the usher. Everything was set for February 20th.

The guys had been on tour for six months and were ready for well-earned break. It had been non-stop concerts, interviews, and press conferences. When they got back, Simon thought it would be a good idea to throw a huge party.

Lots of people came including film stars, Nick and his band, other bands they knew – all sorts of celebs. There was a girl group there, one of the girls was Alison. She'd been seeing Marshall Rogers but that was all over. Now she really had the hots for Danny and she wanted him bad, but then again, a lot of women did. Chris didn't like this one though.

She was a pretty blonde with a good figure and she was always coming on to Danny. She was all over him every time they were in her company. Chris watched while Deborah tried to placate her.

"You've nothing to worry about...Danny isn't like that."

Chris turned to Deb annoyed...

"No? Is that why he's got his hand on her ass?"

Danny was very close to Alison and his hand *was* on her rear, caressing her butt cheeks. No wonder Chris was so angry. Deb's eyes got wider and her lips parted with sheer astonishment. She could not believe what she was seeing. She marched over to Danny, pulling him away.

"Just what are you playing at?"

"What's wrong babe...? You jealous?" he laughed. "I know you are – so why don't you just give in to me?"

"What the hell do you think you're doing Danny. What about Chris... your wife?"

"What about her? You don't wanna play do ya? So Ali will have to do." he shrugged his shoulders as he went back over to Alison.

Danny knew Deb was watching him now. She was really angry and he knew it. He took Alison s hand and took her up stairs. Deb knew where he was going and who with, so she followed him. Danny was on the landing with Alison, his hands moving up her legs and he was just about to kiss her when Deb appeared.

"Danny." Deb shouted abruptly.

Alison scanned Deborah's face intently.

"Next time Dan" she said winking at him.

Danny turned to Deb, sighing.

"What Deb... What is it?"

"What the hell do you think you're you doing?" Deborah screamed at him with pent up frustration.

Danny took hold of her and pulled her to him before pushing her against the wall, moving his body against her.

"What am I doing…? What are you doing?"

Deborah looked at him

"What were you doing with that girl?"

"I'm having some fucking fun. Getting on with it just like you told me to."

He grabbed her by the arms, pressing himself against her so she couldn't move. He ran his fingers through her hair. He kissed her deeply, biting and holding her lip with his teeth.

"I've been having real dirty thoughts about you"

"Stop…."

"I want to touch you and lick every part of your body. I want to make you come over and over again, make you crazy with excitement and Baby, I want you to feel every inch of me"

"Stop it Danny"

He kissed her again, biting her bottom lip. Moving his hand up her leg, her dress rode up as his hand went higher. He pushed his body closer against hers and she could feel the bulge in his jeans pressing against her.

"You're real hot now… I can feel you…you want this don't you?" he whispered in her ear as he jabbed her with his penis.

"Stop it Danny…"

"See what you're missing babe… there's only me that can make you feel like this… You'll never feel the way you do right now with anyone but me." he hissed as he turned and walked away.

Deborah closed her eyes and sighed breathlessly. Nick had been on the stairs the whole time and he'd heard everything.

"Deb… Are you OK?" he asked as he appeared from the top of the steps

Deborah opened her eyes quickly. He'd startled her.

"Nick….You heard all that, didn't you?"

Nick just nodded.

"Are you going to tell Simon?" she asked.

He shook his head.

"Come on… Let's get a drink – I think you need one."

They went down stairs and Danny was back with Alison. By this time, Chris had enough. She told Deb she was going and stormed off, tears streaming down her face. Simon ran after her and Tony and Sue pulled Danny away from Alison.

"What the fuck are you doing?"

"For fucks sake… having some fuckin fun."

Simon made sure Chris was taken home. Danny asked Tony if he could crash at theirs. Everyone started to leave and Deb and Simon went to bed exhausted from the night's events.

Danny finally went home the next day. Chris however was not impressed – she thought he'd been with Alison all night

"Morning," Danny said casually, as if nothing was wrong.

"Fuck you! Have you been with that tart all night?"

Danny slammed his hands down on the counter and informed her that she didn't own him. She looked at him in amazement. She told him they were married and that meant commitment from both parties. Danny gave her a hostile look.

"I'm a rock star!"

"Did you fuck her?"

"What if I did?"

"You may be a rock star but that doesn't mean you can fuck everything that's in a skirt."

"What the fuck do you think fucking happens on tour baby?"

Chris stood up and walked towards him and slapped him across the face so hard she left red finger marks. Danny glared at her and told her she was so lucky she was a woman. He turned and walked away. He jumped in the shower, changed his clothes and jumped onto to his Triumph motorcycle and rode away.

Simon took breakfast up for Deb and, ruffling her hair, he murmured,

"Wake up sleepy head."

He got back in bed and Deb leaned over towards him, kissing him sensuously.

"Thank you…You are so good to me…"

"Are you going to make love to me now or after breakfast?" Simon asked seductively.

Deb looked at him lovingly.

"Oh after breakfast…Definitely,'' she smiled.

"I'll look forward to it… I'll just wait here then till you've finished."

Deborah laughed at him as she ate her breakfast. Simon ran his finger over her shoulders and kissed her neck.

"Simon…What are you doing?"

Simon looked at her longingly and said, "I have told you how much I love you?"

"Yeah…Lots… But unfortunately for you I have to get to the restaurant…I have got orders coming in and I know that you want to get laid."

"Deb… You said after breakfast."

"Sorry. I meant well after breakfast. I'll make it up to you tonight."

"I'll keep you to that… tonight then."

"Maybe!" she said as she got out of bed and jumped in the shower.

"Deb?"

"Maybe…" Deb shouted back.

She had a shower and got dressed. She told Simon, who by this time was sitting in the kitchen, that she was going.

"Deb…"

"Yeah?"

"Tonight?"

"Bye babe…" She laughed

And she left. And made her way to the restaurant. As she pulled up in the car lot she noticed Danny sat on his motorcycle. She got out of the car and went over to him.

"What are you doing here Danny?"

"I just found myself riding here"

"Oh Danny…, come on I'll make some coffee"

They made their way inside through to the kitchen. Deb switched on the percolator as Danny sat on the stool staring at her. You could smell the aroma of fresh coffee as the machine spluttered. Danny stood up, looking her up and down. He moved towards her, slowly trailing his fingers up and down her arm. She could feel his warm breath on the back of her neck.

He kissed her neck gently. She almost gave in, she didn't trust herself alone with him but she turned quickly. He moved his head to hers, he traced his fingers over her lips then wrapped his fingers around a strand of her hair, his lips softly touches hers. Still playing with her hair between his fingers he told her he loved her.

"Danny no" she said interrupting him.

He looked at her and drew his eyebrows together as he scanned her face.

"We have both made decisions, Danny"

"Yeah… stupid ones"

"Whatever, we have to live with them, we can't keep doing this – *you* can't keep doing this"

"Goddamit woman what do I have to do?"

"Stop, please just stop"

"I'll never stop and I'll never give up – you are driving me crazy"

Danny turned and as he walked towards the door, he looked back and mouthed, 'I love you Deb'. She put her head down in despair.

She heard the door slam and his bike screech as he rode away.

Chapter 26

The year 1992

Simon took Deb on a romantic weekend for Valentine's Day. She didn't know anything about it and was totally surprised when he took her to New York. They had a beautiful weekend together – luxury hotel, lavish meals – he made her feel like a princess. All he wanted to do was make Deb happy.

He arranged a romantic meal in their room and gave her the biggest bunch of roses she'd ever seen. A string quartet played for them whilst they were having their meal and he had surrounded the room with candles – he even got her up to dance. He gave the most beautiful white gold diamond necklace, telling her he loved her very much. He took off the pendant she was already wearing and replaced it with the one he had just given her. She loved it. She placed her fingers over his and turned round to smile at him. He had made her feel so good.

"Simon, you have made this weekend beautifully romantic, thank you."

She took hold of his hand and led him into the bedroom. She kissed him as she removed his shirt. Moving her hand down his chest, she started digging her nails in.

"Ah ah umm…" he sighed, breathing heavily.

She was really turning him on. She moved her hands down his body, kissing him and biting him gently, at the same time unzipping his trousers. He felt so excited at this point and he couldn't take any more teasing. He took hold of her and kissed her very passionately, moving his hands all over her body before he made love to her.

The sex was hot and passionate as she dug her nails in his back… he liked it. It turned him on so much.

The next morning Deborah woke up and got in the shower. Simon climbed in with her.

"Have you seen my back?"

"Yeah… But you liked it…You couldn't get enough."

"Yeah… But I have deep scratches on my back – I look as if I've been slashed."

Deb laughed.

"You weren't complaining last night. I heard a lot of moaning and wanting more but no complaining."

"Yeah…."

"You loved it."

"You're an animal."

Deb growled at him as she rang for breakfast before she thanked him for such a lovely weekend.

"No, no – after what you did last night, thank *you*."

"Simon," she said as she growled at him again.

"Oh… Oh Deb…Do you wanna do what you did to me last night?"

Deborah looked at him longingly.

"Get your ass back in that bedroom if you think you can take it."

Simon looked at her and grinned from ear to ear.

'Oooh…, oh… Yeah babe."

They had to get back to Beverley Hills. The next morning they both went back to work. Sue asked if they had a good weekend.

"Yeah it was great. So what's been happening here while we've been away?"

"Well, Danny and Chris have had a big bust up and I mean a very big one too."

"What, again?

"Danny was making out with Alison, Chris went crazy."

"What is it with this Alison."

"They're all coming here after the rehearsals." Sue warned.

Sure enough, Straight after rehearsals they all ploughed in. Deb was in the kitchen making coffee and took it out to the guys. When she went back into the kitchen, Danny followed her. Everyone was in deep conversation so no-one had noticed Danny disappear. Deb turned round quickly.

"Danny… What are you doing?"

"This," he said as he grabbed her and kissed her.

"I want you," he whispered as he kissed her again.

There was a false cough, Tony appeared. Deb broke free and went back in to the others.

"Danny…What the hell were you doing? I could have been Simon."

"And you think I give a shit?"

"Danny…."

"Tony…She's driving me crazy."

"So where does Alison fit in?"

"Nowhere…." Danny shrugged.

"Danny buddy… come on."

They went back in to the others. Tony was really concerned about Danny. This just wasn't like him, he was worse than the last time.

Sue and Tony's big day finally arrived. Sue and Chris went round to Deb's. Sue was so excited, she was talking so fast that Deb had to slow her down.

"I'm I jabbering?"

"Yeah babe."

Sue quickly turned on her heels and went to get ready. When she reappeared she looked so beautiful in her ivory lace dress. Deb placed her veil over vintage curls that swept away from her face. Simon looked at her admiringly.

"Sue…You look beautiful."

Deborah and Chris agreed.

"Do you think Tony will like it?" Sue asked

"Oh yeah babe …he'll like." Simon reassured her.

Chris and Deb got ready. The car arrived to pick them up then went back for Sue and Simon. As the limo pulled up to the church, Simon got out and walked to the other side. He held his hand out to her as she stepped out of the car and Deb and Chris straightened her dress. She made her way in to the church, linking arms with Simon. They smiled at each other and Simon told her how beautiful she was and he winked at her.

Tony and Danny were there waiting at the altar when Sue and Simon arrived. Dave put his thumbs up. Sue and Simon started to walk down the aisle.

Tony turned and was knocked out by Sue. Emotionally he whispered to Dan.

"She's so beautiful man."

"Yeah Tony…You're a very lucky man and look at Daniel…What a handsome little guy."

"Yeah…That's my boy" Tony smiled lovingly at him.

At the reception Danny managed to make Deborah feel uncomfortable yet again. Nick noticed how edgy she was and went over to talk to her. She was pleased to see him and gave him a kiss.

"You look as beautiful as ever."

"Thank you. You are so nice…I think I should have met you first."

"I wish." Nick exclaimed

"We nearly did

He looked at her in confusion and asked her what she meant. She told him that she had come to one of his concerts when she lived in England and she tried to get his autograph. She couldn't get near enough to get it. He gasped and shook his head.

"There's something I want to ask you…Can I come and see you at the restaurant?"

"Yeah …When?"

"In few weeks' time?"

She spent quite some time talking to Nick. Danny and Chris looked as if they were having yet another argument. Sue and Tony only had eyes for each other.

They set off on their honeymoon the next day. They went to Barbados and had a wonderful time.

Little Daniel stayed with Deb and Simon. He had the best time and he got to do all sorts of cool things. Simon, Danny and Dave took him everywhere with them and if he wasn't with the guys he was with Deb and Chris. The papers got their story as ever and lots of photos… and again they were headline news.

ROCK STAR TONY MYERS MARRIES HIS GIRLFRIEND SUE ANDERSON

It wasn't long before they were back and the guys were going on tour again. While the guys were away the girls all got together. Deb made a meal for them after the restaurant closed and they were sat drinking and talking when Deb asked Chris how things were between her and Danny.

"I don't know." she shrugged, "he is so argumentative and bad tempered…I think he's having an affair with Alison or he's on drugs."

Deb was aghast, "No he's not, on both counts."

Sue agreed. There was no way.

"So what's wrong with him then?"

"He's under a lot pressure – The guys do a lot of tours." Sue suggested.

"Yeah… But Simon isn't like that."

"But maybe something is bothering him."

"I asked him if he wanted to start a family but he said no."

"Don't worry…It will sort itself out." Deb comforted.

"I hope so… I don't know how much more I can take… he needs to talk to me."

Chapter 27

Nick came round and they were sat talking over coffee when he asked her if he could use the restaurant for his video.

"Yeah… Why not? My restaurant will be famous."

"It's already famous… *You* could be famous though."

Deb laughed and brushed his face with her fingertips

"You could be the girl in my vid… The girl I get to kiss." he said, giving her cheeky grin

Deborah smiled and said, "Ohm…You are real good."

"Yeah… Doesn't work on you though, does it?"

"Oh Nick… I don't know. You're very charming," she said smiling.

He smiled back at her longingly, "I wish it did…You're so beautiful."

"Oh Nick you say all the right things…You always make me feel good." She said, smiling as she kissed him.

He looked deep into her eyes and moved closer to her, placing his arms round her. There was an attraction there… a big one. He leaned in and kissed her and she kissed him back. They found themselves kissing passionately, more and more intensely and leading to him unzipping her dress.

He pulled her closer and she pulled his T-shirt over his head, throwing it on the floor, moving her hands over his body. Slowly he started to touch her. Things were starting to get very hot between them. They were both turned on and he told how much he wanted her.

"The first time I ever saw you I wanted you."

She found herself wanting him. He laid her down on the table, opening her dress even more as he trailed his hands down her body, over her breasts and down to her navel, followed by his lips. Slowly, he covered her body with lingering butterfly kisses. She could feel his hot, sweaty body pressing against her… he was so turned on… he was so hard. She could feel how turned he was by his body pressing against her. She pulled the zip down on his jeans as she brushed her hands over the bulge that was pressing in to her.

Suddenly he stopped. She looked at him incredulously

"What's wrong."

"I can't," he said, "I want to… Fuck me, I want to – but I can't. Simon is my mate and I think that it would just complicate your life even more. I know Danny is giving you a hard time."

She sat up, fastened her dress and kissed him.

"Oh Nick …."

He zipped his jeans up and put his T-shirt back on.

"I'm a fucking idiot…I *do* want you. I'll be in touch about the video… I'd better go before I change my mind."

Deb smiled at him. "The girl that gets you will be very lucky."

Nick raced out of the restaurant. He was in danger of changing his mind, he want her so much. Deborah sat down thought to herself, 'Oh Shit – what just happened and why did that happen? '

She locked up and went home but she couldn't get the evening out of her head. She couldn't sleep for thinking about what nearly happened.

When the guys got back from their tour Simon went straight home. Deb was at the restaurant. He had missed her so much. He got changed and headed over there. Sue had gone home to see Tony. When Simon got to the restaurant he sneaked up behind her and put his arms round her. Deborah turned round and kissed him. She had missed him and wanted to prove it. After what nearly happened between her and Nick, it was as if she had to convince herself that it never actually happened.

194 | Deborah Caren Langley

She left the chief in charge and they went home for a romantic evening together. Deb made her way to the kitchen and got out some crispy potato skins with a spicy dip, grabbed a bottle of wine and headed up the stairs. Simon had run a hot bubble bath. They had a beautiful, big round bath and he had placed candles all around it and put some soft background music on. He was already relaxing in the tub. He gestured for her to get in and she sat down spooning him. They both relaxed, drinking wine and eating their potato skins. Lightly he kissed her collarbone.

"I love you," he whispered.

She turned herself round in the tub to kiss him tenderly.

The week after was the Spinout Rock Awards night. Danny had been nominated for the 'Sexiest Rock Star' and 'Best Male Performer' and he won both. Deb and Danny were sat at the table together. Danny moved over to her and smiled. Deborah turned to him.

"I'll warn you now Danny. Don't mess with me because I'm ready for you."

"Don't mess with you…You're ready for me?" he repeated insolently.

"Yes I am."

Danny smiled, "Good because I'm ready for you."

He moved in even closer and grinned at her as she looked at him.

"Danny I'm warning you. Smiling at me isn't going to work."

"Why…It always did before."

She spotted Nick and waved. He blew a kiss at her.

"You like Nick don't you?"

"Yeah…he's a nice guy." Danny smiled to himself.

"What are you smiling at?"

"Nothing."

"What Danny?"

"Nothing, babe."

Everyone came back and gathered round the table. Danny was watching Simon. Simon was nestling into Deb, kissing her neck, moving his hands up her legs, stroking them. Danny was breathing heavily and his nostrils were beginning to flare. He was getting more and more frustrated. Chris leaned over to kiss him.

"Chris, just stop making a scene…" he snapped, annoyed at her.

He really hurt her pushing her away, she didn't understand what was wrong. Then she saw Alison heading towards him.

"Hi sexy" he crooned

Alison was really attracted to Danny but his thoughts were just with Deb. 'I'll show you Deborah Carnell... I'll get you to give me your attention. '

"Ali come and sit on this," he smirked, grabbing his groin and making a duck face.

Chris was fuming, she stormed off. Deb, Simon, Sue and Tony just looked at Danny, horrified. Deb gave him such a frosty look but Danny just winked at her. Chris was in the restroom with streams of mascara tears running down her face. Deb went after her, with Sue close behind. Deb took her in her arms.

"Why is he doing this?"

"I don't know – but I'm going to find out."

Sue helped Chris to fix her make up while Deb was pacing the floor. She was so angry with Danny right now, steam was coming out of her ears and she was determined he was going to get piece of her mind.

"What the fuck are you doing Dan?" Simon asked.

"I'm having some fucking fun."

Deb and Sue persuaded Chris that he was just messing about.

"Like I do with Nick." Deb explained. "Come on, let's go back."

Alison was still on Danny's knee and he was kissing her neck, moving his hand up her legs. She had her hands all over him. Tony tried to defuse situation but, by this time, Chris could not contain her anger any longer.

"What the hell are you doing Danny?" Chris screamed at him.

Danny calmly turned to her and told her to chill out.

Chris lunged at Alison, grabbing her by the hair and told her to get away from her man. There was a very loud and public argument – this would be all over the paper tomorrow for sure. Chris stormed out and Sue and Deb chased after her again.

"I'm not going back in there... I'm going home," she began to cry again.

"Why is he doing this to me?" she cried

Alison looked at Danny and then at the rest of the guys.

"I'd better go... Ring me – just not when the wife is with you." Alison smirked.

"What are you doing Dan? Chris is heartbroken."

"I'm fucked off with her. It's time to move on."

"*What?*"

Simon, Tony and Dave all tried talking some sense into him.

"Why don't you all just fuck off? No-one is going to tell me what I can and can't do – I'll screw who I want."

"Dan…What is it with you lately?" Simon asked.

"I don't know what the fuck you're banging on about."

Sue stayed with Chris while Deb went back to the table. She asked Simon to sort a car out for Chris.

"Yeah sure…Is she OK?"

"No, she isn't."

She looked straight at Danny and through gritted teeth she yelled at him.

"Just what the hell do you think you are doing?"

Danny just looked at her calmly.

"Sit down babe."

"Sit down? Is that all you have to say?"

"OK… *Please* sit down babe."

"Danny what is wrong with you?" She shouted so angrily

Danny stood up."Come with me." he said forcefully

He grabbed her hand and took her out to a nearby balcony.

"Why Danny…That was an awful thing to do. If you had done that me…"

Danny interrupted her by putting his finger to her lips.

"That wouldn't have happened. I love you."

"Danny."

"Yeah…But it's true."

"That does not excuse what you did to Chris tonight."

"No… You're right."

He moved closer to her and pressed her against the wall. He brushed his lips over hers and she stammered breathlessly.

"Danny…Stop it."

"You like it…You haven't moved away."

"Well I am now." she stuttered as she tried move.

He pushed her back against the wall and whispered suggestively in her ear.

"I want to get between your thighs, to have hot passionate sex with you…I know you're turned on."

Deb was incensed.

"Danny Brooks…You arrogant bastard… Go home to Chris, apologise. She doesn't deserve to be treated the way you're treating her."

"I know…I know… none of this is her fault. I will apologise."

Danny once again leaned in and kissed her, grabbing her bottom lip with his teeth staring deep into her eyes. He moved his hands slowly up her legs to her hips, wrapping his arms round her waist, bringing her closer to him. She could feel the heat from his body. She really needed to move but he was turning her on so much. She inhaled slowly. A smile flickered across his face, he left Deb stood there. She was quite flustered, taking long deep breaths, inhaling and exhaling. She needed to pull herself together before she went back in to Simon.

"Where's Danny?" she asked.

"He's split… gone home." Simon replied.

When Danny got home Chris was crying inconsolably.

"I'm sorry…You didn't deserve that," he muttered.

"No I didn't. Please Danny, tell me what's wrong? Why are you being like this?"

Danny looked at her and took hold of her hands.

"I'll sort it out…I promise… This should have been sorted a long time ago."

"Danny…Please…What is wrong?"

"I'm going to bed," he replied.

Chris looked very confused, not to mention really worried: Sort what? And why should it have been sorted a long time ago? What did he mean? Was he talking about him and Deb or was it something else?

Chapter 28

Danny went to see his mom and he told her what he had done to Chris the night before.

"Why?"

"In a word… Deb. This is driving me crazy… I'm hurting Chris and it's not her fault"

"I told you Danny… You want her back don't you?"

"Yeah… I love her, mom"

"What about your marriage, Danny?"

"What marriage? The moment Deb came back in to my life there was no marriage. What do I do, mom?"

"Well Danny … You are my son and I love you very much but what you did to Chris was appalling. I know you love Deb. I knew when you married Chris it was a mistake."

"Yeah… I know…I know."

"Well, first you need to be honest with Chrissie… Oh Danny, I knew this was going to happen."

Danny kissed his mom lovingly. "Thanks mom."

He left but whilst he was driving back he thought about what his mom had said and decided that he would take a different approach. No more pressurising Deb, no more hurting Chris to get Deb jealous. He had to win her back with his charm and show her that what was there when they met was still there. He had to be the man she had fallen in love with all those years ago. He knew what he had to do to get her back

A few days later, Nick got in touch with Deb about the video. They hadn't really discussed it properly since the night they were alone in the restaurant and he felt a bit awkward. Deb asked him if he was avoiding her.

"I don't want what happened… I mean…I don't want to make you feel… Oh Deb, I mean…."

"Nick I don't, it's OK – we're friends aren't we?"

"Yeah… But we nearly became something else Deb."

"Yeah," she smiled. "I don't want anything to spoil our friendship…Let's go back to how we were."

Nick smiled and kissed her. "I still want to take you to bed."

Deb laughed. "You're a bad, bad boy."

"You like me being a bad boy. We could have been so good together – not to mention how hot. Scorching. Mmm *scorching*." giving her a naughty grin

"Ooooh Nick."

They both smiled at each other and then laughed in unison.

The video was set to be filmed that week. Deb was so excited. Simon was paranoid about all the time that she and Nick were spending together and it worked out that while Nick was at the restaurant, Simon and the guys had a photo shoot so he couldn't get there. Sam, their photographer, came in and looked over the setting.

"Right guys… Let's get you in position."

"You can get me in any position you want, babe!" Dave said cheekily as he observed Sam's ass when she bent over.

The rest of the guys howled with laughter.

"Come on Romeo," Danny said, playfully thumping Dave's arm, but Dave couldn't take his eyes off Sam with her beautiful figure and blonde hair.

"Dan… What couldn't I do to that."

"Ask her out on a date."

"Ya reckon?"

"Yeah Dave…Go on."

"She's one hot chick."

So Dave asked Sam out and she accepted. They went for a meal and they talked about her job. She told him how she loved it.

"Yeah…All them hunky men I get in my studio and some of them naked… Who wouldn't love it?"

"Yeah… I suppose so."

"hmm…Yeah…Could take some pictures of *you*." she said eyeing him up.

"What…naked?"

"Yeah…"

"As long as you are the one taking my clothes off," he smiled.

She tossed her long blonde hair back as she laughed.

"That can be arranged," she said smiling.

Dave was really into this chick. He asked about her family and she told him about her mom and dad and brother and sister.

"What about you?"

He spoke about his mom, his dad and brother. They had a fantastic evening and she asked him about being a rock star. He told her he loved it

"… Ya know – with all those babes. What's not to like?" he teased, smiling at her. "You have a lovely smile"

"Thanks… So have you."

Dave was a good looking bloke – medium height with longish, light brown hair, brown eyes and nicely toned body. He asked if he could see her again.

"Yeah, love to," she said.

"Good… because I like you… like you a lot."

"I like you too and… I want to photograph that body naked."

"Oh babe, that can be arranged…"

They started to see a lot of each other and they started to get pretty serious.

Meanwhile, Simon had received a call from his dad. He didn't get see his dad much so he was pleased to hear from him. Gary told Simon he was coming to see him as he had something to tell him. Simon asked him when he was coming and Gary told him he'd be on the next plane.

"That's great… Me and Deb will come and meet you." Simon said excited.

Simon thought his dad was going to tell him he had met someone and was going to get married, but he was wrong. When Gary arrived, Simon and Deb met him and took him back home.

"What is it you want to tell us?" Simon asked.

Gary turned to Simon with a serious look on his face and told them both that he had cancer. Simon was devastated, he had already lost his mom to cancer.

"I will get the best doctors to see you dad," he cried.

Gary told Simon he only had a few months to live.

"No… We will get you to another doctor."

"Son… I'm dying."

"No dad…"

Simon booked his dad in with another doctor but the doctor just told them what Gary already knew. Simon told his dad that he wanted him to move in with them and Gary agreed because he wanted to be with Simon as much as he could before he died. Simon was an only child so the rest of the guys pitched in to help him through. If Simon couldn't be at Gary's hospital appointments, Deb took him.

She knew how Simon was feeling as she had done all these trips to the hospital with her mum and knew how hard they were. As the weeks passed, Gary started to deteriorate and was admitted to hospital. They put him on morphine to help with pain. Simon was at the hospital every day to be with his dad.

Danny, Tony and Dave also went to the hospital to support Simon.

The night that Simon had been dreading finally came and when they got the call Simon and Deb dashed to the hospital. Shortly after they arrived, Gary passed away.

Deb rang everyone to let them know as Simon was in pieces. He couldn't talk to anyone and when she finally took him home, she just held him in her arms and let him cry. The next day everyone came round to see them. All the guys threw their arms around him and hugged him just to let him know they were all there for him. Deborah, Sue and Chris left the guys together and went into the kitchen.

Danny came in and asked Deb if she'd make some coffee.

"Yeah Danny… Is he OK?"

"Yeah… he's dealing with it, somehow."

"I'll bring the coffee in…You go back to Simon"

Danny smiled and said, "Thanks."

After the funeral Simon asked the guys if they wanted to get involved in a charity for cancer and, of course, they all said that they would. They contacted the cancer research charity and told them they wanted to get involved by helping raise money for the cause.

They talked about a concert or gala or even raffling one of the guitars off signed by Danny or Simon. They donated some goody bags, CDs, T shirt, posters and keyrings and so on. They started putting together a list of artists they were going to ask to the charity gig. They all were very positive and eager to join in and take part.

The girls went to the *Majestic,* an exclusive night club, where they met up with Nick. He snuck up on Deb while she was dancing and wrapped his arms around her waist, swaying sexily with her. He had just come back from touring and the papers managed to get some pictures of him with Deb.

The pictures showed Nick with his arms around her, kissing her. They were just messing around and being silly with each other, but the photos looked incriminating. They hit the headlines.

ROMA FRONT MAN NICK GRANGER GETS COSY WITH SIMON RICHARDS' WIFE

Simon saw the papers the next day and went ballistic. He tore the papers up and rammed them in the bin

"What are you pissed about? You know Nick and Deb are friends, it won't be how it looks… Deb was with Sue, Sam and Chris last night." Tony said logically.

"Yeah but Nick would love to be in my shoes. He's into Deb in a big way. She spends way too much time with Nick." Simon growled jealously.

Danny laughed.

"So what's so funny?" Simon asked.

"You are… have you heard yourself ?"

"What?"

"You're a prick."

"Fucking hell Dan… Don't hold back… Just say what ya feel."

"Yeah… That's me…and you are still a prick."

"Why?"

"They're just messing about. If you don't know that, you're a bigger fucking prick than I thought you were."

Tony and Dave looked at each other and both agreed with Danny.

Chapter 29

When the guys got back, Danny was talking to Alex. He was telling him he'd written a bunch of songs but didn't know what do with them as they weren't the sort of songs that Decade would do. They were love ballads. Alex suggested that Danny think about doing a solo album. The girl fans would feel like he was singing the songs specially for them as the songs were about love and losing love. One was called *'Missing You'*.

Danny liked the idea of that.

"Yeah, *Danny Brooks Love Songs*… solo album."

"I'll set it up for you." Alex said.

Alex suggested he spoke to the other guys first and so he did. They thought it was a great idea and told him to go ahead and do it.

Alex set it all up for Danny. He got some session musicians and a brass section to give a real classic rock mixed with soul feel. He brought in a couple of top classical pianists and brought Dinah Chesney from the girl rock band *Stratosphere* to duet on a couple of tracks. The album was well anticipated with the press asking if this was the end for Decade.

"Absolutely not – me and the Guys will be back with some new stuff. They thought I needed to do this and they're completely behind me."

The album was snapped up on release and entered the album charts at No 6. When Danny had finished working on it, he came back and started in on the charity event preparation. They asked Nick if Roma would help support the charity. He said they would and with their combined efforts they managed to get lot of bands involved and a lot of film stars and famous people bought tickets. All the money raised was to go to cancer research.

Deb looked stunning that evening. Her dress was stunning. It was black to the floor with a split up the side, revealing her shapely legs. It had a silver edging so she wore silver shoes and purse to match. She wore her hair up with wisps dangling at the sides of face with little diamanté sprinkled through it. It took Danny all his time to keep his mouth shut and his hands off her. Nick had to show some restraint as well.

Alison was there. Chris was dreading it. When she made her way over to Danny, Chris's heart sank.

"Hi Dan," she murmured.

"Well, Hi Ali… how ya doing babe?"

"You haven't called me lately me," she whispered, smiling seductively at him.

"It was fun while it lasted"

She looked at him and gave him such a hostile look.

"She's welcome to you" she said as she stormed off.

Chrissie looked at Danny quizzically.

"It's fine…Everything is fine." Danny shrugged.

"I wish you would tell me"

"I will when the time is right."

Deb and Simon came back to the table and Deb asked Chris if everything was alright. She had seen Alison come over to Danny.

"I don't know…he just keeps telling me everything will be fine."

"I wonder what it is." Deb pondered, shaking her head.

Chris shrugged her shoulders."Will you find out? He might tell you."

"It's not my place Chris…You're his wife."

"Please Deb…I'll get Simon up to dance you can try."

Chris asked Simon to dance. She figured that if Danny was going to tell anyone it would be Deb. Deb moved over to Danny and smiled.

He looked at her longingly.

"You look so beautiful... I'm sure you get more beautiful every day."

"Thanks... so do you... You always were a sexy man with your long streaky blonde hair and those beautiful hazel eyes." She hesitated, looking at him intently.

"Are you OK? Is there something wrong?"

"You've been talking to Chris. All I'm saying is that I'm fixing something. I will say this though... It's something that should have been fixed a long time ago."

Deborah was intrigued and asked if there was anything to worry about. Danny smiled and held his hand out.

"Come on."

"Where we going?" she said taking his hand.

"To dance,." he said simply.

The tension between them had disappeared and Deborah started to feel like she did when she first met him.

He goofed around on the dance floor, whizzing her round and round. He did some real sexy moves – this was the Danny she loved so much They had such a good time laughing and messing around together it was just like old times. A slow song came on and Danny pulled her close.

"I love the feel of your body near mine, the feel of your skin, the smell of your perfume."

She smiled at him. He also mentioned the fact that Nick had fallen over his own feet staring at her and she couldn't help but laugh.

"He did? Oh poor Nick... I do love him."

"He's got the hots for you and Simon is totally paranoid about him."

"Well, Simon is going to have to chill out because I like Nick. We are good friends... Anyway... I saw Alison come over to you."

"Yeah... that's all finished now."

"Oh... good

"I have something really important to fix."

"Oh Danny... Can't you tell me what it is?"

"No... but you'll know soon enough." he said smiling at her.

He took her hand and they went back to the table. Close behind was Nick.

"Hi darling." he said to Deb.

"Oh… I thought you were talking to me, Nick." Danny laughed. Nick laughed.

"If you want me to call you darling, I will Dan."

Danny laughed. He felt so much better now he knew he was going to get what he wanted. All he had to do was stay calm and play it cool.

"I've come to take this lady to dance." said Nick as he held his hand out to Deb.

Simon was seething. He was so jealous of Nick. He was convinced that he was hitting on Deb. She and Nick were on the dance floor but Simon was watching closely. Nick moved his arms tighter around Debs waist, moving closer to her.

"Fucking hell!"

Simon stood up and started to make his way over. Danny stood in front of him and pushed him back.

"Danny…Move."

"No Si…Don't…You're just jealous… That is it…Just jealousy…There is nothing going on."

"Why does he have to touch her?" Si said through gritted teeth.

"They are dancing."

Deb came back and Simon looked at her accusingly.

"What?"

"Nothing!" he said storming off.

Deb looked over at Danny.

"What did he look at me like that for?"

"He was coming over to you and Nick."

"Why? We were only dancing."

"Dan stopped him." Sue informed her.

"Oh God… he really needs to get a grip. Not every man wants to get in my knickers…They don't all think 'Oh there's Deb, I really want to bang her." Danny, Tony and Sue all looked at her and went into a fit of laughter

"What?" she cried.

"You…You're so funny…"

208 | Deborah Caren Langley

"Yeah well... he's getting right on my tits."

That had Danny, Tony and Sue laughing once more. Chris came back and looked at them all inquisitively.

"So what are you guys laughing at?"

"Deb... She's so funny when she's angry." Danny said.

When Simon eventually came back Deb asked him if he'd calmed down. Simon looked at her unforgivingly.

"I'm fine." he mumbled.

Chapter 30

The band were due some time off and Tony and Sue were going to the beach house. The guys had bought the beach house together so they could escape if they needed to. Tony asked the guys if they were interested in going.

"Yeah… Count us in… What about you Dave?" asked Danny and Simon.

"Yeah… Count me in."

The guys were ready for the break. They had done a lot of tours, recording and a lot of charity work. Deb was excited about going to the beach house. She loved it so much there and she knew the restaurant was in good hands with their chef.

After they unpacked, the guys all went down to the beach to play soccer with Daniel. The girls sorted out some food and drinks for lunch. Sam had managed to organize her photo shoots around the vacation. She would have a lot do when she got back but It was worth it. She was looking forward to going to the beach house and meeting up with the girls.

The girls liked Sam and thought she was the one for Dave. They had been seeing each other for a few months now and Sam had fallen for him in a big way. Dave had also fallen for Sam and he was thinking about asking her to marry him but he wanted to talk to the guys first.

While they were down on the beach Danny asked him if he loved her.

"Yeah" he replied

"Well then... Don't hold back."

"Dan's right." Tony interrupted.

"Si...What do you think?" Dave asked.

Simon agreed. "Go for it Dave."

"Yeah...You all think I should?"

"If you don't, something could happen and bite you on the ass and you might lose her. Go for it!" Danny warned.

Dave knew what Danny was referring to. By the time the girls shouted them for lunch, Dave had made his mind up, he'd decided to ask Sam to marry him. Danny was quiet at lunch and Chris asked him if he was OK. He reassured her and smiled at her. He glanced over at Deb and smiled at her. She smiled softly back. Chris leant over to Deb and asked if Dan had told her anything.

"No... nothing ... but he did say he was fixing something."

"Fixing what, though?" Chris asked.

Deborah shrugged her shoulders. "I don't know"

She was concerned though. Meanwhile, Dave stood up and clapped his hands.

"Right guys I have something to say to Sam."

Sam looked at him puzzled.

"What?" she asked.

"Will you marry me?"

Sam's face broke into a big smile.

"Oh god... Yeah... Dave I love you baby..."

Everyone cheered and congratulated them. Tony asked if anyone wanted to have a game of charades. Every one said yeah...they were all up for that.

"My husband, the romantic!" Sue laughed.

The guys were in a deep game of charades when Danny sneaked out and went down to the beach. No–one had been looking but Deb. She went outside and stood watching him. Suddenly Sue came out and asked her what she was doing.

"Watching Danny...."

"Why?"

"There is something bothering him… I know him… Do you know the sex between us was fantastic."

"Where did that come from?" Sue asked incredulously.

"That's what I was thinking about when you come out."

"Deb… Don't do this to yourself again," Sue said, feeling concerned.

"Don't worry Sue."

"But I do…I love you Deb…You are my best friend and I know that you still love him."

"Do I?"

"Yeah and you know it."

Danny started making his way back to the beach house.

"Hi girls…What you doing? Were you watching me?" Danny asked.

"Yeah… We were" said Deb quick to admit it.

"Wow, I wasn't expecting you to admit it."

"We were just wondering what you were doing." Sue said.

"I was just thinking… Come on…Let's go back in otherwise they'll be thinking we're having a threesome," Danny said laughing.

Deb giggled giddily

"Danny…You bad boy." Sue said as she giggled too.

They went back in and Tony noticed them creeping back in.

"Hey…Where have you three been?"

"We have been having a threesome on the beach." Danny laughed.

"You could have said…" Tony said laughing.

The next day they were all on the beach. Dave, Sam, Chris, Tony and Simon were playing volley ball. Sue, Danny and Deb were playing in the sea with little Daniel. Eventually Sue took Daniel and joined in with the volley ball game leaving Danny and Deb in the sea.

They sat in the sea talking. Danny asked where Nick's new single was in the charts.

"I don't know how it's doing…I'll ring him later and find out."

They came out of the water and started a barbecue for the rest of the guys' dinner. Later Deb called Nick and asked him how the single was doing.

"Great Deb…Everything's going great – it's at number 7."

They had been talking for ages when Simon finally noticed and looked quizzically at Danny.

"Who's she talking to?" he mouthed.

"Nick."

Simon wasn't happy and when Deb came off the phone he asked why she had been ringing Nick.

"I wanted to...Why?"

"I don't want you ringing Nick." he shouted angrily.

"*What?*"

"You heard me!" he shouted at her.

"Yeah, I heard you...But I don't give a shit Simon... Nick and I are friends and you need to chill out."

They had a really big argument and Deborah stormed off

"I'm sick of your crap about Nick."

The others all looked at each other.

"Simon...What is your problem?"

"She called Nick and I don't like it." he sulked.

"So you told her?" Dave asked

"Yeah."

Sue shook her head at Simon.

"What? She's my wife! Nick's got the hots for her, he's trying to get her in bed I'm telling you. That's if he hasn't already."

"You are such a prick. Nick's single is the one that he shot in the restaurant and she wanted to know how it was doing... so did I... We were talking about it earlier." Danny said.

"I'll go and find her." Chris volunteered.

She found Deb sat in between the rocks on the beach.

"Do you mind if I sit with you?"

"No... That's OK... sit down"

"Are you OK, Deb?"

"Yeah.... he's such a dick... he is so jealous and I'm getting pissed off with it. Chris, would you go back and get a bottle and bring it out here... we can get pissed... unless you want to stay with the others?"

"No... I'll go and get a bottle."

"Chris, don't say where I am."

Chris went back but Simon had gone in the bedroom to check Debs cell phone to see whether he could find what Nick had been texting her, or what she'd been texting him. Danny went in to the bedroom to see if Simon was going to look for her.

"What are doing Si? You're not checking her cell are ya?"

"Yeah, Why?"

"She'll go crazy."

"She won't know... unless you tell her."

"No...Keep me out of this."

Chris had got a bottle and was heading back to Deb when Sue spotted her.

"Did you find Deb?" she asked.

"Yeah, she wants this..." she smiled, showing Sue the bottle.

"I'll come with you... I'll get another bottle."

Sam asked where they were going. Sue looked at her.

"To get hammered with Deb," she smiled.

"I'm coming too." Sam grabbed another bottle.

And that's exactly what they did – they got wasted and moaned about men.

"We shouldn't put Sam off but its hard going being married to a rock star." Deb slurred.

They all staggered back to the beach house, holding each other up. Tony, Danny and Dave watched them stagger back falling over and just laughing at nothing. The guys put them into bed.

Deb stayed on the sofa and Danny came over to her and asked if she was OK and did she want to share their room with Chris.

"Nooooo... but I'll share with *you*... because you look very sexy tonight. Dooo you know what I would like tooo dooo tooo you? she laughed drunkenly.

"No baby ...I'm fine... go to bed."

Shush" she whispered loudly.

She was really drunk. Danny was really tempted but he just kissed her head and said good night instead.

At breakfast, Deb was a bit fragile , as were Sue, Sam and Chris. They were all sat drinking black coffee while Tony made the breakfast. Deb went looking for her cell phone and called the restaurant to find out how things were just as Simon came out of the bathroom. He looked at Deb on her cell again.

"Are you calling Nick again?"

"No...I am not...Why don't you fuck off ? You're being such a dick."

Simon flew in to a rage. "You fuck off!" he shouted as he got close up into her face. "You bitch!" he ranted.

Danny jumped up and stood in-between, them pushing Simon back.

"Hey... Don't fuckin talk to her like that."

"It's OK Danny." she said grabbing his arm trying to pull him away.

"Don't ever get in her face like that again"

"Danny ... Danny... It's OK, really

"Are you OK?"

"Yeah I'm fine."

Simon gave Danny a dark look. Tony and Dave agreed that he was acting like a total asshole. Simon stomped off to the bedroom were Deb had disappeared.

"I'm sorry Deb... I just get so jealous.""

"You have got to stop this Simon. Nick is my friend – he is no threat."

"I know... I just can't help it... the thought of you with him... Well...I can't even..."

She interrupted him. "Stop Simon, just stop."

Chapter 31

That night, they had a barbecue round the beach house pool. Simon and Deb were talking again and Simon was all over her. They had all had plenty to drink and Deb was tipsy. Simon was kissing her trying to make up for the morning outburst, but she was watching Danny.

It was driving him crazy watching them together so he disappeared onto the beach, he just needed to get out of there. Deb noticed him go and, when everyone was occupied, she sneaked out too.

"What are you doing sneakin off?" she asked Danny when she caught up to him.

"I just need to be by myself for a while?"

"Why?"

"I just do!"

"Danny what's wrong? Please tell me?" she begged.

"There's nothing wrong, Deb"

"You're not in trouble, or ill?"

Danny laughed, "No, Babes… everything is fine."

"Promise me Danny"

Danny changed the subject altogether and remarked how nice the beach was.

"Yeah… It is…It's nice and secluded…It reminds me of some place back in England."

"Does it?" he paused before adding, "Why do you have to be so beautiful?"

"You are too, Danny."

"You're hammered"

"Yeah… Maybe I am… but you are sooo sexy."

She moved closer to him reaching for his face. She kissed him passionately, forgetting herself for a moment. He wrapped his arms round her and held her tight, kissing her back longingly. Suddenly she pulled away.

"Danny… I'm so sorry… I shouldn't have done that…What was I thinking?" she gasped and shook her head.

"Deb… Calm down… It's fine."

"No… No it isn't!" she said as she ran back to the beach house.

Danny smiled to himself. He knew it was just a matter of time. He headed back in as well.

"Where have you been?" Tony asked

"On the beach"

"You've been spending a lot of time on the beach on your own."

"Yeah I like the beach…It helps me think and I must say everything seems crystal clear now."

"What are you up to Dan?"

"Nothing."

"Really, Dan?"

"Really, Tony," he smirked

The next morning they were all sat at the table having breakfast apart from Deb who was really low. She had the hangover from hell and felt like crap. When she appeared from the bedroom she was holding her head.

"Good morning." she managed at last.

"Good morning… You were wasted last night. They all said in unison.

"Oh yeah… Go on…take the piss." she smiled

"We will." Dave laughed.

"Did I make a fool of myself and say anything stupid?" she asked.

"No...I understood you perfectly." Danny smiled.

"You did disappear for a while," Simon said

"Did I?" she asked, trying not to look at Danny.

"No point asking were you went, I suppose?" Simon asked

"No... I don't know... can't remember .... I came back ...."

Danny smiled at her, stroking his lips. She smiled at him coyly.

They finished breakfast and started to load the cars up. Everyone said their goodbyes and the girls told Sam that if she needed any help with the wedding she only had to ask. She replied that she would ring them and they could all get together. They all drove off and headed home.

When Simon and Deb arrived home, Deb rang the restaurant to make sure everything was OK. The head chef told her everything was fine and she told him she would be back in the next day.

The next day, Deb and Sue both went back into work. Deb did some of the paperwork that had got behind while she'd been away and then they both sat down and sorted the new menus with the chef.

"Did you have a good time at the beach house?" Sue asked.

"Yeah...It was great, did you?"

"Yeah it was good," Sue hesitated a minute."Is everything alright with you and Simon?" she asked, concerned.

"Yeah... Why?"

"Oh things seemed a little tense between you both – that's all."

"No Sue... we're good... Everything is fine."

Chapter 32

Chris, Sam and Sue went round to Deb's with Daniel and were all sat by the pool in their bikinis on sun loungers, soaking up the sun and watching Daniel playing. They already had beautiful tans from their vacation but they thought they would get a top up. They were sipping Dom Perignon and rosé wine when Simon and Danny came back.

Only thing was, they weren't alone. They had brought with them a very sexy friend, Dominic, a bit younger than themselves. Sue had gone in to take Daniel upstairs for a nap. Deb, Chris and Sam were still sitting on the sun loungers outside. Deb was sitting back, calmly smoothing suntan lotion in to her legs. Dominic couldn't believe his eyes. All these beautiful women.

Deborah and the girls had never seen this one before. He was the front man for the new upcoming band *Lazar*. He was English and extremely good looking, tall with long dark hair and big green eyes and had a beautiful tanned, muscular body. Simon introduced him to the girls. Deb smiled at him

"Hi Dominic"

He looked at her wide-eyed, "Hmm... You are a beauty... Call me Dom."

He couldn't take his eyes off her. He was a real ladies man, hormones on legs. Danny was not amused at all. He didn't like the way Dom was looking at Deb.

Dominic turned to Chris and Sam.

"My… You're all stunning… Who are you with?" Dominic asked Chris

"I'm Danny's wife."

"Oh… and what about you babe?" he asked Sam. "I'm with Dave," she smiled.

"Shit – is there no-one free?"

Simon urged Deb to put something over her bikini because he didn't like the way Dominic couldn't keep his eyes off her. She slipped on a beach dress but you could see straight through that. Sue came back and looked around at the guys, taking in the added guest.

"Hi guys." she said

Dom turned round and looked Sue up and down.

"Wow babe! Where have you been hiding?"

Sue looked at him flattered.

"And who are you?" she asked.

"Yours, if you want me!"

Sue laughed … she was quite flattered.

"This is Tony's wife, Dom." Simon told him, not impressed.

"Fuck me all these gorgeous women and not one for me?"

"No." replied Danny bluntly.

Simon and Danny took Dom into the study to talk business while the girls had other things on their mind.

"He's a real charmer…" Sue said.

"Yeah… and he's hot for you babe." Deb said laughing.

"Don't laugh…It's not funny."

Deborah cried with laughter. "He is gorgeous, though," she mentioned casually, still giggling.

"Yeah isn't he? Did you see his body through that string vest, those abs?" Chris asked.

"Oh yeah…Very nice. I would love to take photos of him," Sam chimed in.

"He is just my type. I wouldn't mind that piece of ass."

"Chris! Remember Danny, your husband?" Sam said, slightly shocked.

"Oh, umm, Danny who…?" Chris said laughing. "Deb, I'm going to the bathroom."

Deb, Sue and Sam all looked at each other astonished, they were speechless. Chris headed for the bathroom followed by Sam. Danny shouted for Sue. Daniel had woken up and he brought him out to Sue.

"Hi my little darling." Sue crooned.

Danny smiled and said 'Hi', coyly.

Sue smiled and said, "Isn't Uncle Danny silly?"

"Yeah" said Daniel"

"Shall we go home and see daddy?"

Sue left and headed home to see Tony. Danny sat with Deb.

"What do you think of Dom?" he enquired.

"He's very sexy." Deb smiled.

"Really?… your type?"

"Yeah… But he's not a patch on you Danny."

"That's good to hear," he grinned.

"Nnobody has got a smile like you… that's one very sexy smile I might say."

Danny flashed that sexy smile at her

"See… *sexy*."

Simon and Dom came out to the pool followed by Chris and Sam.

"I'm going and I'll see you again darling." Dom said as he kissed Deb's hand.

"Yeah… See you again Dom."

"Oh babe… you can count on it," he said smiling, showing his piano key smile and his beautiful high cheek bones.

Danny said he was going too and he planted a kiss on Deb's cheek.

"Hey…Can I get one of those?" Dom asked cheekily.

"No!" said Simon and Dan in unison.

Chris and Sam headed off with Danny and Dom. Chris was very flirty with Dom. She had taken a shine to him and thought he was very hot.

The beginning of 1993

At the beginning of 1993 Simon was playing in another famous band, *Crash*. They had asked him to join them for the weekend but the gig was out of town. He told Tony that Deb was going to the beach house and that she was going alone. What he didn't realise was that Danny had overheard their conversation and so he knew where Deb was while Si was away. This was Danny's chance.

Deb had left the restaurant in Sue's capable hands and drove up to the beach house. That night Danny drove up there too. She was sat on the beach with a bottle of wine. As she lit a cigarette and poured a glass of wine, she watched the sea splashing onto the sand. The beach house was in a secluded spot, as if the sea had purposely cut it out of the rocks.

It was the most romantic of places. She remembered telling Danny it reminded her of something she'd seen in England. She trawled her mind and remembered what it was. The scenery was like the backdrop of an artist's painting she had seen back in England.

Danny arrived and stood on the top of the rocks watching her. He started to make his way down to her. Deb was deep in thought and when Danny touched her shoulder she jumped.

"Oh shit… Danny," she said turning round quickly. "You startled me."
She sighed with relief, pleased to see him.

"I'm sorry." he murmured apologetically as he sat down beside her.

"Glass of wine?" she asked shaking the empty bottle at him.
She went into the beach house and came out with another bottle and an extra glass. She poured it out for him.

"How did you know I was here?" she asked.

"I heard Simon telling Tony," he replied.

"You shouldn't be here, Danny…" She shook her head. "Why are you here?"

"I wanted to see you. I can't do this anymore… I love you… I always have…and that's never going to change."

She looked into his eyes and put her fingers to his lips stopping him talking. She kissed him and whispered, "I love you Danny."

This was going to be so much easier that he thought because now she had admitted that she still loved him.

"I told you this would never go away Deb."

She leant over and kissed him again.

"Make love to me."

He started to kiss her passionately and she started to breath heavily. She ran her hands through the hair that fell casually over his face making him look sexier. She moved her hands down his body and as he got harder and harder, she teased him more. She removed his shirt and moved her hands, caressing his body. She kissed his bare chest moving her lips down his body, unzipping his jeans and pulling them off.

He laid her on her back and started sliding his hands up her legs, pushing her dress up and over her head. He moved his hands down the curves of her body, followed by his lips. She arched her back. She started to breath heavier. Her feelings were intense and she wanted him so much. Their bodies were hot and sweaty as he moved his hips between her thighs and pushed down on her, moving in rhythm.

She moaned, "Ohm… Oh you feel so good"

"Oh baby, you're so hot."

He made love to her right there on the beach lovingly and tenderly… She had missed him so much. They lay on the beach in each other's arms, gazing into each other eyes.

Danny took her hand, grabbed their clothes and ran inside with her. They just couldn't keep their hands off each other and as their hands explored each other yet again they had to make mad passionate love again. This time it was hot and frenzied, pure lust. They had missed each other so much. They lay in bed caressing each other bodies.

Danny asked her why she had married Simon.

"I thought I could fall in love with him."

"I told you… I knew you didn't love him. I only married Chris because I thought I would never see you again."

"It's a mess Danny"

"Don't you change your mind about us now, Deb."

"I can't Danny… I can't fight this anymore… I've missed you so much."

"Deep down I think Simon and Chris both know that we still want each other."

"Do you?"

"Yeah…I do…Even though Si has got a thing about Nick…but that is my fault anyway."

"Why…What do you mean?"

"I sort of put that in his head." he admitted.

"Danny?"

"I know…I know…I was jealous."

"What time do you need to get back?" she asked.

"I don't want to go Deb… I want to stay with you."

"No…You had better go home."

Danny climbed out of bed and got dressed. Deborah put her robe on and walked him to his car. He took hold of her and started to kiss her again.

"I don't wanna go… I'll ring you tomorrow and come down."

"I'll be waiting for your call" she confessed.

He kissed her again, got into his car and drove away. She waved to him and strolled back to the beach house. She thought of Simon and how much it would hurt him if he found out about her and Danny. She felt an overwhelming guilt pass through her but she couldn't stop herself – she wanted Danny as much as he wanted her. She made herself a cup of hot chocolate and went to bed. She tossed and turned for a while before falling asleep.

The next day Danny rang her and told her he was on his way. She prepared some lunch and then waited on the beach for him. When he arrived he made his way down to her. She threw her arms around him and kissed him deeply. He kissed her back, caressing her long dark hair.

"You're happy to see me then," he smiled.

"Yeah…I am."

"Good… That's what I wanted to hear," he laughed. "Come on, let's walk."

They walked hand in hand along the beach talking and smiling at each other.

"Do you feel guilty Danny?" she asked.

"No I don't… not at all – please don't say you do."

"A little… we will cause so much hurt if they find out," she said sadly.

"It will come out…and I hope it does."

"Danny… Why?"

He started to splash her with water, taking her away from the subject for a moment before he stopped and looked at her intensely.

"I want you to be with me, that's why. I don't just want an affair."

He picked her up and ran into the sea with her.

"Wouldn't it be funny if I dropped you." he said teasing her.

"Danny. Danny. Don't you dare!" she laughed.

He kissed her and then dropped her into the sea. As she went under she grabbed him and pulled him under too. He jumped out quickly.

"Ohh...Jesus...That's cold."

"Is it?" she said teasingly as she laughed at him.

They both started shivering at the same time. He grabbed her hand and they ran back to the beach house. They fumbled around trying to get each other's wet clothes off. They both jumped into the bath, sending water splashing everywhere. Danny rubbed soap all over her. Moving his hands all over her body he brushed his lips over her ears and neck, pulling her closer.

When they got out they put robes on. Deb put lunch on a tray and grabbed a bottle of champagne she'd been chilling. They stayed in bed all day, making love and just chilling. It was just like how it had been all those years ago when it had been just the two of them, in the beginning... minus the champagne, of course.

Danny had got what he wanted. All he had to do now was bring up the question of divorce. Leaving Deborah alone that weekend was Simon's biggest mistake.

Chapter 33

Monday came and Simon went straight to the beach house. He had missed Deb and couldn't wait to see her. She was on the beach where she had spent most of her time, apart from being in bed with Danny of course.

He shouted down to her and she turned and saw him heading towards her. She realised how excited he was to see her and suddenly felt very guilty.

"Hi babe," he said as he moved towards her to kiss her. She moved away guiltily.

"You OK?" he asked bemused.

"Yeah… 'course."

"No kiss, no hug… or sex?" he asked joking.

"Not everything is about sex, Simon,." she snapped.

Simon looked at her confused and wondered what was wrong. Was she mad with him for leaving her?

"We'd better get back… Sue will want to spend some time with Tony."

"Yeah…I'm sure she does…But, but what about us, Deb?" he asked.

"I'm going to get my stuff." she said as she flounced back towards the beach house.

She packed her stuff into the car.

"I'll see you back at home," she said as she got into the car.

Simon was still trying to work out what was wrong as he got into his car and headed back home. Deb hit the dash board while she was driving, 'Shit. Shit. Shit. I can't do this,' she said to herself.

When they got back Deb got out of her car and went over to Simon's.

"I'm sorry," she muttered.

"It's OK."

"No... no it's not."

"It's OK...Really...Something is obviously bothering you."

"No... it's not," she said forcefully.

"Deb..."

Before he could say another word she shouted, "Why do you have to be so bloody understanding?"

She stormed off, got back into her car and drove off. Simon stood there totally shocked, speechless. He wondered what exactly he had done. She was so angry... *why* was she so angry? She just lashed out at him, for what seemed to be for nothing. He'd been away for the whole weekend – shouldn't she be happy to see him, missed him or something? He went inside, got a cup of coffee from the percolator and sat at the counter rubbing his forehead trying to work out what her sudden outrage was about. It was driving him crazy.

He drove to the restaurant to find out what was wrong.

Sue was still there and she welcomed him, "Hi Simon"

"Hi Sue...you still here?"

"Yeah ... why? Is there something wrong?"

"Oh no nothing... is Deb here?"

"Yeah, she's talking to chef."

Deb came out of the kitchens and saw Simon stood talking to Sue.

"What are you doing here?" she asked.

"I wanted to talk to you." he said

"Why" she asked

"I have clearly upset you."

"No, Simon...you haven't... it's me."

"Are we OK?" he was still confused

"Yeah…I'll see you at home."

Sue looked at Deb intrigued, wondering what had happened

"Sorry Sue," Deb apologised.

"It's OK… If you want to talk you know where I am."

"I know… and thanks"

"Is everything alright, Deb?"

"Yeah… Go home and see Tony and Daniel, Sue."

"OK…See you later……Deb if you need me…"

"Yeah"

Simon was at home waiting for her to get back. He thought he should find out what was wrong. So when Deb got home he fixed her a drink and asked her about earlier. She looked at him and apologised. Simon wasn't worried about the apology… he just wanted to know what was bothering her. He asked her again if it was because he had left her over the weekend but she told him it wasn't. She said she didn't know what was wrong. Here come the lies, she thought… She hadn't planned to be a wife who had an affair with her ex… She felt bad but she wasn't giving Danny up now.

With the wedding getting closer, Dave had asked Danny and Chris if they could hold it in their garden. They had a beautiful built-in gazebo and Sam had said she really wanted a big garden wedding. She had worked out exactly what she wanted. She wanted the gazebo decorated in mint and white and all the chairs to be in white with big mint bows on the back of them.

She had found the wedding dress she wanted when she went to wedding boutique with the girls. She had picked a floor length, white strapless satin A-line wedding dress. She stood on the catwalk and posed for the girls. She looked beautiful. She was wearing her hair up with mint and white flowers placed in her hair.

Chris had picked a pink halter neck while Sue had picked a sky blue, A-line spaghetti-strapped dress. Deb picked up a lilac V-neck, chiffon minidress with diamanté around the waist. It looked stunning when she tried it on. They all had their moment on the cat walk and they had a lot of fun posing and drinking champagne until they all got a little tipsy. When they went to lunch, the press seemed to be two steps behind them all day.

All the guys were wearing suits with mint cravats. Dave's brother was his best man and Sam's sister's little girls were her bridesmaids and were wearing little mint dresses. The wedding got even closer and Sam had a little surprise for Dave. She had just found out she was pregnant and was going to tell him after the wedding ceremony.

Finally, It was the day of the wedding and everyone was running about like crazy getting the garden ready. It looked stunning. Dave and his brother stood and waited. When Sam appeared she looked beautiful. She walked up the aisle with her dad towards Dave. She smiled at him confidently. He smiled back at her and whispered, 'I love you.'

They said their vows staring in to each other's eyes. The press was invited in to take some photos. Sam whispered in his ear.

"You…are going to be a daddy!"

Dave was delighted and he announced it in his speech. He was so proud of himself, he couldn't wait to be a dad, Meanwhile, the celebrations were in full swing. Danny and Deb got up to dance.

"You look stunning, Deb"

"So do you."

From nowhere Dominic appeared, "Can I cut in?"

"Yeah…I suppose so." Danny said, looking at Deb.

Deb smiled at Danny. Danny went straight over to Chris and took her onto the dance floor. It was just an excuse to keep his eye on Dom. Tony and Sue were already up dancing. Simon was at the bar with Nick and Brad Cannon. He hadn't noticed Dom with Deb. Dom moved his arms tighter around Deb's waist and pulled her closer to him.

"It's a shame you're married." he grinned.

"I thought you had the hots for Sue?"

"Yeah…She's hot…But so are you."

"You're a real charmer."

"Hey babe… it normally works. I'd be a fucking fool not to want fuck you."

"Dom… shouldn't that be make love."

"If that's what you wanna hear babe."

The song finished and Deb headed off to see Simon. Simon put his arms round her waist.

"Deb... Meet Brad Cannon"

"Oh My God... Brad Cannon. I'm such a big fan of yours."

"Are you really? I'm glad to hear that"

Deb talked to Brad for some time. She had always had the biggest crush on Brad Cannon. He was tall with short black hair, sexy blue eyes, smouldering good looks and a really sexy smile. Apart from Danny, he was the only one who could get to her with his smile and he had the sexiest voice. When he spoke he sent her dizzy. She just went starry eyed when she looked into those baby blue eyes and that sexy voice sent shivers down her spine. Right from being a child she'd always had a crush on him. She couldn't believe she had got to meet him, let alone speak to him. She had wanted to meet him for so long.

She spotted Nick and made her way over to him.

"Hi sexy... I thought you'd gone off me," he said as he put his hand round her waist.

"Nick... Never! Come on, dance with me."

She grabbed his hand and dragged him to the dance floor. Chris was already on there with Dom and she seemed to be flirting with him. Nick asked her how things were going and she told him things were great and she was pleased to see him. As he turned her on the dance floor he told her she looked fantastic, suggesting that she should marry him as she was so intoxicating. She smiled at him and asked him how everything was with him. He told her he was all the better for seeing her.

"Oh, I do love you, Nick"

There was a tap on Nick's shoulder. It was Dave and Sam.

"Hi guys... this is one hell of a wedding."

Dave asked were the rest of his lot were.

"At the bar getting wasted"

Simon came over. "I'm cutting in bud."

Nick left Simon and Deb on the dance floor and he made his way over to the bar to join his friends. Simon moved closer to Deb and nuzzled in to her neck, kissing her gently. They swayed together to the music. He held her so close he feel her body next to his.

"You look fucking fabulous."

"Why thank you, Simon"

"I just want to make love to you," he murmured.

As the music finished, they strolled off the dance floor. Deb and Sam headed over to the bar where Sue and Chris were with Nick, Danny and Tony, leaving Simon and Dave talking. Deb flung her arms round Sue and Chris.

"Hey girls, what ya doin?"

"Getting hammered!" they both said in unison.

"Well girls … I'm one of you now…" Sam announced happily.

"Yes you are," Deb said, putting her arm round her shoulder.

All four girls headed for the dance floor. They put their arms around each other and danced together.

Brad came over and said, "Which one of you beautiful ladies would like to dance?"

Sue, Chris and Sam looked at Deb. Sue pointed towards Deb.

"This one." Sue giggled.

Brad smiled at Deb and took her hand and pulled her close. She could not believe that she was now dancing with Brad Cannon. He looked deep into her eyes. She was like putty in his hands.

A charity event came up and everyone got together. Danny and Deb had been seeing each other every chance they had. Nick had seen Deb, got a drink and went over.

"Hi gorgeous… you're looking good. That white dress shows off your body beautifully." he said.

"Nick… Hi… you're looking very handsome tonight yourself." She said, putting her arms round his neck and planting a big kiss on his lips.

"Does this mean that you have finally fallen for me?"

"You'll take some lucky girl's breath away."

"Have I taken your breath away?"

Danny and the rest of the guys came back.

"Hi Nick." Danny said.

"Hey Dan…My man…how ya doin?"

"Fucking awesome…What about you, buddy?"

"Not bad… met this bird last night – got laid…Ya know what I mean."

Danny laughed, "Way ta go!" and he high fived him.

"You guys…" Deb exclaimed. "The way you talk about ladies."

Both Danny and Nick smiled at her.

"Not you babe…" Danny smiled.

"No… not you," Nick repeated.

The charity raised a substantial amount of money for Cancer Research and everyone was having a good time. Danny grabbed Deb's hand and led her on to a very crowded dance floor. He pulled her close and asked her if she could feel anything. He pulled her even closer against him and smiled at her. She felt the bulge in his trousers

"Danny Brooks!"

"You make me feel so horny. What are you going to do about this?" he asked as he moved her hand to his crotch. "Let's sneak out." he suggested.

"Where are we going to sneak to?" she giggled.

"Meet me at the end of corridor."

"OK," she said grinning at him.

"That didn't take me long." he laughed.

"No…it didn't." she smiled sexily.

Deb met Danny at the end of the corridor and he pulled her into an empty dressing room. He locked the door and began to kiss her very passionately. Frantically, he tried to get his trousers undone as Deb wriggled out of her panties. He pushed her against the wall, moving his hands up her legs, pushing her dress up. He was so turned on, he wanted her so badly. They stumbled over to the table with some urgency. She braced herself against it as Danny eased himself between her thighs and pressed down on her, making love to her. She pulled him closer.

"MMMM" she sighed.

"Hmm… I just can't get enough of you. You excite me like no other woman can," he groaned.

Breathing heavily, he built up a steady rhythm.

"Good…Keep it that way!" She said giving him a whopping big smile.

Pulling his trousers back up, Danny left Deb fixing her hair and make-up and made his way back to the party. So as not to cause suspicion, he joined Nick and his friends. Deb reappeared and went to talk to a group of film stars.

Danny looked over at her and winked. She just gave him a naughty grin.

Chapter 34

A few weeks later Danny and Chris turned up at Simon's to party. Simon was quite happy to go along with it.

"Hi Si"

"Dan… What are you doin here?"

"Here to party, bud."

"Great… but there's only me, you and Chris."

"Not for long," Dan said confidently.

Tony rang Sue at the restaurant and said that he and Daniel were going to Simon's and told her to come back with Deb. Dave and Sam had already arrived when Deb and Sue got back. Danny had everyone in the party mood – even little Daniel was joining in. Danny was playing games with Daniel when Tony said, "Right guys listen up!"

"We all hear you."

"We are having a baby!" he announced, looking lovingly at Sue."

Oh wow!" Deb said. "That's two babies… no more work for you."

"Oh well…OK If you insist." Tony said smiling

"Not *you*… Sue!" she laughed.

Everyone congratulated them and the conversation turned to baby talk. Deb went into the kitchen to get some more wine, beer and nibbles and Danny followed her.

"Deb," he breathed sexily. "I wanted to see you and this was the only way I could think of. So here I am."

"You are dangerous," she whispered.

"Hmm, good," he replied, raising his eyebrows.

Deb pulled him close and kissed him, moving her hand up and down his thigh.

"Hmm… Oh Deb no…We can't." He was stiffening as she touched him.

"No? Are you sure?"

She moving her fingers to the zip of his jeans and pulling it down. She moved her hand to the inside of his jeans. She could feel he wanted her badly. She was really turning him on.

"*I'm* dangerous?" he whispered excitedly.

She winked at him, biting her lip and smiling seductively.

"You're a tease…I am really horny now."

She laughed at his unease.

"I love you." she said, her green eyes gleaming with mischief.

"Yeah and I love you," he answered kissing her.

Deb went back into the others who were sat drinking and eating and having a good laugh, leaving Danny to readjust himself. Daniel had fallen asleep on the chair so they put him to bed.

"Does anyone want to hear this song I wrote?" Danny shouted from the back of the room.

"You've written a new song?" the guys asked.

"Well, yes and no… I wrote this a long time ago."

Danny got his guitar and sang the song.

He had written the song for Deb a long time ago and he'd called it '*Always have… Always Will'*. Deb knew it was for her but so did Simon.

"That was great… Why haven't you released it as single?" Sue asked him.

"I don't know."

"Yeah Dan…Why not release it… or is there some reason you don't want to?" Simon asked.

"No...no reason."

"Well I think there is... That song is for..." he was interrupted by Deb snapping at him.

"Shut up Simon."

"Do you like it Deb?" Simon asked her moodily.

"Yeah, every girl will think that the song is for them."

"Do you like it Deb?" Danny asked

"Yes I do...it's a beautiful ballad Danny."

"We should release it Dan" Tony said excitedly.

"OK, we will."

As everyone started to leave Sue asked if they could leave Daniel and pick him up in the morning.

"Yeah... no need to disturb him," Deb answered.

When everyone had left Simon started grabbing Deb trying to kiss her.

"I want a baby," he said ,trying to kiss her again.

"Go to bed Simon." Deb said exasperated.

"That song...It was for you and you know it."

"Go to bed" she said firmly.

He grabbed her and tried to kiss her again but now he was getting very rough.

"I want you!" he demanded.

"Get off me ...Simon."

"Are you fucking Nick?"

"What...?"

"I said...Are you fucking Nick?" he said poking her in the chest."Is Nick giving you it? Because...You sure don't want to fuck me."

Deborah slapped his face.

"Fuck off to bed... You are drunk and disgusting."

Simon raised his hand to hit her back.

"Go ahead. What's stopping you?" she said as she turned round and walked away. He ran after her and grabbed her.

"I'm sorry."

She looked at him angrily. "Let me go!"

There had been a lot of tension between them for some time now, but things had started to fall apart for Simon. He felt he was losing her bit by bit. He thought Nick was the reason but he should have known better.

The next morning Deb was sat down stairs drinking coffee and giving Daniel his breakfast when Simon came down. He sat down at the table and looked sadly at Deb.

"I'm sorry," he muttered.

"No you're not."

"Yeah…I'm sorry… I didn't mean any of that last night."

"Oh you did , Simon." she said and turned her back on him.

When Daniel had finished his breakfast she put him in the car and they went to the restaurant. She called Tony to tell him Daniel was there with her. Tony said he would collect him. Sue had an appointment then she was meeting Chris and Sam. After Tony had collected Daniel she had a busy day with the deliveries. They all came at once and then Sue, Chris and Sam arrived.

"She's been nagging to come here all morning." Chris said pointing at Sue.

"You can't stay away can you?" said Deb.

Just then another delivery came. She always flirted with the delivery guy and he would flirt right back with her. Garret liked Deb, he thought she was so down to earth for a rock star's wife. He loved it when she was there. She went back to the girls.

"Now Sue, Sam. Go buy baby clothes."

"Are you trying to get rid of us?" they asked.

"Yeah…. Chris… take them shopping."

She finished the deliveries and sorted out menus and then told the chef that she would be back later. She was going to meet Danny at the beach house.

He had made some lunch by the time she arrived and he kissed her passionately.

"Simon was right about that song."

"I know." she sighed.

"Simon rang me this morning."

"I don't want to talk about Simon, Danny."

"OK…OK."

"Make love to me Danny." She smiled at him.

"Well if you insist…"

He smiled showing his perfect white teeth, his eyes alive and on fire.

"Yes…I do," she oozed

He kissed and took her to the bedroom. He laid her on the bed where she flicked her shoes off. He moved his hands up her legs slowly, running his fingers along the inside of her thighs. She lost her breath when he reached the apex of her thighs. Her fingers began to toy with his chest. He slowly made his way up her body using his tongue. She was breathing heavily, the sexual tension building up between them. They were skin to skin. He brushed his lips over her. She forcefully grabbed him, kissing him deep and passionately, moving her hand down his body, moving her lips slowly down his body.

He was so hard he thought he would explode. They took their time, savouring every minute. They made love passionately, exploring every part of each other. The sex between them was fantastic and explosive… it had always been fantastic. When they were done, they lay in bed and just cuddled each other, making the most of the time they had left.

"I want you to be with me,." Danny said.

"I know and I want to be with you… but at the moment we need to get up and go."

"Deb, be serious… we need to talk about what we do next… I know what I want to do."

"I know…We need to talk…but please not today…Please!" she said wearily.

"OK, but soon… promise me."

Deb nodded. They got up and had a shower. They kissed each other goodbye and Deb went back to the restaurant. By the time she arrived, Simon was there.

"Where have you been?" he asked sulkily.

"Out…Are you starting about Nick again?"

"No." shaking his head

"I'm going home to get ready for tonight."

As she passed him he grabbed her arm, yanking her back.

"We need to talk"

"No Simon."

"I'm sorry."

"OK… You're sorry."

"What's happening to us? You have changed… Do you not love me anymore? That's if you ever did."

"Simon…just stop! You are becoming so hung up about Nick and it's getting real boring. You're driving me crazy with it."

Chapter 35

The girls all arranged to meet up with Sam. By this time she was heavily pregnant and ready to drop so Deb decided they should make it into a baby shower. She prepared a lunch at her house and then went off to the mall to do some serious shopping. In the end, she found she had bought lots of baby gear and designer baby outfits for Sam. It didn't take long to find out that Sue and Chris had done exactly the same! They were really enjoying their lunch when Sam's waters broke.

Chris rang Danny and told him to tell Dave, and the girls took Sam to the hospital.

Dave and the guys raced to the hospital and met the girls there. Dave went into the delivery suite with Sam while the rest of them just waited.

As the baby was born Dave came out shouting with excitement.

"I've got a son…A boy… 7lbs 2oz… and he's beautiful." he cried.

The next day they all went to see the baby and he was beautiful. Danny asked them what they were calling him.

"Alan… after our Alan."

The guys thought that was great tribute to their mate Alan and to his memory.

The year 1994

The band went on tour – this time around Australia. When they arrived at the airport they were stopped and arrested on suspicion of possessing drugs. They were searched and the concert got cancelled. That night the papers had great time with the story.

ROCK BAND *DECADE* ARRESTED LAST NIGHT
ON SUSPICION OF DRUGS.

Finally everything was sorted out and they were able to get on with the tour. Before they went on stage they would do breathing exercises and voice practice. Costumes would be checked, equipment would be checked and they would go and meet their fans before the show. They always had an after party too and they would get very drunk and very loud.

On the last night of the tour at the after party Simon got very drunk. He took a girl to his room. He wanted no strings attached… just good, dirty sex.

"Bend over babe," he whispered as he lowered his zip.

With a moan, he pulled out the throbbing bulge in his jeans. The beautiful redhead's eyes looked down towards his penis and moved her hands round it, stoking it. Dropping to her knees she went down on him, wrapping her mouth round it.

"Oh…Oh … yeah keep doing that sweet cheeks… That's so fuckin good."

His eyes started to roll to the back of his head as he felt himself coming. He bent her over, pulled her skirt up and slapped her ass.

"You like that don't you baby?" he asked.

He pushed his hand between her legs, moved her panties to the side and gave her what she'd gone there for. She moaned and groaned as he banged her.

"Oh fuck yeah …yeah… that's it, Yeah babe!"

He was so drunk he passed out and when he woke up the next morning, the very attractive red head was lying next to him. Simon tried to sneak her out but he bumped straight in to Danny.

"Danny," he muttered, surprised.

"Did you have good night?" Danny asked casually.

"I don't remember taking that girl to my bed… you can't tell Deb."

"Nothing to do with me, Si – but I knew you'd do it eventually." he smirked."

"Danny, you can't tell Deb."

"No...I won't say anything."

This was just perfect for Danny.

"Thanks, buddy."

Breakfast arrived but Simon was so quiet that Tony asked him what was wrong.

"He's got the mother of hangovers." Danny laughed.

"Oh right, nothing to do with the redhead, then?" Dave asked casually.

"Do you all know about the girl?" Si asked.

"Yeah...You were all over her." Tony remarked.

"Shit. I was fucked... I'm surprised I even got it up."

"Oh...You got it up alright...We all fucking heard you. 'YESSSS... Ohhhh YESSSS...'" Dave teased.

"What about Deb?" Tony asked, more seriously.

"It was a mistake."

"Fuckin hell, Si," Dave said.

Danny just sat there and listened, not saying a word.

When the guys got back home they began work on some new material. They also released the Danny's song – the one that he had written for Deb.

(*Always have, Always Will*) went straight to number one

Deb decided to throw a dinner party to celebrate. She invited the guys and she invited Nick with his band and their girlfriends. Nick told her he was bringing a girl and she was so pleased that he was coming.

Deb and her chef sorted out a great menu for the evening. He got everything started but he couldn't stay because he had to be at the restaurant. He asked her if she was happy with everything and she told him she was more than happy and he would get a big bonus on wage day.

She had a shower and got ready. Simon came back and she told she'd put his clothes out on the bed.

"Oh...OK...I'll get a shower then."

He moved over to her putting his arms around her. He started to kiss her neck and asked if she wanted to get in the shower with him.

"I've just got ready, Simon."

"Oh…not so long ago you would have got in with me and we would have made love."

"Simon!"

"OK…OK…I'm going."

Simon got into the shower and Deb went downstairs. Her guests started to arrive. Tony, Sue, Dave and Sam were the first to arrive, then Steve, Mike, Jake and Wayne, Nick's band members with their partners. Deb asked where Nick was and Steve said he'd be here soon. Then Danny and Chris arrived. Danny took hold of Deb and kissed her on the cheek. Simon came down and smiled at them all.

"Hi guys."

Nick finally arrived with his new girlfriend. He went straight over to Deb, put his arms round her kissed her. Simon nearly choked on his drink but Danny stopped him going over.

"Don't Si."

Simon looked at Danny. Danny shook his head. Nick introduced his girlfriend to Deb and the rest of the guys.

The waitress came out with a tray of drinks and Simon grabbed a glass in each hand. She asked if everything was to Deb's satisfaction.

"Why, yes… Thank you Alice."

"When would you like me to serve dinner Mrs. Richards?"

"In about a half hour… Oh, and Alice…"

"Yes Mrs. Richards?"

"Please call me Deborah."

"Yes Mrs. Richards…I mean Deborah." she smiled."

"That's better."

Dinner was served and everyone enjoyed the meal.

"You must have the best chef in Beverly Hills." Chris remarked.

"Yeah… I have… he's fantastic."

Coffee and mints were served and everyone made their way to the lounge. Tony had been watching Danny and Deb closely all night. He had noticed the way they were with each other, the way they kept looking at each other and the little subtle touches that nobody else would notice.

Simon was drunk again and very loud. Nick told them all that he was getting a house in Beverly Hills.

"That's great... We'll get to see you more often, then." Deb said, excited for him.

"Fucking hell... how much more of him do you want to see?" Simon asked sarcastically.

Deb threw him a cold look. Tony watched what was going on, thinking '*I don't think its Nick you need to be hung up about, Si.*' The evening went really well and everyone loved it. They all started to leave and Nick gave Deb a big kiss before he left. Danny and Chris thanked her for a great night and Danny kissed her.

"See you soon?"

"Yeah...You will."

Tony and Sue said they were going. Sue gave her a big hug and Tony gave her a kiss. Tony mentioned to Sue on the way home about Danny and Deb and the way they were around each other.

"You don't think there's something going on, do you?" she gasped."

Yeah I do."

"What makes you think that?"

"The way they are with each other... and poor Si thinks it's Nick he has to fuckin watch.

Simon was sat on the chair when Deb came back into the lounge.

"You are beautiful."

"Come on Si...Let's get you into bed."

Simon clapped his hands together.

"Now you're talking." he grinned drunkenly.

"Simon...Come on."

She took his hand and led him to the bedroom. He sat on the bed looking at her.

"Do you know how much I love you?" he asked.

"You're drunk, Simon."

"No...no... I know what I'm saying... I love you and I'm so sorry."

With that he passed out. Deborah put him in to bed and gently stoked his hair. She wasn't sure what he meant by, 'he was so sorry,' but she put it down to him being drunk. Little did she know Simon was talking about the redhead that he had slept with on tour.

She went downstairs where Alice was cleaning up.

"Alice, why are you still here?"

"I thought I'd better do this first."

"No... go on home."

Deb asked the driver to take Alice home and then she went in to the kitchen and made some coffee. She started thinking about Simon. She knew he loved her and she felt bad. She shouldn't have married him. She knew she was going to hurt him and that was wrong... but she did love Danny. She knew he was the only man she had ever really loved

She didn't know what she was going to do... It was a mess.

Chapter 36

That night, Sue went into labour and gave birth to a beautiful baby girl, 6lb 12oz and they called her Debra after Deb. Tony called Deb in the morning. Simon was feeling really fragile when Tony called.

"I'll be in to see her today." Deb screamed.

"Deb… Please don't scream." Simon moaned.

"Sue and Tony have a little girl."

"That's great… but…"

"Simon are you feeling rough?"

"Sure am, baby."

Deb went upstairs and jumped into the shower and got dressed. Simon was still in the kitchen.

"See you later."

Simon asked where she was going.

"Going to the restaurant first, doing some shopping, then off to see the baby."

"Oh…right OK."

"Do you want to come?" She said, holding her breath.

She could feel herself burning up as she was lying – she was actually meeting Danny.

"No Deb…I don't think so. I'll meet you at the hospital."

"OK…See you later." she said sighing with relief.

She went to the restaurant, Fran was already there.

"Morning, Mrs Richards"

"Good morning Fran… I believe we were very busy last night?"

"Yeah…Brad Cannon, the movie star, was here."

"Brad Cannon?"

"Yeah…."

"Oh God… he is so sexy."

"Yeah." Fran agreed.

They agreed that they couldn't dream about Brad Cannon all day so they went through the menus for that night with the chef. Deb told them all that Sue had had a baby girl and they all wished her their best and asked Deb if she would take the presents that they had bought for her when she went.

"Yeah, course I will… give them to me before I go"

Deb went off to meet Danny. He told her he wanted to bring everything out into the open. She told him that they couldn't yet. He wanted to know why.

"Whatever we do or say it's gonna hurt. Deb, I m sick of sneaking around. I want to marry you."

"I know…I know."

Danny leaned over and kissed her. She kissed him back and she told him she loved him.

'Why doesn't she want to tell them?' He couldn't understand. She loved him and she wanted to be with him and he wanted her to get divorced. So why was this so hard for him to get her to do? It kept going over and over in his head while they sat having lunch.

When they left, Deb went shopping and then she went on to the hospital to see the baby. Simon was already there and so was Danny with Chris. Deb saw the baby and picked her up and gazed down at her. Danny watched Deb with the baby and smiled.

"She's so beautiful." Deb crooned

Dave and Sam had already been earlier. Chris was getting broody.

"Oh Danny, don't you want a baby?" she asked.

"Yeah...not yet."

"Oh Deb, aren't you broody?" Chris asked

"I'm not ready yet so no... Sue...I've got to go. I've got to get back to the restaurant but I'll see you tomorrow."

She gave Sue a kiss and told her that little Debra was beautiful. She gave Tony a big kiss and got hold of little Daniel, giving him a big cuddle and telling him he had to help mommy look after his little sister. She told everyone she would see them later and left and headed back to the restaurant.

That night Deborah was quite busy at the restaurant when two men came in causing a disturbance. Deb asked them to leave as they were very abusive. One of the men called her a stuck up bitch. She eventually got them to leave but they waited until she had closed up and she was on her own. They thought they would teach her a lesson.

Deb opened the door to leave and they pushed her back in. She was petrified. One of the men thought he would have some fun with her and took hold of her and ripped her dress open. Deborah struggled so he hit her and grabbed her again. He tried to kiss her but she hit him and stuck her nails in his face.

He got really angry and hit her really hard, so hard she flew over the table hitting her head on the corner of the table in front of her. She lay unconscious on the floor. There was blood everywhere.

"Shit...You fucking dick...You've killed her..."

"Fuck. Let's get out of here."

They ran out of the restaurant so fast they knocked a woman over. The woman wondered why they'd run out of the restaurant so fast and so she went in and found Deb on the floor bleeding.

"Oh my God!" she cried and called 911 for the medics.

Deb was rushed to the hospital and they informed Simon who rushed straight over. When he got there, the doctors were in with Deb. Simon asked the nurse who had brought her in and she told him that a lady brought her in and had stayed with her until the doctors came to her.

He rang Danny and told him what had happened. Danny was dumbfounded and very worried. Simon told Danny he didn't know what was going on, but that the doctor was still in with her.

Danny said he would be right there. Chris could see Danny was in shock and asked what was wrong. Danny told her that Deb had been attacked.

"Oh my god…Is she alright?"

"I don't know… Come on, we'd better get to the hospital."

Chris could see how worried Danny was. On the way he rang Tony and Dave and they all met up there. Tony had not long left the hospital but turned round and came straight back. When the guys got there the doctor was with Simon. He told him she had lost a lot of blood and that she had concussion, and that she had lost the baby."

"Baby, what baby?" Simon asked.

"Yeah… She was pregnant… Didn't you know?"

"No… Has…has she been told about the baby?" Simon asked in shock.

"No, not yet. We have sedated her."

With tears rolling down his face he asked if she was going to be alright

"Yeah she's going to be fine…no reason why you can't try for another baby in time. She needs plenty of rest at the moment."

"Can I see her?"

"Yeah…But not too many in at once." he smiled.

The doctor left and Danny asked what he had said.

"She's lost the baby."

"What baby?" he asked.

Danny's mind was working overtime and all he could think was this must have been his baby.

"She was pregnant… We were having a baby." Simon cried, interrupting his thoughts.

"Is she going to be alright, Simon?"

"Yeah"

They went in one by one so they didn't disturb her as she was heavily sedated. Simon just looked at her. Her face was black and blue and her lips were swollen and cut about.

When Danny went in to see her tears rolled down his face. He couldn't hold them back as he took her hand, kissed it and whispered.

"I love you, I'm here baby."

Danny came out of the room and spoke to Simon

"The police better get to those bastards before I do."

The guys went home but Simon stayed with her and when she woke the next morning Simon told her about the baby. She was devastated. Simon just held her and told her everything would be OK.

When Tony went to see Sue he told her what had happened. She wanted to go and see her.

"How can you Sue?" he asked.

"Tony… She needs me. I want to see her. Take me to her."

"OK babe. Just let me see what I can do."

Sue went down to see Deb who was still a bit groggy from being sedated. Deb just burst into tears when she saw her.

"I thought he was going to kill me."

"I'm so sorry about everything, Deb" She just held her and let her cry.

Later Danny and Chris went to see her and told Simon to go and get some rest. Chris asked if he'd eaten anything.

"No." he replied

"Come on Simon I'll take you for some breakfast"

"No…I can't leave her." he replied.

"Danny will stay with her."

"Yeah – Go on Si… I'll stay here."

Chris took Simon to give him a break and something to eat and a change of clothes. Danny took Deb's hand and kissed it

"Danny…I'm so sorry."

"Why?"

"The baby was yours I know, I know it was."

"I know"

"I was scared Danny" she said as tears streamed down her face again. Danny took hold of her and held her tenderly.

"They'll get the bastards or I will," he threatened. "Deb…I love you so much. I was so scared. I thought I'd lost you"

"It's not that easy to get rid of me Danny."

There was a knock on the door and it was Nick

"Hi Dan... Is she awake?"

"Nick, buddy – Yeah, come on in."

"Hi babe."

"Hi Nick"

"Deb...I have just heard. I would kiss you but I don't want to hurt you. Have they caught the fucking wankers?"

"I don't know what's happening." she replied."Where's Simon?"

"He's gone to get some rest... he's been here all night."

Nick and Danny stayed till Simon came back.

"Nick." Simon said wondering how he knew about Deb.

"Hi Si."

"How did you know." he asked.

"It's all over the papers."

Chris went to get a paper and there it was on the front page.

ROCK STAR SIMON RICHARDS' WIFE ATTACKED
LAST NIGHT IN HER RESTAURANT AS SHE WAS LEAVING
LADY PASSING BY SAVED HER LIFE

Chapter 37

Eventually, everyone left – even Simon. Deb had told him to go, telling him she was fine. The nurse popped her head round the door and told her there was a lady to see her. Deborah asked who it was and the nurse told her it was the lady who had brought her in.

"Tell her to come in." Deb said.

"Hello" she said popping her head round the door.

"Come in."

"How are you, Mrs. Richards?"

"Good, thanks to you. What's your name by the way?"

"Amarika"

"I'm very pleased to meet you Amarika. What a beautiful name."

"You're not American are you, Mrs. Richards?"

"No, I come from England. Do you come from here?"

"No. I'm from Jamaica" she smiled.

"Oh please… call me Deb. You saved my life and I owe you for that."

"No you don't. I'm just glad you are alright."

"Well I think I do… Tell you what, I'd like you to come to the restaurant as my special guest. Anything you and your family want is on me."

"You don't have to do that"

"Yes I do… It's the least I can do…I will get the invitation sent out to you if you let me have your address.

"Well thank you. You are a very lovely lady. I will leave you to get some rest… Bye, Deb."

She wrote her address down, gave it to Deb then said bye.

"Bye Amarika…And thank you very much."

A few days later Deb left the hospital still battered and bruised. Simon wanted to sell the restaurant but Deborah wouldn't – she loved the restaurant.

When she went to meet Danny they just sat on the beach talking. Danny could see Simon's point on this one and suggested that she bought another restaurant if it meant so much to her. She could buy another one, a better one. She mulled it over and decided she liked that idea. She would sell the restaurant and buy another.

She told him that Simon wanted to try for a baby. He wanted to start a family. He told her that Chris also wanted a baby. It was getting difficult. They needed to tell them and get it out open.

"I think it's time Deb."

It was getting harder. Deb did need to think about the future. She wanted to be with Danny, she would have to think about telling Simon. She wanted a divorce but she really didn't want to hurt him – or Chris, for that matter.

Deb had decided she would hire two more members of staff – someone to manage the restaurant, and a doorman. She would only go in when she had to.

She was at the restaurant talking to her staff when she told them she was selling the restaurant. She reassured them that they would all be going with her if they wanted to when she found the new place. Sue wanted to get back to the restaurant too but Tony wasn't sure he liked that idea after what had happened to Deb.

Deb told Sue she was getting a manager and a doorman and that they would just go in when they absolutely needed to, hosting special events and stuff like that.

"Yeah we'll do it together," Sue said excitedly. "No more being on our own in here!"

"When those men came in that night they frightened me so much. I don't ever want to be here on my own again. It needs a man here at night. I don't want anyone alone here at night."

"OK, Deb – I understand."

"I can understand why Tony doesn't want you to come back."

Sue smiled.

"Come on. Let's have a coffee."

Then Deb told Sue all about Amarika and she'd had invited her to the restaurant. She asked her if she would come for that because she would like her to meet her. Sue said she would love to.

Amarika received the invitation that Deb promised her. Deb told her chef that she had a very special guest arriving and wanted her treated in the VIP manner. Two days later, Deb went to the restaurant greet her. She had bought a big bouquet of flowers for Amarika.

"Welcome Amarika." she said as she kissed on the cheek.

"Oh Deborah, this is wonderful…Thank you."

She introduced Deb to her husband Sebastian and her family.

Amarika's son Delray was a fan of Decade and her daughter Centrica had a crush on Danny so Deb had asked the guys to come in and meet them. They were over the moon especially when they gave them tickets for one of their concerts. Amarika and her family had a wonderful time. Deb, Sue and the guys made sure that they did. Deborah was so grateful to Amarika.

She didn't want to think of what could have happened if Amarika hadn't come in and found her as she lay bleeding on the floor.

Chapter 38

Simon and Deb thought it would be good to have a pool party. They invited lots of people. There was lots to eat and drink and loads of loud music with glorious sunshine and to top it off, Marshall Rogers was there. Sue, Chris and Sam had been drooling over his muscular, tanned body as he stood there showing his beautiful six pack off. He knew how good he looked and women would go in frenzy over him. All three of them gazed into those big brown eyes of his.

Deb however was more interested in the sexy Brad Cannon. She was waiting for him to arrive. She couldn't wait.

Everyone was having a good time and everyone was soaking up the sun around the swimming in the pool. Danny went over to Deb and told her she looked sexy in her bikini and sarong.

"Do I?" she said smiling at him.

"Yeah… You are really turning me on."

"Oh good! Well, you have really turned me on with that sexy smile of yours," she whispered.

"OK… So we are both turned on. What we going to do about it?" he asked huskily.

"Well Danny…You are going to meet me up in the bathroom in five minutes time."

"OK… I'll see you there."

Deb went up to the bathroom and waited for him. Danny made his way up and knocked on the door. She opened it and grabbed him, pulling him in to her. He kissed her passionately.

"Oh Deb…You really get me horny." he said as he proceeded to remove her sarong.

She wriggled out of her bikini bottoms and he gradually eased out of his shorts. Their hands were all over each other and she felt dizzy with excitement. She ran her hands down his chest and down to his thighs.

" Mmmm, Deb." he sighed she moved her lips down his body. He gave out a groan.

"Ooh baby… I like that… ohh."

She looked up at him licking her lips gave him a naughty smile.

"Ohh… ahh… don't stop, Umm," he took hold of her and turned her round

She braced herself with her hands on the wall he bent her over and parted her legs with his knee. She suddenly gave a moan.

"Ohhhh ahhh Danny"

There was no stopping them and they made love in the bathroom while everyone partied downstairs. Afterwards, Danny got dressed, watching every move she made.

"Mmm. You're such a bad girl." He murmured as he kissed her.

"You like it," she said licking her lips.

"Hmm. Oh baby…You know I do. And please don't lick your lips like that."

Danny went back to the party while Deb put her sarong back on, straightened her hair and re-applied her makeup. By now, Simon was looking for her. He spotted Danny and asked if he'd seen her.

"No" he said shaking his head. "Why, have you lost her?" he grinned.

"Yeah"

Nick came over and Danny asked, "Have you seen Deb?"

"No… I've been talking to Sue, Chris and Sam."

Nick glanced around the room, "She's over there… She's with Tony."

Simon excused himself and went over to her. Nick looked suspiciously at Danny.

"Was she not in the bathroom, then?"

Danny looked at Nick and winked at him.

"You are playing a dangerous game Dan but I've got to say you are one lucky bastard." Nick said, shaking his head.

"Nick… I love that woman with everything I've got and I don't give a shit if it comes out."

Sue came over.

"Brad Cannon has just arrived. Chris and Sam are over there with him."

"Oh Boy…Lock up your women. Wait while Deb sees him. He's her favourite actor." Danny laughed.

"She thinks he's hot. She's crazy about him." Sue agreed.

"Seriously…?" Nick asked, "he's about twenty years older than her."

"Wait and watch." Danny said.

Deb excitedly ran over to Sue.

"Come on…Brad Cannon is here… here at my house…Can you believe it?" She was so excited and very giddy.

"Hi guys… Brad Cannon is here…Sue come on." She pulled at her sleeve impatiently.

Sue turned to Dan and Nick and grinned at them.

"She is going to have multiple orgasms now, guys."

Danny laughed when he saw Nick's face. His mouth was wide open, he couldn't believe Deb's reaction to Brad Cannon.

"See…I told you."

"Wow…She's like a teenager. Look at her… I wish I had that effect on her."

"I have buddy."

"Fuck off Dan. Just rub it in."

Deb pulled Sue over to Brad

"Hello again …. Mr. Cannon" she said playing with her hair, wrapping it round her fingers.

Brad looked at her.

"Hi… Aren't you Simon's wife, Deb? I always remember a pretty face."

"Do you?" she said as she drooled. "This is Tony's wife."

"Hi Mr. Cannon."

"Oh, hey… call me Brad."

They had been talking awhile, mostly about Brad's next film, when Sue made her excuses. She made her way over to the children leaving Deb still talking to him. They talked for quite some time and Simon was beginning to get uncomfortable with it. He mentioned that she'd been standing with him for ages. Danny pointed out that she had the hots for Brad Cannon. Simon was flabbergasted.

"You're joking, right?"

"I think he's got the hots for her, too." Tony observed.

Danny looked over at Sue and nodded. He pointed out that Brad was not the only one that was attracted to someone. Simon agreed with Danny. Dom had been preoccupied with Sue for some time.

"Well he can Fuck off!" Tony fumed.

Simon, Danny and Nick laughed with amusement at Tony's jealousy

"Don't know what the fuck you're all laughing at…WANKERS."

With that he went over to Sue. He was quite jealous and warned her off Dom.

"Oh." Sue laughed.

"Well he can fuck off. You're mine baby." He said winking at her.

"Oh Tony, you were jealous baby."

"Yeah…have I got plans for you." he said kissing her seductively."Ohm baby, stop it."

Brad and Deb were in deep conversation. Deb just gazed at him while he was talking, watching his lip as they parted as each word came out of his mouth he had such a sexy voice. All she could think was 'God. You are so sexy. '

Brad was really attracted to Deb and she loved it. He asked her to have dinner with him.

"Oh Brad I'd love to but I'm married."

"It's only dinner."

"But…. I"

"But…I want you to have dinner with me…."

"I'll ask Simon when he's free."

"Oh no, darling... I would prefer it if it was just you and me."

"Oh" she blushed, her big green eyes gleaming.

By this time she was quite flustered. He put his hands around her waist and pulled her close and whispered in her ear.

"I would love you to come," he said, winking at her and flashing that sexy smile.

She couldn't believe that Brad Cannon was hitting on her. Someone came over and grabbed Brad to introduce him to a movie producer. He turned to Deb.

"Catch you later babe?"

"Yeah." she replied giddily.

"Good...Maybe we can hit the dance floor."

"Yeah...I'll keep you to that."

Brad went over to a group of people but kept his eyes fixed on Deb. Sue came scurrying over and pointed out that she looked flustered. Deb looked at her and told her she thought Brad had just hit on her. He had just asked her to dinner

"He would *love* me to come," she laughed.

Sue laughed back, "What to dinner... or just to come?" she giggled.

"Hmm I'm not sure – do ya know what's scary? I'm really tempted."

"Oh Deb... No you can't."

"Ohhhhh Why?"

"Deb... No you can't, can you?"

Deb rolled her eyes and smiled.

Chris and Sam came over and wanted to know all the gossip as she was with Brad for quite some time and they wanted to know he had said to her.

"He is so sexy."

"She wouldn't mind banging him, would you babe?"

"Chris? Where is this coming from? Is this the new you?"

"Yeah...And... guess where I've been?"

"Where?" the girls asked sounding really intrigued."Chris. Come on tell us."

"Well...I've been with Dom. He followed me into the bathroom."

"You didn't!" Sue shrieked.

"We nearly did but we heard someone coming."

"Chris, what are you doing?"

"I'm having fun. Danny has gone off the boil and I'm getting pissed off with it.

"You're hammered." Sam said smirking at her.

The party went off really well. The kids had had a good time too and they ended up sleeping as the party went on really late – Deb had had all the kids up dancing for ages. She had got really drunk and now had Chris dancing. They were so drunk they were cuddling each other and then they got Sue and Sam up as well.

Brad had been watching Deb and decided to go over.

"You owe me a dance."

He had purposely waited until it was a slow one.

"Yesss…I do… don't I?" she said, slurring her words.

He put his arms around her, pulling her close and was whispering in her ear.

"You look hotter than hell. I'd love to get hot and sweaty with you baby," he kept kissing her neck.

Simon and Danny were watching Brad. Simon asked Danny if Brad was actually kissing her.

"I don't know…he's so fuckin close to her I can't tell."

Nick, Tony and Dave came over and asked what they were looking at.

"Brad." said Danny.

"Wow… Brad's full on…Fucking Hell," Nick blurted out

The others agreed and Simon said, "Fuck this… I'm stopping this right now."

Simon made his way over to Deb and Brad.

"Brad buddy… I'm cutting in… I want to dance with my wife."

Brad reluctantly released his grip from Deb's waist and took her hand and kissed it. His big sexy blue eyes looking straight in to hers.

"Simon." Deb said, astonished, as he took Brads place.

"You're hammered, baby,." he said kissing her.

Everyone was having such a great night.

The paparazzi were desperate to get some sneaky shots. They were climbing up trees, sitting on walls, anything to get shots of the celebs.

Danny watched Deb laughing and messing around. She saw him watching her so she went to him and pulled him up to dance. She pressed herself against him seductively.

Danny smiled at her and whispered huskily.

"Please don't do that Deb. Your gonna give me a hard on."

Deb bit her lip"Am I turning you on baby?" she said swaying drunkenly.

"Yep…."

"You're so freakin hot Danny."

"Yeah… so are you babe. I just wanna take you now. You drive me wild."

She smiled at him her eyes glowing. Her smile was so inviting. Danny just wanted her more and more.

Chapter 39

The next morning she was a bit fragile but she gave the kids their breakfast. They love being at Aunty Deb's and Uncle Simon's. Tony and Dave picked the kids up and then Deb went to the restaurant. Sue was already there and was sat waiting for Deb with a pot of coffee.

"Morning, Sue"

"Morning ... Someone was wasted last night... Cosying up to Brad." Sue laughed

"Oh Sue... Don't... Give me some coffee."

"What was that all about last night with Brad on the dance floor?"

"What? I don't remember."

"Simon had to come over. Brad was all over you. Kissing you... God knows what else he said to you."

"Really...Jesus...."

Sue looked at Deb closely and asked her just when she was going to tell her about Danny. Deb just looked at her friend. She didn't know what to say. She asked what she meant. Sue said that she knew and she was worried about her. She knew how much Deb loved Danny.

Deb put her head down and told Sue she wanted to tell her but she couldn't. Sue just wanted Deb to be happy and she didn't want her to get hurt. She wanted to know what was going to happen and asked if she was planning to leave Simon. Deb nodded. She told Sue that Danny was leaving Chris.

"It should never have come to this" Deb said sadly, "…but it has".

The phone rang and it was Simon. He told her he was going to Coasters and to meet him there. Tony asked Sue to meet him there too.

"Oh and Deb – Chris and Sam are coming to the restaurant to you first."

Deb and Sue were closing and Phil, the new manager, was locking up when Chris and Sam arrived. The cab arrived and they all jumped in and headed for Coasters. They left Phil and Eddie, the doorman to lock up. They all shouted bye to them.

"Bye girls…have a good night." Phil and Eddie shouted back.

Coasters was the place to go if you were rich and famous – or if you were connected to anyone rich and famous. When they arrived, Deb bumped straight into Nick. He put his arms around her and kissed her. Sue, Chris and Sam found the guys. Simon asked were Deb was.

"Oh she's talking to Nick" Chris answered.

"Who's she talking to?" Danny asked.

"Nick…Fucking Nick…." muttered Simon.

Danny looked at his stony face

"Oh Simon," he sighed.

"What's wrong?" Chris asked.

"Nothing…." Danny said shaking his head.

Deb eventually made her way over.

"Hi guys." she said cheerfully.

"Where have you been?" Simon asked abruptly.

"I've been talking to Nick."

"So talking means you fuckin touch each other?"

"Simon…Fuck off." she said walking away.

She was heading back to Nick. Tony grabbed hold of her arm as she passed.

"What is his problem?"

"I don't know but he is starting to piss me off."

Simon's eyes were firmly fixed on her. She knew he was watching her and purposely took hold of Nick's face and kissed him passionately. As much as he liked it he was speechless. Simon stormed over angrily asking what she thought she was doing. She pointed out that this was what he wanted to believe. Nick pushed him back.

"Fuck off, Si"

Dave and Tony grabbed Simon and pulled him away before things could get worse. Danny, however, grabbed Deb's arm and asked what she was doing.

Chris went over and sat with Simon.

"Are you OK Si?

Simon looked at Chris and said, "I'm losing her."

Simon looked around and saw Dom dancing very close to Deb. They were dancing very suggestively, Dom's hands roaming all over her body. Deb was on fine form. She'd had enough and decided to have some fun. Sue and Sam looked at Tony and Danny. Tony shrugged his shoulders as he noticed the look on Danny's face. Danny wasn't amused! Tony thought he was going to burst a blood vessel. Deb was behaving out of character and while Dom loved every minute, Danny didn't like it at all.

"Fuck me…is it just me? Or am I that jealous" Simon said putting his hands to his head.

"She's just having a good time" Chris interrupted. "Look – Sam, Sue, Tony and Danny are up dancing as well.

The next day Deb was at the restaurant doing the orders with Sue, Phil and the chef. She'd been there all day as things were pretty tense at home after last night's events. She'd managed to get a lot of paperwork done but she still had the accounts to do. She decided to take them home with her as she needed to have some quiet to go through them.

She doubted she would get much quiet when Simon finally arrived back from his meeting with Alex. She had to face the music at some point. Chris and Sam came in to see her and Sue. Sam had got little Alan with her. He went running over to Deb and Sue and they both gave him a big kiss and cuddle.

Sue asked him where he was going and Sam answered.

"We're going shopping now with Aunty Chris aren't we?"

Deb and Sue both smiled at him. Alan said goodbye and kissed them.

Chris and Sam said, "See you later girls."

Sue and Deb decided to call it a day. They went home but when Deb got home she realized she'd forgotten her paperwork. She called Phil and told him she would be back in later to collect them. When Simon got back he walked passed her as if she wasn't there, he was so angry with her.

"OK Simon," she yelled.

She told him she was wrong for kissing Nick like that and she was sorry. He had made her so angry with his crazy thoughts about them. He turned and walked back to her. He told her he loved her so much and she had really hurt him last night. She apologized again and he leaned forward to kiss her, smiling softly at her.

Danny, on the other hand, wasn't going to forgive that easy. He didn't understand why she needed to kiss Nick the way he did.

That evening Brad Cannon went to the restaurant hoping to see Deb.

"Good evening, Mr. Cannon," Phil greeted him.

"Good evening… Is Mrs. Richards here?"

"Not at moment, but she is coming in later."

Brad was disappointed that she wasn't there as he wanted to see her again.

"Ah well…I will have a table for two then, in the corner please and I'll have a bottle of champagne"

"Yes Mr. Cannon"

Phil took Brad to his table and a little later Deb arrived.

Phil said, "Hi Deb, Mr. Cannon is here and he has been asking for you."

"Oh right…Thanks Phil."

She made her way over to where he was seated.

"Hello Mr. Cannon"

"Mrs. Richards…Sit down and join me."

"Why…Thank you"

"Have some champagne"

"Are you celebrating something?" she asked.

"No…I like champagne. You have not called me."

"Oh…was I supposed to?"

"Yes… for our dinner date remember."

"Oh… I see. I'm so sorry."

"So why didn't you ring?"

Deb was speechless and didn't know what to say.

"Hmm." she stuttered.

Brad asked were Simon was and Deb told him he was at home. He told her if she was his wife he wouldn't let her out of his sight. She pointed out that he was not just a handsome man, he was also very charming.

"Of course…What else would you expect? I think we should become lovers." he cajoled as he took her hand and kissed it.

Deb laughed and he smiled at her. He had such a beautiful smile. Very sexy… Deb loved that smile…The only other person that had a smile like that was Danny.

"I think we will be lovers… You make me feel alive."

"Brad, I'm married…We can't be lovers."

"I'm divorced and we can be lovers."

"But I'm in love Brad…If I was not in love this could be very different."

"Beautiful and faithful, Simon is a lucky guy… if you ever change your mind call me."

He wrote his number down for her and then swiftly placed it in the palm of her hand.

"Don't lose it," he said winking at her

"I'm very flattered." Deb said smiling at him.

"Well you are a very beautiful woman"

"And you are a very nice man and extremely sexy and now I've really got to go."

Brad gave Deb a kiss.

"I'm going back to New York tomorrow but remember what I said…If you change your mind we could be lovers. You take my breath away."

Deborah went for her paperwork, waved to Brad and left.

Chapter 40

A few days later, Simon bumped into Nick and decided to have it out with him. He asked what was going on with him and Deb.

"What the fuck are you talking about?"

Simon pushed him against the wall and told him to stay away from her.

"Screw you, Si."

"I'm warning you Nick"

Nick looked confused."Why?" he asked.

"I don't want you near her."

"Why? And what the fuck are you talking about?"

"I know about you and her."

"Yeah… and what the fuck do you think you know."

"Ya fuckin prick!" Simon got more aggressive and started getting in Nick's face. "You are screwing my wife."

"What the fuck?" Nick laughed, "You think me and Deb are having an affair?"

"Come on Nick… Do you think I'm fucking stupid?"

"Yeah…I fucking do… It's not me that Deb wants…I wish it was. But if you think that Deb is having an affair you should look closer to home."

"What?"

"Now… if you've fucking finished"

Nick walked away leaving Simon frozen to the spot. He knew exactly what Nick meant by closer to home. An affair with Nick was bad enough but an affair with Danny only meant one thing. He didn't want to think about it, never mind believe it.

He went to the restaurant and he saw Deb and Dan together. Simon's world had just crashed and died.

"No…No…This is not happening." he whispered.

He stood there watching them. He saw their closeness and the way they laughed together and he knew…

He went home and sat in the dark waiting. When Deb arrived home she put the light on and jumped when she saw him sat there.

"Simon…What are you doing in the dark?" She asked confused.

"Where have you been?"

"I was at the restaurant."

"Were you on your own?"

"Yeah…Why? Oh shit Simon, not this again…I was not with Nick."

"I'm going to bed," he growled.

She looked at him closely. His eyes were serious and dark. A chill ran down her spine.

"Simon what's wrong?" she said, trying to placate him.

"Nothing."

His tone was harsher and he frightened her. Simon didn't know what to do. He could confront her but that might make her choose and he didn't want that.

He didn't want to lose her, he loved her.

A few weeks later the guys were touring around Europe when Simon started feeling really odd. He was really lethargic, no life in him and he was really white and clammy. Tony asked him if he was OK but Simon said that he just feeling a bit unwell. On the second night of their tour, Simon collapsed on stage and was rushed to hospital.

They had to cancel the rest of the tour. The doctors found that he'd caught some sort of a virus and he was quite sick. Tony rang Deb to let her know. She flew out on the first flight she could get. She was really worried about him. He was her husband, after all, and she did care about him.

She stayed at the hospital and when he woke she was the first thing he saw, asleep at his bedside. He put his hand out and stroked her forehead. She woke up and smiled at him.

"I can't turn my back for a minute."

Simon smiled back at her.

"I'm gonna go back with Dave to get changed then I'll be back."

"Deb." he murmured taking hold of her hand, "Thank you"

"For what?"

"Caring."

"Simon. Please don't be silly…You're my husband."

"Deb…Please don't be long."

Deb went back to the hotel with Dave. Danny and Tony were sat talking to Alex about what happened next. Alex gave them the alternatives.

"We can put the concert on hold and when Simon gets better we can either do later dates or we can give refunds."

They mulled it over.

"Later dates are probably the best." Danny said and Tony agreed.

They asked Dave what he thought.

Dave said, "Yeah, later dates."

"Right. I'll organize a press conference. I'll go and sort that out now. Oh Deb … How's he doing?" Alex asked.

"Yeah, how is he?" Danny and Tony asked.

"Not too good," she replied. "He's awake…"

"Yeah he's not so good though…" Dave told them

"Did the doctor say what had caused it? How long will he be out of action?" Alex asked.

"I honestly don't know Alex. They've put him on some really strong antibiotics to try and get rid of the virus."

"Right… Well I better organise this press conference" Then he left.

"Right guys I'm going to the restaurant... Anyone coming?"

Tony said he would and Deb and Dan said they would follow. Danny asked Deb if she was OK.

"Yeah...I'm fine."

Danny moved towards her and kissed her. She kissed him back longingly.

"So... what happens now?" he asked.

"I don't know Danny. We need to put things on hold. He needs to get better... he looks so weak. I was worried about him."

"Yeah I know...he didn't do much for us either."

"No I bet he scared you all."

"Yeah...he did...Come, let's get something to eat"

They went to the restaurant and ate with Tony and Dave and then they all went the hospital all went to see Simon.

Meanwhile Alex had sorted out the press conference. When they got back, he told them they had 20 minutes before the press arrived.

"Fuckin hell Alex" Dave grumbled.

"Come on guys"

They made their way to the conference room where the press was waiting for them.

"How is Simon?" one reporter shouted

Another yelled, "... Is Decade's tour cancelled?"

Danny, Tony and Dave answered all their questions then left, heading back to their suite.

When Simon was well enough to move they travelled back home but he was ordered to rest. Deb took time off from the restaurant to look after him and she didn't see Danny for a while. They'd decided to put their plans on hold.

Nick was on tour in Japan but called Deb to find out if Simon was any better.

"Yeah...he's got to rest but he seems OK."

Nick told her about the fight that he and Simon had. About the affair that they were supposedly having and he might have dropped her in it.

"What do you mean Nick?"

"He thought we were having an affair... I wouldn't mind if we were but I know about you and Dan and I think I dropped you in it."

"You know what, precisely?"

"I saw you and Dan go to the bathroom at your pool party."

"Shit Nick."

When she got off the phone she sat thinking. Simon knew. So why had he not said anything? Why had he not gone mad or maybe he doesn't know?

She went up to the bedroom with some lunch for Simon. She smiled at him.

"Lunch is ready"

Simon looked at her.

"You know I love you…I know you don't love me like…" he hesitated. "I just want you to love me."

"Simon please do we have to keep going over this?"

"No…I'm sorry"

When Simon was back in action they went back on tour and did the dates they had cancelled before he'd become ill.

He was trying to think how he could win Deb back from Danny but he knew that this wasn't just an affair. He knew Danny and Deb really loved each other.

He knew he was going to lose her.

Chapter 41

June 1995

Danny turned up at the restaurant. Deb was so pleased to see him, she threw her arms around him and kissed him. He kissed her back passionately and told her he'd missed her. She told him she'd missed him too but she didn't have long.

"Why, you got something on?"

"I said I'd be home." she said nervously.

"Why?"

"Simon's making dinner."

"What? No… I have had enough of sneaking around. Catching an hour here and there… I want to tell them."

"Danny"

"No…We tell them tonight."

"Danny…Please."

"No Deb… No, tell him tonight!"

They got in to a big fight and Danny told her he was telling Chris tonight.

He stormed out of the restaurant. She got into her car and sat there for a moment. She started the engine and drove. She found herself heading towards Nick's. She needed to talk to someone. She pulled up outside and just sat there until Nick noticed her car and went out to her.

"Deb. What are you doing out here?"

She started to cry.

"Come on Deb."

He took her into the house and got her a drink putting his arms round her. She told him everything about her and Danny.

"You should be with the person you love and that's clearly Dan."

"Oh Nick… I don't want to hurt anyone"

"Simon might be married to you but he doesn't have you"

"I know…I have to tell Simon…but…"

"Deb, there is no easy way of doing this."

"Oh… Nick, I know." she sighed with a heavy heart.

She knew what she had to do

"You love Dan, anyone can see that and I know that Dan loves you… he told me a long time ago."

Deb kissed Nick

"You are a special man and whoever gets you will be a very lucky woman. I know I keep saying this but it's true."

She kissed him again, then headed home to tell Simon about her and Danny.

When Danny got home he was so angry. He didn't like fighting with Deb and he started slamming things about. Chris appeared and asked him what was wrong. Danny turned round suddenly. She startled him.

"Oh Shit, Chris."

"What's wrong?" she asked.

He looked at her, searching her face. He felt bad for what he was about to say.

"I'm so sorry…"

"What for…? What do you mean?"

She was beginning to feel uneasy. She knew what he was going to say

"I'm so fucking sorry… This is not your fault…I never meant to hurt you… You don't deserve this."

"Danny... Please tell me what's wrong."

"I want a divorce."

"What? Why? What have I done?"

Tears started to fill up in her eyes and to roll down her face.

"You have done nothing... It's me...

"Danny?"

"I can't do this anymore and there's no easy way of saying this."

"Danny...It's Deb, isn't it? I know you still love her – you never stopped did you?"

"No... and I'm sorry." he said shaking his head.

Chris started to sob harder.

"I love you Danny... Why did you marry me?"

"Chris, please don't."

"Why... Are you sad? You're the cheating bastard here... how long, Danny?" Chris shouted changing her tone.

"Chris...I do feel bad"

"How long have you been sleeping with her"

"I've always loved her"

Chris started to cry even more and tried pulling Danny close to her to kiss him. Danny pushed her away.

"Chris Stop. Stop..."

"No...I love you."

"Well I don't love you... I probably never did."

She slapped him hard across the face and took hold of his shirt collar.

"I hate YOU...I hate YOU... I could have had Dominic if I'd wanted"

"You think that makes a difference? You think I'm jealous?" he sniggered"I don't give a shit... Fuck who you want."

She went to hit him again but he pushed her back and she fell over and ended up on the floor sobbing.

"You can have your divorce but I want this house," she screamed.

"You money grabbing Bitch! OK, Have the fuckin house!"

"You'll be with her. That's all you wanted anyway, I always knew that."

"YEP… It always has been Deb… you so fuckin right."

She went upstairs and started packing his bags, throwing them down at him. He left and went to Tony's.

Tony sat talking to Danny.

"What you going to do Dan?" he asked.

"Deb should be telling Simon as we speak."

"Oh shit, Dan."

"Tony, I don't want to be without Deb anymore."

"No…I know…She really is the girl for you"

Sue came in. She'd heard what they'd been talking about.

"Is Deb going to be alright with Simon when she tells him?"

"Yeah…Simon wouldn't hurt Deb…" Danny said confidently.

"I hope not."

Tony and Danny looked at each other.

"He wouldn't hurt her would he?" Danny asked Tony, less confident now.

"No Dan…He loves her…No… ," he replied, shaking his head.

Chapter 42

Deb entered the house to the smell of cooking. The lights were low and Simon had put candles on the table. He had made dinner and he had made everything romantic. He smiled at her lovingly as she entered the room."

Hi Deb... Sit down babe...I've made an omelet with a side salad and I've chilled us a bottle of white wine"

Deb sat there quietly, trying to work out the best way of telling him about her and Danny. Simon moved over to her and bent forward to kiss her but she silently moved away.

"So...What's wrong?" he asked concerned.

"I'm just tired" she shrugged.

"Tired?"

"Yeah... Sorry. I need to tell ...." she muttered guiltily.

"Sorry my ass."he interrupted her abruptly.

Simon's mood and tone changed. Deb jumped up from the table and tried to move but he pushed her against the wall aggressively, pinning her against it. He tried to kiss her, forcefully pulling at her clothes, ripping them open. Her buttons flew across the room.

"Stop it, Simon." she managed to scream.

"I want you." he shouted huskily.

"Stop it… Let go… Simon let me go…."

"All I want is for you to love me." he cried.

"Let me away from the wall."

No… stay there." he yelled slamming her back against the wall. "We haven't had sex for fuck knows how long." he said aggressively pointing at her. "No – correction – *I* haven't … but you have, haven't you?"

"What?" she asked as a cold shiver ran through her.

"Yeah… I know about you and Danny… I know you have been screwing him."

His eyes were so angry and cold as he started hitting his head with the palm of his hands.

"I should have guessed if it was gonna be anyone it would be Danny – All the women want to fuck Danny, he must be fuckin great in the sack"

"Simon… I…"

You… You…" he was so angry he couldn't get his words out

Deb put her hands to her mouth and tried to move away from the wall.

"I'm so sorry"

She could feel herself shaking. She was terrified as Simon forcefully slammed her against the wall again.

"Doesn't fuckin move." he yelled.

His eyes were frosty and cold as he forcefully kissed her again pushing her down on the floor pulling at her clothes again.

"Simon…You're hurting me."

He stopped and looked at her coldly.

"Fucking bastard." he yelled as he hit the wall.

He looked at her frightened face and suddenly seemed to come to his senses.

"Deb… I'm sorry," he cried as he let go of her.

"I'm sorry Simon, but I want a divorce."

"No. No. No. Deb please…I love you."

"Simon I know you love me…but I love Danny…I always have."

"No. No. No." He started to shout again. "You will tell Dan it's over and this will never happen again."

"No Simon...I won't."

"It was him that started this wasn't it? He made you."

"No."

"Yeah he did."

"Simon."

"When did this start" he asked.

"That doesn't matter"

"Yes it fucking does...When...?" he demanded

"Simon"

"When, DEB" he shouted at her again through clenched teeth.

"The first time anything happened was two days before we got married."

"WHAT?"

Simon slid down the wall and started to cry.

"I love you." he sobbed.

"Simon please... I'm so sorry."

"When did it start again." he asked.

"The weekend you went away."

Simon put his hands to his head and cried. Deb felt so bad, she moved over to him and told him she had never wanted to hurt him. Simon put his hands down and looked at her with tear-filled eyes.

"We can work this out... I can forget this," he said as he grabbed hold of her again and kissed her.

"Simon...No...I want a divorce."

"No...Stop saying that...You never really loved me did you?"

"Simon please...Let's end this now."

"Go to bed please... Deb please.... Please!"

Deb went to bed but Simon had frightened her so she locked the bedroom door. She had never seen him like that before. She knew she had hurt him deeply.

Simon stayed downstairs. He poured himself rather large vodka and drank it in one gulp, and then got another, then another.

He started mulling things over his in head. He decided to go to Danny's. He jumped in his car and drove like a maniac. He screeched up Danny's drive. Leaving the car door open, he stagger to the front door. He hammered loudly, shouting and sobbing.

"Come out you fuckin bastard"

The lights went on and Chris opened the door. She had been crying, her eyes were red and puffy,

"Where the fuck is he?" he screamed at her.

"I don't know Simon"

"Yeah, you fuckin do"

"No I don't" as tears started to run down her face again.

"You know what he's been doing don't you?"

"Yeah I kicked him out" she spluttered

Simon looked at Chris realizing that she must be hurting too.

"I'm sorry Chris"

As he went to get back in the car, Chris ran after him grabbing his arm, begging him to come inside. He was so drunk and she was worried about him.

"No, I need to find Danny now."

"Please come inside

"No!"

Simon pulled his arm free, shutting the car door. He spun it round screeching the tyres as he drove off. He knew that Danny would be headed to Tony's but when he got there, Tony told him to go home.

"No, I want Danny out here now." he shouted angrily.

"Fuck off Si, my kids are sleeping." Tony shouted back.

Danny came to the door and told Tony he was sorry and he would take this away from the house. Simon lunged at Danny.

"You fuck"

"Come on Si, let's do this"

Danny started to walk away from the house, out of sight. Tony rushed back in and called Dave.

"I'm gonna need you bud. Si has found out that and Dan and Deb are having an affair. Si is here and he and Dan are going for it"

"Oh Fuck... I'll be right over"

Dave shouted to Sam and explained what was going on.

"Oh shit." Sam cried

"Yeah... this going to be messy, they've always loved the same woman. Si has found out that Danny has been sleeping with Deb.

"Yeah Sue told me the story, it's very sad." Dave kissed her and left for Tony's.

Sue wanted to know were Deb was. She was really worried about her. Tony said he didn't know but he was sure she would be alright

"Why... Dan why."

"She's mine, Si. She always was, you fuckin prick. You really didn't think I was going to let you keep her did you?"

"She's my wife."

"I told you a long time ago I would do whatever it took to get her back"

Simon lunged again at Danny, hitting him in the face. Danny swung back at him. By the time Dave got to Tony's they were in a full scale fight with fists flying in all directions. Tony and Dave ran down to them. Tony grabbed Danny and Dave grabbed Simon.

Quickly they pulled them apart, they were both dripping in blood. They had busted lips, black eyes, and torn clothes. Dave forced Simon back in the car. Simon crumpled but managed to shout, "You're not fucking getting her!"

Dave drove Simon home. They sat in the car

"Why... Dave, why has he done this to me? We're best buddies"

"Oh Si... You knew he always loved her"

"Oh so that makes it alright that he's fucking my wife then?"

"I didn't fuckin say that, it's a fuckin mess"

"I'm not letting her go," he said getting out of the car.

He was trying to work out how he could keep her. He didn't want to lose her but deep down he knew he had.

She was and always would be Danny's.

Epilogue

JUNE 5 1995

Deb woke up and went downstairs. Simon was already there having breakfast.

"Deb"

"Simon"

"I don't want to fight again, Deb."

"No I don't either."

Simon, how did you get that black eye?" She sounded very concerned.

He had scared her so much last night she hadn't even realised he'd gone out. She was shocked to see the state of his face.

"Danny… we had a fight."

"Simon. You and Danny had a fight Oh my God… when… ? Where …?"

"When you tell Danny it's over, we can start again."

"I want a divorce. I want to be with Danny… I always have… I'm so sorry, Simon."

"NO. Tell Dan it's over. Tell him Deb…PLEASE."

Deb poured herself some coffee and went back upstairs. She got into the shower. When she climbed out, she just stood there gazing into the mirror, remembering when she first arrived in America.

She knew what she had to do, she needed to see Danny. She realised that this was it and she needed to get hold of him. She got dressed and packed some stuff in a bag and headed to the restaurant. She called Danny's cell as soon as she got there.

"Danny, I've done it… I've left."

"Yeah… So have I… I'll meet you at the beach house."

Deb got there first and she sat on the beach waiting for Danny. There was a lady on the beach with her husband. Deb watched them wistfully. They looked very much in love and they were messing around with their dog. The dog had been in the sea and ran straight over to Deb, jumping all over her. The lady apologised.

"That's fine."

She laughed as she stroked the dog and made a fuss of him. He was a beautiful big Alsatian. The lady mentioned that they were on honeymoon.

"Congratulations… I hope you are both very happy"

They thanked her and carried on walking. Dark clouds had started to roll in and the rain had started to pound the beach. Deb was covered in wet sand and decided to have a bath. As she ran the water she poured in some of her favourite scented bath salts. The smell of the lavender calmed her and as soaked she relaxed, breathing a sigh of relief.

When Danny arrived he shouted out to her.

"Deb?"

"I'm in the bath" she shouted back.

As she got out she wrapping the towel round herself. Danny looked at her and smiled. Deb looked at his lip and his cheek.

"Oh Danny, that looks painful"

"It is"

"How did Chris take the news?"

"She didn't take it well."

"No… Simon didn't either – as you can see.

"He wants me to tell you it's over."

"Deb, please tells me you're not going to do that."

Deb took his hand and led him in to the bedroom and dropped her towel.

"Danny, just hold me," she cried.

Danny moved closer to her and put his arms round her naked body, kissing her.

"All this is mine?" he asked as he moved his hands up and down her body.

"Always has been… always will be…" she whispered as she started to remove his clothes.

"I never want to lose you again Deb."

"And you won't…We will never be parted again."

They kissed passionately. His lip hurt but he didn't care. Their mouths locked together. His hands slowly, moved down her body, followed by his lips. He moved his lips up her thighs and she sighed breathlessly, running her fingers through his hair. Caressing her body he pressed down on her. His hips were firm as he made love to her. They moved together in frenzy.

Her hands reached up and Danny clasped them. Her body arched to his every touch, she groaned loudly. They were so hot and sweaty their sweat mixing together. She tightened her legs round his waist. Their breathing became heavier and ragged until they both climaxed. She grabbed the sheets twisting them round her hands. Then they suddenly relaxed and they lay in bed cuddling and caressing each other.

"I love you Deb," he said as he drew his fingers through her hair and kissed her. "Will you marry me?"

"I love you too Danny…Yes I will, as soon as we get divorced"

"We need to think about where we are going to live but we can stay here tonight." Danny said, trailing his finger over her skin.

"What about the band?"

"If the band splits up, it splits up… all I want is you."

"Are you sure this is what you want?"

"Yeah…I've never been surer about anything. Now come on…Tonight we are going to celebrate…Let's go to that little restaurant up the road."

"OK then."

They were so happy.

Deb went in to the bathroom to freshen up while Danny called Tony.

"Hey Dan, where are you?"

"At the beach house with Deb. We are going to get married as soon as we are both divorced."

"I'm happy for you both."

"Look if you want me to leave the band I understand, but I will never give Deb up."

"Dan I ..."

"Hey man, it's OK."

As Deb got dressed, Danny sat on the bed and watched her putting her make up on. She could see him though the mirror.

"What you doin?

"I just love watching you...You're so beautiful"

She moved over to him and kissed him tenderly.

"Ouch." he flinched

"Oh sorry baby, that lip looks so painful," she smiled apologetically as she kissed his nose.

"Are we ready?" she asked.

"Yeah...we have wasted so much time, Deb"

"Not anymore baby."

He looked at her, giving her a whopping big smile. She smiled back at him, her eyes glowing.

"Do you know what that smile does to me?" she asked.

"Yeah I do... Come on lets go for dinner and I'll flash you my smile later."

They took Danny's car and headed for the restaurant. It was very foggy and from the earlier down pour it had made the roads treacherous. Suddenly a car light appeared out of the fog causing Danny to swerve violently.

"Oh Shit!...I've lost control!" he cried.

The rear tyre blew out, causing the car to go full circle. Danny was trying to gain control of the car when it smashed through the safety barrier. They were hurled off the side of the mountain, dropping about thirty feet. The car landed and rolled twice before it came to an abrupt stop, throwing Danny through the windscreen.

The car that had appeared out of the fog turned round to see if there was anything they could do.

"Oh my God… I think they're dead… Phone for help!" The driver said turning to his wife, grabbing his first aid box as he tried to make his way down to them.

The mountain was very steep but the man tried never the less

When mountain rescue got there Deb was barely breathing and there was blood everywhere. Danny had died on impact.

The rescue team had to cut Deb out of the car. Her legs were stuck and her head was bleeding badly. They had to work quickly because there was smoke coming from the engine. Deb was rushed to the hospital by helicopter.

It didn't take long for the media to find out what happened and soon they were all over it.

By the time Simon and Chris were told of the accident, it was breaking news everywhere, on every channel. Tony had gone with Chris to identify Danny's body.

Simon rushed to the hospital. Deb was in theatre when Sue, Dave and Sam got to the hospital. Tony waited with Chris until her brother came to get her. She was in shock. She'd said some dreadful things to Danny.

Tony then rushed to the guys and found Simon pacing the floor, up and down. Tony got hold of him and hugged him.

"I can't lose her Tony," he cried as he started pacing again.

Tony asked how Deb was doing and Sue told him she was still in theatre.

"Danny and Deb were at the beach house all day."

"How do you know that?"

"Danny rang me and told me… he sounded so happy."

"Oh Tony… Deb is going to be devastated when she is told about Danny."

After some considerable time the doctor came out and told Simon that she was in a poor way and that the next seventy two hours were going to be critical.

The surgeons had to operate on Deb to remove metal fragments from her lungs. She had internal bleeding, severe head trauma and her legs, some ribs and one of her arms were broken. She'd had been put on a life support machine. There were tubes and wires everywhere. They didn't hold out much hope.

Simon could go in and sit with her but when he saw her he wept. He looked at her and sat talking to her, knowing she couldn't hear him but hoping all the same.

"I LOVE YOU... We will be alright... Danny would want you to be happy..."

The media was congregating outside the hospital waiting for news about Danny and Deb. Alex Parks arrived to make the announcement about Danny.

"It is with deep regret I have to announce that Danny Brooks died earlier this evening and also Deborah Richards is fighting for her life"

The press started firing questions from everywhere.

"How bad is Deborah?"

"She is currently in theatre... she's in a critical condition."

Then one reporter yelled out.

"Is it true that Danny was having an affair with Simon's wife?"

"Did Simon know about the affair?" another reporter shouted.

"No comment. Thank you that's all now. No more questions"

"Were there a fight between Danny and Simon?"

"No more questions"

"How long had they been sneaking around?"

"No more questions!" he snapped.

This was difficult enough without all this hassle. He pushed his way through the media and cameras and made his way in to the hospital to find Simon and the rest of them. Alex sat with them for hours. They all just sat and waited and waited then suddenly the alarm on the life support machine went off.

Simon was asked to wait outside and Sue asked what was going on.

"She's gone into cardiac arrest." Simon said, just stunned.

"No. No." she cried. Tony took hold of her.

"What...?" Dave asked putting his hand to his mouth.

"No..." Sam cried.

The crash team rushed in to revive her. They were losing her, the machine just continued the stomach churning 'beeeepppp'. They attached pads to her chest and began shocking her.

"CLEAR!" the doctor shouted.

The shock made her body lift from the bed. 'BEEEEEPPPP…

It was a desperate race to get her back.

"CLEAR!"

They shocked her again. They shocked her three times but they couldn't get her back. They removed the pads and turned to Simon.

"No… No… No!" he screamed, dropping to knees

Tony and Dave sat Simon down. The shock had knocked him for six and he was a bit wobbly on his legs. Sue and Sam hugged each other for consolation. They were all devastated. They had lost two people they loved.

Simon went back in to see her. He sat and stroked her hair and kissed her. Over and over He told her how much he still loved her and how he always had and always would.

– BREAKING NEWS –

ROCK STAR DANNY BROOKS AND FORMER LOVE DEBORAH RICHARDS BOTH DIED TONIGHT IN A CAR CRASH.

DECADE FRONT MAN DANNY DIED ON IMPACT

DEBORAH RICHARDS, WIFE OF FELLOW BAND MEMBER SIMON RICHARDS, DIED A FEW HOURS LATER IN HOSPITAL FROM HER INJURIES. IT'S BEEN RUMOURED THAT THE PAIR WERE HAVING AN AFFAIR AND HAD REKINLED THEIR LOVE FOR EACH OTHER.

IT IS CLAIMED THE PAIR HAD NEVER REALLY
GOT OVER EACH OTHER

Deborah and Danny were destined to be together. Nothing was going to keep them apart.